GIVE
WAR
A
CHANCE

'He is wickedly good'

Sebastian Faulks, INDEPENDENT ON SUNDAY

'His sentences have the economy and timing of a proficient
stand-up'

Laura Page, SUNDAY TELEGRAPH

'For the jokes alone, *Give War A Chance* is worth a read'

Jeremy Paxman, SUNDAY TIMES

'The US needs an unapologetic hedonist like P. J. O'Rourke
on the literary scene, flashing two fingers at the forces
behind random drug-testing and neutered lager . . . an
exuberantly malevolent collection of journalese'

Douglas Kennedy, LITERARY REVIEW

'Not only the best title for years, but funnier than a billion
politically correct comedies'

THE FACE

'A riveting read'

TIME OUT

ALSO BY P. J. O'ROURKE IN PICADOR

Republican Party Reptile

Holidays in Hell

Parliament of Whores

P. J. O'ROURKE

EYEWITNESS
ACCOUNTS
OF MANKIND'S
STRUGGLE AGAINST
TYRANNY,
INJUSTICE AND
ALCOHOL-FREE BEER

GIVE
WAR
A
CHANCE

PICADOR

First published 1992 by The Atlantic Monthly Press, New York

First published in Great Britain 1992 by Picador

This edition published 1993 by Picador
a division of Pan Macmillan Publishers Limited
Cavaye Place, London SW10 9PG
and Basingstoke

Associated companies throughout the world

ISBN 0 330 32536 1

9 8 7 6 5 4 3 2 1

A CIP catalogue record for this book is available from
the British Library

Phototypeset by Intype, London
Printed and bound in Great Britain by
Cox & Wyman Ltd, Reading, Berkshire

Like many men of my generation, I had an opportunity to give war a chance, and I promptly chickened out. I went to my draft physical in 1970 with a doctor's letter about my history of drug abuse. The letter was four and a half pages long with three and a half pages devoted to listing the drugs I'd abused. I was shunted into the office of an Army psychiatrist who, at the end of a forty-five-minute interview with me, was pounding the desk and shouting, 'You're fucked up! You don't belong in the Army!' He was certainly right on the first count and possibly right on the second. Anyway, I didn't have to go. But that, of course, meant someone else had to go in my place. I would like to dedicate this book to him.

I hope you got back in one piece, fellow. I hope you were more use to your platoon mates than I would have been. I hope you're rich and happy now. And in 1971, when somebody punched me in the face for being a long-haired peace creep, I hope that was you.

CONTENTS

CONTENTS

'The Death of Communism', 'Return of the Death of Communism, Part III', and most of the Gulf War section of this book originally appeared in *Rolling Stone*, where I am the 'Foreign Affairs Desk Chief', a title given to me because 'Middle-Aged Drunk' didn't look good on business cards. I would like to thank Jann Wenner and the staff of *Rolling Stone*, especially Bob Wallace, Eric Etheridge and Robert Vare for good editing, better ideas and best paychecks.

Although the Gulf War dispatches appeared in *Rolling Stone*, it was ABC Radio that actually sent me to Saudi Arabia. The General Manager of News Operations, my friend John Lyons, called me from Dhahran and said, 'I noticed your bylines on the Kuwait invasion story were Jordan and the UAE, and this tells me you haven't been able to get a Saudi visa.' John got me one and got me a job, too (my first real one since 1980), doing commentary for his radio network. The 'Gulf Diary' entries and much of the material in the *Rolling Stone* dispatches are drawn from my radio pieces. I know nothing about radio, and John was a patient boss – though his patience was sorely tried when I wound up, briefly, as the only ABC Radio reporter in liberated Kuwait City and was sending back live reports such as: 'Uh, uh, uh, uh . . . oh my gosh, blown-up tanks'. Many thanks go to

John and to the equally patient real ABC Radio reporters in the Gulf, Linda Albin, Chuck Taylor and Bob Schmidt.

'Return of the Death of Communism', 'Fiddling While Africa Starves', 'The Deep Thoughts of Lee Iacocca', 'The Very Deep Thoughts of Jimmy and Rosalynn Carter' and 'Mordred Had a Point – Camelot Revisited' all appeared in the *American Spectator*, as did 'Notes Toward a Blacklist for the 1990s'. This last was expanded, with the aid of the *Spectator*'s readers, into a book-length proscription called *The New Enemies List*. Copies are available from *The American Spectator*, P.O. Box 549, Arlington, VA 22216. My thanks to R. Emmett Tyrrell, Jr, Wladyslaw Pleszczynski, Andrew Ferguson and the rest of the staff of that fine publication.

'Second Thoughts About the 1960s' was originally a speech, given in October 1987 at the Second Thoughts conference in Washington, DC. Second Thoughts was a gathering of former New Leftists and other people who had successfully recovered from the sixties. The conference was put together by Peter Collier and David Horowitz, and we all had a great time chastising our former selves. Part of my speech was published in the *New Republic*, then under the brilliant (even if he does call himself a liberal) editorship of Michael Kinsley. The entire text was printed in the book *Second Thoughts*, edited by Collier and Horowitz and published by Madison Books (Lanham, Md) in 1989.

The Second Thoughts conference was organized with the help of Jim Denton, Director of the National Forum Foundation, one of Washington's more thoughtful think tanks. The National Forum Foundation has worked hard and even successfully to aid pro-liberty forces in Central America and Eastern Europe. It was Jim Denton who convinced me to go to Nicaragua for the 1990 elections. Jim even went so far as to claim Violeta Chamorro might win.

'A Serious Problem' was commissioned by the intelligent and beautiful Shelley Wanger, then Articles Editor of *House and Garden*. But Ms Wanger left, *House and Garden* became *HG* and my piece was judged to contain too few photographs of celebrity bed linen.

'Studying for Our Drug Test' appeared in *Playboy*, assigned by sagacious Articles Editor John Rezek. 'The Two-Thousand-Year-Old US Middle East Policy Expert' was published in *Inquiry* at the behest of its excellent Managing Editor, Jack Shafer. 'An Argument in Favor of Automobiles vs Pedestrians' saw print in *Car and Driver* when that doughty publication was being run by the as-doughty or doughtier David E. Davis, Jr. And 'Sex with Dr Ruth' came out in *Vanity Fair*, Executive Literary Editor Wayne Lawson being the only person on earth who could convince me to go see Dr Ruth, let alone admit it later.

Additional thanks are due to Morgan Entrekin, my editor and publisher, who paid me again for all these articles even though I'd been paid for them already, and to Bob Dattila, my agent, who made Morgan do that. And I must sincerely – though sincerity is not my forte – thank my wife. She had been my wife for only a month when the air war started in the Gulf and I headed there for the duration. She didn't cry, she didn't complain, she didn't let the car insurance lapse. And, when she heard about the way I almost set off a booby trap by fooling around with a box of Iraqi ammunition, she said – in even, measured tones – those words which elucidate so well the content and the style of all my journalism work: 'P.J., that was really stupid.'

' . . . and from the nothingness of good works, she passed to the somethingness of ham and toast with great cheerfulness.'

– Charles Dickens
BARNABY RUDGE

HUNTING THE VIRTUOUS – AND HOW TO CLEAN AND SKIN THEM

This book is a collection of articles about – if I may be excused for venturing upon a large theme – the battle against evil. Not that I meant to do anything so grand. I was just writing magazine pieces, trying to make a living, and evil is good copy.

Various types of evil are battled here. Some are simple. Iraq's invasion of Kuwait is a case of bad men doing wrong things for wicked reasons. This is the full-sized or standard purebred evil and is easily recognized even by moral neophytes. Other malignities – drugs in America, famine in Africa and everything in the Levant – are more complex. When combating those evils people sometimes have trouble deciding whom to shoot.

Anyway, it's a book about evil – evil ends, evil means, evil effects and causes. In a compilation of modern journalism there's nothing surprising about that. What does surprise me, on rereading these articles, is how much of the evil was authored or abetted by liberals.

Now liberals are people I had been accustomed to thinking of as daffy, not villainous. Getting their toes caught in their sandal straps, bumping their heads on wind chimes – how much trouble could they cause, even in a full-blown cultural-diversity frenzy? (I mean if Europeans didn't discover North America, how'd we all get here?) But every iniquity in this book is traceable to bad thinking or bad government. And liberals have been vigorous cheerleaders for both.

'Liberal' is, of course, one of those fine English words, like lady, gay and welfare, which has been spoiled by special pleading. When I say _liberals_ I certainly don't mean openhanded individuals or tolerant persons or even Big Government Democrats. I mean people who are excited that one per cent of the profits of Ben & Jerry's ice-cream goes to promote world peace.

The principal feature of contemporary American liberalism is sanctimoniousness. By loudly denouncing all bad things – war and hunger and date rape – liberals testify to their own terrific goodness. More important, they promote themselves to membership in a self-selecting elite of those who care deeply about such things. People who care a lot are naturally superior to we who don't care any more than we have to. By virtue of this superiority the caring have a moral right to lead the nation. It's a kind of natural aristocracy, and the wonderful thing about this aristocracy is that you don't have to be brave, smart, strong or even lucky to join it, you just have to be liberal.* Kidnapping the moral high ground also serves to inflate liberal ranks. People who are, in fact, just kindhearted are told that because they care, they must be liberals, too.

Liberals hate wealth, they say, on grounds of economic injustice – as though prosperity were a pizza, and if I have too many slices, you're left with nothing but a Domino's box to feed your family. Even Castro and Kim Il Sung know this to be nonsense. Any rich man does more for society than all the jerks pasting VISUALIZE WORLD PEACE bumper stickers on their cars. The worst leech of a merger and acquisitions lawyer making $500,000 a year will, even if he cheats on his taxes, put $100,000 into the public coffers. That's $100,000 worth of education, charity or US

---

*It was that talented idiot Percy Bysshe Shelley who first posited this soggy oligarchy when he said, 'Poets are the unacknowledged legislators of the world.' Modern liberals are no poets, however, and are hardly satisfied with legislating in the unacknowledged manner. Today's liberals love politics as much as they love disappearing rain forests, homelessness and hate crimes, because politics is one more way to achieve power without merit or risk.

Marines. And the Marine Corps does more to promote world peace than all the Ben & Jerry's ice-cream ever made.

Liberals actually hate wealth because they hate all success. They hate success especially, of course, when it's achieved by other people, but sometimes they even hate the success they achieve themselves. What's the use of belonging to a self-selecting elite if there's a real elite around? Liberals don't like any form of individual achievement. And if there has to be some, they prefer the kind that cannot be easily quantified – 'the achievement of Winnie Mandela' for example. Also wealth is, for most people, the only honest and likely path to liberty. With money comes power over the world. Men are freed from drudgery, women from exploitation. Businesses can be started, homes built, communities formed, religions practiced, educations pursued. But liberals aren't very interested in such real and material freedoms. They have a more innocent – not to say toddlerlike – idea of freedom. Liberals want the freedom to put anything into their mouths, to say bad words and to expose their private parts in art museums.

That liberals aren't enamoured of real freedom may have something to do with responsibility – that cumbersome backpack which all free men have to lug on life's aerobic nature hike. The second item in the liberal creed, after self-righteousness, is unaccountability. Liberals have invented whole college majors – psychology, sociology, women's studies – to prove that nothing is anybody's fault. No one is fond of taking responsibility for his actions, but consider how much you'd have to hate free will to come up with a political platform that advocates killing unborn babies but not convicted murderers. A callous pragmatist might favour abortion *and* capital punishment. A devout Christian would sanction neither. But it takes years of therapy to arrive at the liberal point of view.

Since we're not in control of ourselves, we are all vulnerable to victimization by whatever *is* in control. (Liberals are vague about this, but it's probably white male taxpayers or the Iran–Contra conspiracy). Liberals are fond of victims and seek them wherever they go. The more victimized the better – the best victims being too ignorant and addled to challenge their benefactors. This is why animal rights is such an excellent liberal issue. Not even a Democratic presidential candidate is as ignorant and addled as a dead laboratory rat.

The search for victims of injustice to pester explains why liberals won't leave minorities alone. 'The minority is always right,' said that pesky liberal Ibsen. And, when it comes to minorities, there is none greater – or, as it were, lesser – than that ultimate of all minorities, the self. Here the liberal truly comes into his own. There is nothing more mealy-mouthed, bullying, irresponsible and victimized than a well-coddled self, especially if it belongs to a liberal.

Liberal self-obsession is manifested in large doses of quack psychoanalysis, crank spiritualism, insalubrious health fads and helpless self-help seminars. The liberal makes grim attempts to hold on to his youth – fussing with his hair, his wardrobe, his speech and even his ideology in an attempt to retain the perfect solipsism of adolescence. He has a ridiculous and egotistical relationship with God, by turns denying He exists and hiding in His skirts. Either way – as God's special friend or as the highest form of sentient life on the planet – liberal self-importance is increased. The liberal is continually angry, as only a self-important man can be, with his civilization, his culture, his country and his folks back home. His is an infantile world view. At the core of liberalism is the spoiled child – miserable, as all spoiled children are, unsatisfied, demanding, ill-disciplined, despotic and useless. Liberalism is a philosophy of sniveling brats.

There! It was good to get that off my chest. Now that I've had my say, however, you may be wondering – don't I sometimes get called a Nazi? Yes, name-calling, in which conservatives such as myself are so loath to indulge, is a favourite tactic of the liberals. I have often been called a Nazi, and, although it is unfair, I don't let it bother me. I don't let it bother me for one simple reason. No one has *ever* had a fantasy about being tied to a bed and sexually ravished by someone dressed as a liberal.

THE BIRTH,
AND SOME
OF THE
AFTERBIRTH,
OF
FREEDOM

THE
DEATH
Berlin, # OF
November 1989 # COMMUNISM

A week after the surprise-party opening of East Germany's borders people were still gathering at the Berlin Wall, smiling at each other, drinking champagne and singing bits of old songs. There was no sign of the letdown which every sublime experience is supposed to inspire. People kept coming back just to walk along the freshly useless ramparts. They came at all sorts of hours, at lunch, dawn, three in the morning. Every possible kind of person was on promenade in the narrow gutter beside the concrete eyesore: wide hausfraus, kids with lavender hair, New Age goofs, drunk war vets in wheelchairs, video-burdened tourists, Deadheads, extravagant gays, toughs become all well-behaved, art students forgetting to look cool and bored, business tycoons gone loose and weepy, people so ordinary they defied description and, of course, members of the East German proletariat staring in surprise – as they stared in surprise at everything – at this previously central fact of their existence.

Even West Berlin's radicals joined the swarms. West Berlin had the most dogmatic agitators this side of Peru's Shining Path, but that was before 9 November. Near the restored Reichstag building I overheard a group of lefties amicably discussing nuclear strategy with a half dozen off-duty US GIs.

'Ja, you see, tactical capability mit der cruise missiles after all vas not der Soviet primary concern . . . '

'Sure, man, but what about second-strike capability? Wow, if we hadn't had that . . . '

All in the past tense. A British yob, who certainly should have been off throttling Belgians at a football match, came up to me apropos of nothing and said, 'I fucking 'ad to see this, right? I 'itched 'ere from London and got these chunks off the wall. You think I can't pay for the fucking ferry ride back with these? Right!'

At the Brandenburg Gate the East German border guards had shooed the weekend's noisy celebrators off the Wall. But the guards weren't carrying guns anymore and were beginning to acknowledge their audience and even ham it up a bit. Somebody offered a champagne bottle to a guard and he took a lively swig. Somebody else offered another bottle with a candle in it, and the guard set the candle on the wall and used a plastic cup to make a shield around the flame.

The people in the crowd weren't yelling or demanding anything. They weren't waiting for anything to happen. They were present from sheer glee at being alive in this place at this time. They were there to experience the opposite of the existential anguish which has been the twentieth century's designer mood. And they were happy with the big, important happiness that – the Declaration of Independence reminds us – is everybody's, even a Communist's, unalienable right to pursue.

The world's most infamous symbol of oppression had been rendered a tourist attraction overnight. Poland's political prisoners were now running its government. Bulgaria's leadership had been given the Order of the Boot. The Hungarian Communist Party wouldn't answer to its name. Three hundred thousand Czechs were tying a tin can to the Prague Politburo's tail. And the Union of Soviet Socialist Republics was looking disunified, unsoviet and not as socialist as it used to. What did it mean? The Commies didn't seem to know. The Bush administration didn't either. And you can be certain that members of the news media did not have a clue. Ideology, politics and journalism, which luxuriate in failure, are impotent in the face of hope and joy.

I booked a hotel room in East Berlin. When I arrived at the West Berlin airport a taxi dispatcher said the border crossings were so busy that I'd better take the subway to the other side. The train was filled with both kinds of Berliners, and stepping through the car doors was like walking into a natural history museum diorama of Dawn Man and his modern relations. The Easterners looked like Pleistocene proto-Germans, as yet untouched by the edifying effects of Darwinian selection. West Germans are tall, pink, pert and orthodontically corrected, with hands, teeth and hair as clean as their clothes and clothes as sharp as their looks. Except for the fact that they all speak English pretty well, they're indistinguishable from Americans. East Germans seem to have been hunching over cave fires a lot. They're short and thick with sallow, lardy fat, and they have Khrushchev warts. There's something about Marxism that brings out warts – the only kind of growth this economic system encourages.

As the train ran eastward, West Berliners kept getting off and East Berliners kept getting on until, passing under the Wall itself, I was completely surrounded by the poor buggers and all the strange purchases they'd made in the west. It was mostly common, trivial stuff, things the poorest people would have already in any free country – notebook paper, pliers and screwdrivers, corn flakes and, especially, bananas. For all the meddling the Communist bloc countries have done in banana republics, they still never seem to be able to get their hands on any actual bananas.

The East Berliners had that glad but dazed look which you see on Special Olympics participants when they're congratulated by congressmen. The man sitting next to me held a West German tabloid open to a photo of a healthy fräulein without her clothes. He had that picture fixed with a gaze to make stout Cortez on a peak in Darien into a blinking, purblind myope.

At the Friedrichstrasse station in East Berlin, passport examination was perfunctory and the customs inspection, a wave of the hand. I walked outside into a scene of shocking, festive bustle. Though, to the uninitiated, I don't suppose it would look like much – just squat, gray crowds on featureless streets. But there are never crowds in East Berlin. And the crowds had shopping bags. There's nothing to shop for in East Berlin and no bags in which to put the stuff you can't buy. Taxi drivers saw my luggage and began shouting, 'You want taxi?!' 'Taxi, ja?!' Imagine shouting that your services are for hire in East Berlin. Imagine shouting. Imagine services. I heard laughter, chatting, even giggles. I saw a cop directing traffic with bold and dramatic flourishes. I saw border guards smile. It was a regular Carnival in Rio by East Berlin standards. And, the most amazing thing of all, there was jaywalking.

I had been in East Berlin three years before. And I had been standing on a corner of a perfectly empty Karl-Marx-Allee waiting for the light to change. All Germans are good about obeying traffic signals but pre-1989 East Germans were religious. If a bulb burned out they'd wait there until the state withered away and true communism arrived. So I was standing among about a dozen East Germans, meaning to follow the custom of the country, but my mind wandered and without thinking I stepped out into the street against the light. They all followed me. Then I realized I'd walked into the path of a speeding army truck. I froze in confusion. They froze in confusion. Finally I jumped back on the curb. And they did too, but not until I'd jumped first.

In 1986 I'd come through the border at Checkpoint Charlie, and getting in was a dreary and humiliating experience similar to visiting a brother-in-law in prison. There was much going through pairs of electrically locked doors and standing before counters fronted with bulletproof glass while young dolts in uniforms gave you the fish-eye. There were an inordinate number of 'NO EXIT!' signs, and I remember thinking the exclamation points were a nice touch.

You had to exchange twenty-five perfectly good West German marks, worth about fifty cents apiece, for twenty-five perfectly useless East German marks, worth nothing. I thought I'd see how fast I could blow my stack of East marks on the theory that the test of any society's strength and vigor is how quickly it Handi-Vacs your wallet.

I walked to Unter den Linden, old Berlin's Champs Elysées. The city was empty feeling, no construction noise, no music, no billboards or flashing lights. There were plenty of people around but they all seemed to be avoiding one another like patrons at a pornographic movie theater and, although it was a beautiful spring day, the East Berliners were moving with their shoulders hunched and heads turned down as though they were walking in the rain. The women were frumps but the men bore an odd resemblance to trendy New Yorkers. They had the same pallor and mixing-bowl haircuts. They wore the same funny, tight high-water pants with black clown shoes as big as rowboats and the same ugly 1950s geometric-patterned shirts buttoned to the neck. Except the East Berlin guys weren't kidding. This wasn't a style. These were their clothes.

Unter den Linden's six lanes served only a few deformed East German Wartburg sedans and some midget Trabant cars. The Trabants had two-cycle engines and made a sound like a coffee can full of steel washers and bees. They looked like they were made of plastic because they were. Other than that the traffic was mostly blimp-sized double-length articulated buses progressing down the vacant avenue at the speed of Dutch Elm disease.

The store windows were full of goods, however: a fifty-bottle pyramid of Rumanian berry liqueur, a hundred Russian nesting dolls, a whole enormous display devoted entirely to blue plastic toothbrushes with the bristles already falling out. The huge Centrum department store smelled as though the clothes were made from wet dogs. The knit dresses were already unraveling on their hangers. The sweaters were pilling on the shelves. The raincoats were made out of what looked like vinyl wallpaper. And there were thirty or forty people in line to buy anything, anything at all, that was for sale.

I went to a bar in the showplace Palace of the Republic. It took me thirty minutes to be waited on although there were two bartenders and only five other people in the place. The two bartenders were pretty busy washing out the bar's highball glass. I was amazed to see 'Manhattan' listed on the drink menu and ordered it and should have known better. There was some kind of alcohol, but definitely not whiskey, in the thing and the sweet vermouth had been replaced with ersatz sloe gin.

Next, I stood in line for half an hour to see what Marxism could do to street-vendor pizza. It did not disappoint. The word *cottony* is sometimes used to describe bad pizza dough, but there was every reason to believe this pizza was really made of the stuff, or maybe a polyester blend. The slice – more accurately, lump – had no tomato whatsoever and was covered in a semiviscous imitation mozzarella, remarkably uncheeselike even for a coal-tar by-product. Then there was the sausage topping. One bite brought a flood of nostalgia. Nobody who's been through a fraternity initiation will ever forget this taste, this smell. It was dog food.

I went back to Checkpoint Charlie. You weren't allowed to take East German money out of the country. I don't know why. It's not like there was anything you could do with it in the west. The bills are too small for house-training puppies. But East Germany was so total in its totalitarianism that everything was banned which wasn't compulsory. Anyway, when I went through customs a dour official in his early twenties said, 'Have you any currency of the German Democratic Republic?'

'Nope,' I said. 'I spent it all.'

He looked skeptical, as well he might have. 'Empty pockets, *bitte*,' he ordered. I had twenty-one marks left over.

'Well, I'm coming back tomorrow,' I said.

His expression changed for a moment to boyish amazement. 'You *are*?' He resumed his governmental frown. 'This once I will allow you to retain these currencies because you are coming back tomorrow,' he said and rolled his eyes.

I did come back and this time couldn't find anything at all to spend money on. The only excitement available in East Berlin seemed to be opening the subway car doors and getting off the train before it came to a complete halt. But I couldn't figure out how to pay the subway fare so I couldn't even spend my money on this. I walked back toward Checkpoint Charlie with forty-six marks in my pocket. Then I did something my capitalist soul had never allowed me to do before in my life. I crumpled up money and threw it in a garbage can.

There was no question of throwing money away on my 1989 visit to East Berlin. The glimmering new Grand Hotel, standing on that very corner where the garbage can had been, accepted only hard currency. In return you got food you could swallow and Johnnie Walker Scotch at the bar (although something described as 'cod liver in oil' still lurked on the restaurant menu).

There had been changes for the regular citizens of East Berlin as well. There were three or four times as many shops on the streets, some with pseudo-boutique names like 'Medallion', 'Panda' and 'Joker'. The stuff for sale was awful enough, but there was more of it. Thus at least half the law of supply and demand was being obeyed – if something's lousy, it's always available. The first line-up of shoppers I saw turned out to be waiting for an antique shop to open. The new Wartburg 353 models even had styling – not much styling and that borrowed from 1960s Saabs, but styling none the less.

However, the real change was the lack of fear, a palpable physical absence like letting go of your end of a piano. My note-taking – which in 1986 would have sent passers-by scuttling like roaches surprised in a kitchen – now went unremarked. American reporters were all over the place, of course. And in every hotel lobby and café you could hear East Germans griping loudly to the reporters while the reporters loudly explained how all this was feeling to the people of East Germany.

There were pictures everywhere of the new East German leader, Egon Krenz, just as there'd been pictures everywhere of the old East German leader, Erich Honecker. But these weren't the lifted chin, stalwart forward-looker vanguarding the masses photos. Egon – who resembles a demented nephew of Danny Thomas's – was shown spreading hugs around, tousling toddler mop-tops and doing the grip-and-grin at various humble functions. He was politicking, plain and simple. The Commies didn't

9

quite have it right yet: they take office and *then* they run for it. But they're trying.

Personally I missed the old East Berlin. The only thing East Germany ever had going for it was a dramatic and sinister *film noir* atmosphere. When you passed through Checkpoint Charlie the movie footage seemed to switch to black and white. Steam rose from manhole covers. Newspapers blew down wet, empty streets. You'd turn your trench coat collar up, hum a few bars of 'Lili Marlene' and say to yourself, 'This is me in East Berlin.'

That's gone now and the place is revealed for what it's really been all along, just a screwed-up poor country with a dictatorship. The dictatorship part is understandable, but how the Commies managed to make a poor country out of a nation full of Germans is a mystery. The huge demonstrations that had shaken East Germany for the past several months had one characteristic which distinguished them from all other huge demonstrations in history – they never began until after work. I went to one of these at Humboldt University. The students were demanding economics courses. It was hard to reconcile this with my own memories of student protest. We were demanding free dope for life.

The students were also protesting the opening of the Wall. Not that they were against it. But they were furious that the East German government might think this was all it had to do. One picket sign showed a caricature of East Berlin's party boss, Gunther Schabowski, naked with a banana stuck in every orifice and a balloon reading, 'Free at last!' No one made any attempt to break up the rally. Soldiers and police were there, but they were applauding the speakers.

Even though the guard dogs and the machine-gun nests were gone, the east side of the Berlin Wall was still pristine, smooth whitewashed pre-cast reinforced-concrete slabs a foot thick and ten feet high and separated from the rest of the city by thirty yards of police. On the west side, the Wall was in your face and covered with graffiti paint as thick as ravioli.

I went out Checkpoint Charlie – with nobody worrying over

what I might do with my East German marks – and turned right on Zimmer Strasse, what Berliners call 'Wall Street' because the Wall runs along the old curbstone, leaving only a sidewalk in front of the West Berlin buildings. There was a steely, rhythmic noise that, for a moment, I thought might be some new Kraftwerk-style European synthesizer music (Berliners are horribly up-to-date with that sort of thing). But it was the sound of hundreds of people going at the Wall with hammers, chisels, picks, sledges, screwdrivers and even pocket knives. The chipping and flaking had progressed in a week until long, mouse-gnawed-looking ellipses were appearing between the slabs with daylight and occasional glimpses of East German border guards visible on the other side. I saw thirty schoolchildren on a class excursion with their teacher, all beating the Wall in unison with rocks, sticks and anything that came to hand.

I talked to a man in his sixties who was going along the Wall with a rucksack and a geologist's hammer. He'd escaped from the East in 1980. He'd been in prison over there for his political opinions. He gestured at the layers of spray-painting, the hundreds of symbols, slogans and messages ranging from John Lennon quotes to 'Fuck the IRA'. 'I want one piece of every color,' he said.

A twenty-year-old West German named Heiko Lemke was attacking the Wall with a set of professional stonemason's tools. In two days he'd made a hole big enough to pass a house cat through, even though the police had twice confiscated his cold chisels – the West German police. During a one-minute breather Lemke said he was an engineering student, a supporter of the Christian Democratic Party, didn't want history to repeat itself and was going to come back to the Wall on the weekend with some serious equipment.

. Two American teenagers, Neville Finnis and Daniel Sheire, from Berlin's English-language JFK high school, were attempting to rip the top off one section of the Wall with their bare hands. The Wall is capped with six-foot-long two-hundred-pound half pipes cast in ferroconcrete. These need to be lifted nearly a foot in the air before their edges clear the cement slab and they can be heaved to the ground. Neville and Daniel straddled the wall, in postures that would bring dollar signs to the eyes of any hernia surgeon, and lifted. When that didn't work, two more JFK students got up on the Wall and lifted Neville and Daniel while Neville and Daniel lifted the half-pipe. 'Go for it! Go for it!' they yelled at each other. It was an American, rather than a scientific or methodical, approach. The half-pipe landed with a great thump. The political message was clear to all the JFK students. 'Yeah!' shouted one. 'Let's sell it!'

The East German border guards didn't interfere. Instead they came up to openings in the Wall and made V signs and posed for photographs. One of them even stuck his hand through and asked would somebody please give him a piece of concrete to keep as a souvenir.

The hand of that border guard – that disembodied, palm-up, begging hand . . . I looked at that and I began to cry.

I really didn't understand before that moment, I didn't realize until just then – we won. The Free World won the Cold War. The fight against life-hating, soul-denying, slavish communism – which has shaped the world's politics this whole wretched century – was over.

The tears of victory ran down my face – and the snot of victory did too because it was a pretty cold day. I was blubbering like a lottery winner.

All the people who had been sent to gulags, who'd been crushed in the streets of Budapest, Prague and Warsaw, the soldiers who'd died in Korea and my friends and classmates who had been killed in Vietnam – it meant something now. All the treasure that we in America had poured into guns, planes, Star Wars and all the terrifying A-bombs we'd had to build and keep – it wasn't for nothing.

And I didn't get it until just then, when I saw that border guard's hand. And I think there are a lot of people who haven't gotten it yet. Our own President Bush seems to regard the events in Eastern Europe as some kind of odd dance craze or something. When I got back to the United States, I was looking through the magazines and newspapers and it seemed that all I saw were editorial writers pulling long faces about 'Whither a United Germany' and 'Whence America's Adjustments to the New Realities in Europe'. Is that the kind of noise people were making in Times Square on V-E Day?

I say, Shut-up you egghead flap-gums. We've got the whole rest of history to sweat the small stuff. And those discredited peace creeps, they can zip their soup-coolers, too. They think Mikhail Gorbachev is a visionary? Yeah, he's a visionary. Like Hirohito was after Nagasaki. We won. And let's not let anybody forget it. We the people, the free and equal citizens of democracies, we living exemplars of the Rights of Man tore a new asshole in International Communism. Their wall is breached. Their gutstring is busted. The rot of their dead body politic fills the nostrils of the earth with a glorious stink. We cleaned the clock of Marxism. We mopped the floor with them. We ran the Reds through the wringer and hung them out to dry. The privileges of liberty and the sanctity of the individual went out and whipped butt.

And the best thing about our victory is the way we did it – not just with ICBMs and Green Berets and aid to the Contras. Those things were important, but in the end we beat them with Levi 501 jeans. Seventy-two years of communist indoctrination and propaganda was drowned out by a three-ounce Sony Walkman. A huge totalitarian system with all its tanks and guns, gulag camps and secret police has been brought to its knees because nobody wants to wear Bulgarian shoes. They may have had the soldiers and the warheads and the fine-sounding ideology that suckered the college students and nitwit Third Worlders, but we had all the fun. Now they're lunch, and we're number one on the planet.

It made me want to do a little sack dance right there in the Cold War's end zone. We're the best! We're the greatest! The only undefeated socio-economic system in the league! I wanted to get up on the Wall and really rub it in: 'Taste the ash-heap of history, you Bolshie nose-wipes!' But there was nobody to jeer at. Everyone over there was in West Berlin watching Paula Abdul videos.

DEMOCRACY
IN

Paraguay, # ITS

April 1989 # DIAPERS

Asunción, Paraguay, is farther from New York than Moscow. Not that it matters how far away a thing is if you don't know where it's at. My friends couldn't quite place Paraguay. Most of them thought Paraguay was where Uruguay is. Others thought it was between Colombia and Peru. And one young lady – a college graduate – had it confused with Papua New Guinea. Paraguay is the difference between a B and a B– on a geography exam, or would be if people took geography anymore, which they don't. United States diplomats privately refer to Paraguay as 'the Tibet of South America'. (Though the mystical religion of Paraguay has never caught on with New Age types because there's no such thing as Tantric Catholicism.) Paraguay is nowhere and it's famous for nothing.

Or almost nothing. Paraguay has been a popular hiding place for Nazi war criminals such as Josef Mengele because when a Nazi war criminal hides in Paraguay everybody goes looking for him in Uruguay and Papua New Guinea. And Paraguay used to have this classic of a tinpot dictator, General Alfredo Stroessner, who'd been *El Sleazo Caudillo* since 1954. They don't make them like the Stroess anymore. Stroessner was so old and nasty that if Latin America were a soap opera – and some argue it is – you could cast him as the cold, disciplinarian dad that young,

14

sensitive, caring Augusto Pinochet rebels against. Stroessner was all wizened and drooly and spent his days reviewing troops, sitting in the stands in a uniform copied off the cover of *Sgt Pepper's Lonely Hearts Club Band* and wearing one of those great big general hats with two pounds of brass macaroni on the brim which would fall down over his eyes while he snoozed to the lulling sound of goose steps.

In Latin America – as in any good soap opera – the worse a situation is, the longer it lasts. So it came as a surprise and a shock to everyone when Man-Mummy Stroessner got a *coup* in the *état* from his own army chief of staff, the porky, affable and corrupt General Andrés Rodríguez.

General Rodríguez promptly called for elections. Elections are a fad in the developing world for the same reason portable tape decks are a fad in the inner city. Elections and tape decks both make a lot of noise. They both attract attention. And having an election, like having a tape deck, is crucial to achieving job skills and social justice.

Suddenly Paraguay was news. Page 8, one-paragraph, wire-service-filler-item-news, but news. Dozens, okay, one dozen American reporters flew to Asunción. And US diplomats began privately referring to Paraguay as 'the *former* Tibet of South America'.

I was not prepared to love Paraguay. I was not prepared to do anything but upchuck and die after the eight-hour night flight from Miami on an Air Paraguay DC-8 older than most second wives that flew through the center of five Dr Frankenstein-your-lab-is-on-the-phone lightning storms and aboard which I was served a dinner of roast softball in oleo. But as we shuddered down out of the atmosphere dawn cut loose with that annoying beauty which I never get to see except when I'm sick to my stomach from some life disruption. Mists soft and transparent as excuses flapped across pastures the color of crap-table felt. Out on the tarmac the air was cool, moist and floral – God's Wash'n' Dri. The Paraguayan customs inspection was a most informal formality. The taxi cab, an Alfa-Romeo sedan, was old and dented but rubbed to a shine. And the taxi driver was the only taxi driver on earth able to drive from an international airport to a downtown hotel without opening his yap.

There was nothing Latin American about the ride into Asunción, no litter, no shanty towns, no remains of horrendous bus wrecks. Traffic stayed in its lane and obeyed the posted speed limit – phenomena unusual enough to trigger a police investigation in most places south of the Rio Grande. Every street was lined with palms and frangipanis and pink-blossoming bottle trees. Every street was also lined with children going cheerfully, even willingly, to school. Each face was scrubbed, each head combed just so. Uniform blouses were as white and stiff as typing paper. The little boys wore shorts. Bigger boys wore ties with all-thumb four-in-hand knots. Teenage girls moved with the first wiggles of self-consciousness inside their modest frocks. I felt a completely unprofessional sense of cheery peace descending upon me. This is *tranquilo*, a very Paraguayan state of mind. The hotel was good. The breakfast was better. I poured myself a small restorative from the mini-bar and slept until siesta. Then I got up and took a nap.

Journalists aren't supposed to praise things. It's a violation of work rules almost as serious as buying drinks with our own money or absolving the CIA of something. Not only that, but if a journalist shows a facility for praise he's liable to be offered a job in public relations or advertising and the next thing you know he's got a big office, a huge salary and is living in a fine home with a lovely wife and swell kids – another career blown to hell. So I'm wrestling with the angel of reportage here, fully aware that good news is no news, but I can't help myself. Even a person with the soul of a foreign correspondent has to like something sometime, and I like Paraguay.

Asunción is a city with about the same population as Austin, Texas. It is built on unassuming hills overlooking a New York Harbor-sized backwater of the River Paraguay. This is the third largest river in the western hemisphere and even here, one thousand miles from its mouth on the Atlantic, its waters are so broad and calm that Paraguay hardly seems to be a landlocked country. You'd think you were in some balmy coast, Florida maybe. Paraguay's climate is almost identical to Florida's but more comfortable since nobody has to wear a giant mouse costume to make a living.

Zoning is not a concept hereabouts, so Asunción is a pleasant jumble of buildings – office towers next to mansions next to little shops next to big hotels. Some of the architecture is the Río de la Plata Argentine type, a distant cousin of the Taco Bell school. And the newer buildings are that kind of modernistic which is looking so old-fashioned these days. But most of Asunción was built around the turn of the century in what's called the 'academic style', where elements of the classical, baroque and beaux-arts were gathered higgledy-piggledy and set down hodgepodge in painted stucco instead of carved stone. It's a kind of imitation European façade I've only seen in one other place – Russia. The design influences are French and Italian but the effect is subtropical Leningrad, a very relaxed subtropical Leningrad.

Asunción is *so* relaxed that there are no traffic lights or stop signs at the downtown intersections. Cars just noodle up to the corners and wave one another by. I accidentally ran a road block by the Presidential Palace and the soldiers shrugged. The whole city closes, firmly and without exception, at noon. People go out and have a few drinks and a big lunch. Then they go home, make love, doze, take a shower, change clothes and return to work – refreshed to the point of exhaustion – at three. Stores and offices stay open until seven. Or six. Four-thirty, anyway.

Paraguay is a poor country. Twice as poor as Mexico, if you believe in statistics. Yet the people are tall and sleek. You don't see goiters or toothless mouths or milk-white eyeballs. The old women in the market stalls are well turned out. The shoeshine boys are clean and kempt. Asunción has so few beggars that they're known by name. There are slums. One of the worst is a squatter settlement on the mud flats below the cathedral. But the hovels have small yards and flowers and trees, and there's a clipped and chalk-lined soccer field in the midst of them. The cars on the streets are mostly old, but they're interesting old cars, like my airport taxi, the kind you used to see in American college towns – Volkswagen Beetles with Baja Bug front ends, comical 2CV Citroens, out-of-tune 914 Porsches with Bondo on the fenders and plumply dignified little Mercedes sedans from the 1950s. I was told that a lot of these cars were stolen in Brazil. If so, it's a tasteful and understated kind of car theft.

Another of Paraguay's happy surprises was seeing the US State Department going about its business there without a foot in its mouth or a thumb up its butt. This is because Paraguay is not a vital nation. Therefore the State Department is allowed to send a first-rate ambassador to Paraguay. Vital nations get political-appointment-type ambassadors – Arizona condominium developers who think the earth is flat but who are uniquely qualified to be ambassadors to vital nations because of the statesmanlike wisdom they exhibited in donating a jillion dollars to the Willie Horton Appreciation Day PAC in 1988. Actually, this is about what most vital nations – such as France, Israel and Japan – deserve. Anyway, the American ambassador to Paraguay, Timothy Towell, is not that type. He is educated, amusing, well-mannered and a career diplomat who even – and I'll bet this shocked the natives – savvies the lingo.

Ambassador Towell invited the American press to the embassy residence for a briefing and little sandwiches with the crusts cut off. Timothy Towell is a fine human, and the invitation proved his beautiful wife, Dane Towell, is another. Imagine having journalists in your own home and not even covering the furniture with plastic sheets first.

I'm afraid we weren't exactly the media's A team, either. None of us had the kind of wit, vision and heartfelt empathy for the underdog which characterizes, for instance, a Jane Pauley. The more important journalists were off reporting on more important elections, in Panama, Argentina, Bolivia and other countries that Americans know the whereabouts of or, anyway, get their dope from. We in the Asunción press corps called Paraguay 'The Land That Time Forgot – also *Life* and *Newsweek*'.

18

And this was one more nice thing about Paraguay, no important journalists. The clatter of rented helicopters, the yammer of electronic up-links, the hiss of inflating egos – it's impossible to get a decent siesta when important journalists are around.

I'm a particularly *un*important journalist. I can't even remember the 'Four Ws' or whether four is the number of Ws there are supposed to be. Which? Whatchamajigger? Whoa? What the fuck? It's something like that. So I was confused by the embassy briefing. Ambassador Towell kept going on and off the record. That is, sometimes when he said something he was 'Ambassador Towell'. And sometimes when he said something he was 'a highly placed diplomatic source'. True, it does make you feel mature and privileged to be spoken to off the record, like when you were a kid and your dad took you into a bar with him and on the way home he said, 'I don't think your mother has to know about this.' On the other hand it's a big responsibility trying to make sure the attractive and hospitable Towells don't wind up in the US embassy on the Ross Ice Shelf. Thus it was Ambassador Towell who said, 'I genuinely like this country,' and a highly placed diplomatic source who called it 'the former Tibet of South America'.

The gist of the briefing was that the coup had been fun. Paraguay's Presidential Palace, its Defense Department and the home of Stroessner's mistress (where the old goat was finally run to ground) are all within a few blocks of the American embassy. The diplomats got to stay up all night and use the embassy's emergency bunker and all its communications bells and whistles while mortar shells flew overhead. Maybe this doesn't sound like entertainment to you, but you have to understand that Asunción is a dull place.

'When Rodríguez came to power we assumed we were just getting a new general for an old one,' said a highly placed diplomatic source. 'Then Rodríguez did things that he said he was going to do.' The ambassador shrugged. His staff shrugged. The members of the press all shrugged.

Rodríguez has canceled the country's perennial state of emergency, eliminated censorship, legalized opposition parties, released political prisoners and welcomed exiled dissidents home. He has ordered prison torture cells destroyed, begun dismantling state economic controls and even launched a couple of corruption investigations (though not of himself). It's part of a worldwide trend in unaccountable and irrational dictator behavior.

Gorbachev, Jaruzelski, Roh Tae Woo, Pinochet – they're all acting nutty, and there have been outbreaks of freedom and democracy in such unlikely places as Estonia, Namibia, Hungary and the New York City mayoral race. Did somebody dip the International Monetary Fund debt notices in XTC? Don't tell me the CIA has finally done its job and infiltrated all these governments and is making them be good. 'Are diplomats supposed to be optimistic or cynical?' asked a highly placed diplomatic source.

That night I went out to a *parrillada*, a commercial version of that exotic Paraguayan custom known as a backyard cookout. I had a big piece of steak and a big glass of whiskey and more steak and more whiskey and a salad made out of a quarter head of iceberg lettuce – my kind of cuisine. Then I had an excellent cup of coffee, a cognac about the same vintage as that DC-8 and a big, smelly Cuban cigar. All told, it cost me eight dollars.

I walked back to the hotel with an American who'd been coming to Paraguay for a decade. At ten p.m. the downtown streets were mostly dark and wholly deserted. 'Don't worry,' said the American, 'it's safe to walk around at night. There's virtually no street crime. It has to be one of the last really safe places left in the world.' He paused as an ugly thought crossed his mind. 'I wonder if that will survive democracy, huh?'

There were some things about Paraguay which *did* make ugly thoughts cross your mind: a Nazi helmet for sale in a downtown antique store, ominously large embassies from naughty nations such as South Africa and Nationalist China, reports in the newly legal opposition press of 'secret graves' where Stroessner opponents were said to be numerous and a sign in Spanish advertising 'Von Stroheim's Tae Kwan Do Parlor' – the last an apparent effort to bring together a little bit of the worst in all the world's cultures. Also, for a country with only four and a half million people, a country that's been out of the Realpolitik loop for more than three centuries, Paraguay has a lot of war memorials, way too many.

Paraguay is a pleasant place all right, but not for the right reasons. It's not like the United States. It wasn't hard work, good luck and vigorous immigrant stock that made Paraguay nice. Paraguayan *tranquilo* is the product of a horrible and ridiculous history.

The conquistadors ignored Paraguay. It didn't have any gold. Wealth was to be gotten in farming, but the colonial Spanish were rarely tempted by manual labor. Madrid let missionaries do whatever they wanted with the place. In 1609 the Jesuits began gathering up the nomadic Indians, the Guaraní, and putting them into *reductions*. These were theocratic agricultural communes of about three thousand people where the Indians could be drilled in the use of Christian sacraments and the moldboard plow. Eventually some hundred thousand Guaranís were 'reduced'. The Spanish Jesuits, who wanted the Indians' souls for God, were quite brave about fighting off the Brazilian *banderiantes* who wanted the Indians' bodies for slavery. For this reason, and because the Jesuits didn't kill Guaranís or rape their women very often, the *reductions* of Paraguay became famous examples of utopia and the subject of a Robert de Niro movie, *The Mission*. Voltaire, Jesuit-hater though he was, called the *reductions* 'the triumph of humanity, expiating the cruelties of the first conquerors' and set part of *Candide* in Paraguay. Robert Southey, one of England's less talented poet laureates, wrote an immense poem about this alleged paradise:

> For in history's mournful map, the eye
> On Paraguay, as on a sunny spot,
> May rest complacent: to humanity,
> There, and there only, hath a peaceful lot
> Been granted, by Ambition troubled not . . .
> Etc., etc., etc., etc.

The *reductions* preserved Guaraní culture. Today ninety per cent of Paraguayans speak the Guaraní language. But at what cost, nobody ever bothered to ask the Guaranís. Perhaps the *reductions* were as pleasant as the collective farms we've seen in this century in the Ukraine and China. Anyway, when the Jesuits were kicked out of the New World in 1766, the Guaranís skedaddled and the *reductions* collapsed. This is generally called a tragedy in Paraguayan history, but it's hard to say where tragedies leave off and benefits begin in Paraguay.

The nation achieved independence in 1811 without firing a shot at the Spanish. There's some doubt if Spain even noticed. Paraguay was promptly taken over by a lunatic (and national hero) named Dr José Gaspar Rodriguez Francia. Dr Francia – elected *El Supremo* for life in 1814 – forced the Spanish upper class to intermarry with the *mestizos*. He forbade newspapers, fiestas and foreign trade. The clergy was suppressed. No one was allowed to emigrate. Immigrants were arrested and put to forced labor. Francia leveled Asunción and laid new avenues in a formal grid for fear conspirators might lurk in twisty back streets. He dressed all in black except for a scarlet cape and was fanatically honest with the national treasury – possibly the reason he was never known to smile. *El Supremo* died in 1840. More than a quarter century of his loathsome rule left Paraguay culturally homogeneous, economically self-sufficient, well-defended and possessed of a large budget surplus.

The next leader, Carlos Antonio López, freed political prisoners, granted citizenship to Indians, encouraged education and foreign investment, built one of South America's first railroads and is not nearly as well thought of today as Dr Francia.

Carlos López's son, Marshal Francisco Solano López, was another hero. *El Mariscal* is revered for destroying the nation. He was trying to play Argentina off against its traditional rival, Brazil, and he somehow managed to get into a war with Brazil and Argentina both and Uruguay besides. The War of the Triple Alliance lasted from 1865 to 1870. When it was done there was hardly a Paraguay left. Fifty-five thousand square miles had been conquered and annexed and the rest of the country was occupied, razed, starved, burned and pillaged. More than half the population was dead, including *El Mariscal* and eighty per cent of the adult males. To this day one of the nicest things about Paraguay is that there's no overcrowding.

Paraguayans are very proud of the War of the Triple Alliance. 'We fought desperately because we loved our land insanely,' as one war veteran too aptly put it.

It took Paraguay more than sixty years to recover. As soon as it did, it got into another amazingly bloody conflict you've never heard of – the Chaco War. This was fought with Bolivia from 1932 through 1935. One hundred thousand soldiers were killed battling over non-existent oil deposits in the Chaco, an immense region of grassland and thornbush populated mostly by dead soldiers.

Paraguay spent the following nineteen years recovering again while having ten presidents and the odd civil war and helping make Latin America the world's governance laughingstock. Then Stroessner arrived, bringing tyranny with shelf life; and for thirty-five years Paraguay had *tranquilo* (unless, of course, you were some kind of Commie or agrarian reformer or civil libertarian big-mouth, in which case you became permanently tranquil).

I was getting pretty tranquil myself. Paraguay was making me so mellow and content that I could feel my social conscience dribbling out my ears and IQ points flaking off my head like dandruff. Before long I had the brain of a tourist. I even caught myself getting interested in church architecture.

Paraguayan church architecture is no-nonsense stuff. The churches look like horse barns with verandas. But, inside, they're real retina-thrashers. The eighteenth-century church in the town of Yaguarón contains two thousand square feet of crazed whittling, a masterpiece of Paraguayan baroque. It's as ridiculously detailed as anything from the Europe of that era but with fun Guaraní Indian touches such as drug-trip color combinations and altar chairs with armrests that turn into snakes. I took a close look at some of the carved portraits of saints, and I think the Guaranís were pulling the padres' legs vis-à-vis conversion to Christianity.

Nearby in the town of Capiatá a modern woodcarver had created a one-man museum of Guaraní mythology. The front rooms of a large Spanish colonial house were filled with life-sized, that is, living-dead-sized Guaraní bugaboos such as the Plata Yryguy, a headless dog; the Corupi, a smug, plump fellow with his penis wrapped three times around his waist; the Kaaguy Pori, which has a big tentacle for a body, another tentacle for a leg, a bunch of tentacles for arms and tentacles growing out of its nose; and the Ao-Ao, which is too terrible to discuss. How convenient for the Guaranís that they had a mythology all ready to describe the conquering Spaniards and the subsequent history of Paraguay.

Paraguay is the size of California, so I didn't tourize it all. But I put five hundred miles on the rental car and was unable to find an ugly place except the Asunción Zoo. It was a very casual and dirty zoo where most of the cages were made of chain-link fence and fastened closed with twisted bits of wire. The hippo was chewing determinedly on its chain links and seemed three-quarters of the way to an escape. I don't know much about hippos. Are they one of those animals, like alligators, that look slow but *Wild Kingdom* always tell us can run faster than a horse? A lot of other cages had birds in them. There were cages full of chickens, ducks and pigeons as though the zookeepers just caged up whatever was handy. The bear cage smelled disgusting, and the bear looked dead. The puma cage smelled worse. The female puma was sleeping something off and the male puma was trying to get romantic but didn't seem to know what part of him he was supposed to stick in what part of her, romantically speaking. One small cage in a corner had a large ugly bird in it labeled 'Yryvu' with a small placard underneath reading '*Alimentación: animales putrefactos*'. And how.

If it weren't for *tranquilo* I could probably tell you what the

Asunción Zoo says about Paraguayan society and the Paraguayan political system. But, as it was, it was just a dirty zoo.

In truth, I can't even tell you what *Paraguay* says about Paraguayan society and the Paraguayan political system. I was doing for journalism about what the puma was doing for his mate. I did look up Martin Bormann in the phone book, but I guess he had an unlisted phone number. These Nazi war criminals are getting so old anyway, what would you do with them? Shorten one leg on their walker? Put a frog in their colostomy bag? Stick a playing card in their wheelchair spokes so they make a lot of noise and are easier for the Mossad to find?

I did finally go to a campaign event, in spite of myself. I got stuck in traffic in front of one.

A speech was being given by the principal opposition leader, Domingo Laino, presidential candidate of the Authentic Radical Liberal Party. This as opposed to the Fake Conventional Stingy Party, which, I guess, is what Rodríguez represents. Laino, a youthful-ish fifty-three, bewhiskered and just slightly thick around the middle, looked like a former college activist, which is what he is. Rodríguez supporters call him 'the detestable beard'. Stroessner used to throw him in jail a lot, so he can't be all bad. On the other hand, Stroessner never killed him, so maybe he's not *that* good.

Having covered the US presidential campaigns all through 1988, I was profoundly relieved to have absolutely no idea what the issues were in this election. The usual choice in Latin America is oppression combined with economically disastrous corruption causing a left-wing insurgency versus incompetence combined with economically disastrous social programs causing a right-wing coup. Laino has a Ph.D in economics, so he probably favors incompetence.

He's an impassioned and highly indignant orator, whatever his platform. The rally had begun at 2:00 p.m. I happened by at four and the Beard was still going strong. Whenever he said anything particularly indignant, the crowd would respond with the Jesse Jackson 'The People United/Will Never Be Defeated' chant. That was about all I could make out with my bar-floor Spanish. I stood below the podium trying to imagine what was being said with such vigor.

> MY OPPONENT WEARS UNDERPANTS WITH LITTLE BUNNIES ON THEM!
> HIS DAUGHTERS KISS BOYS THEY ARE NOT ENGAGED TO!
> HE PUTS SINK WASHERS INTO THE POOR BOX AT CHRISTMAS AND HAS GIVEN INSULTING AND RIDICULOUS NAMES TO HIS DOGS!
> VOTE FOR ME, I WILL TIE THE POINTS OF HIS SHIRT COLLAR TOGETHER UNDER HIS NOSE!
> I WILL WIGGLE MY BEHIND AT HIS HOUSE!
> I WILL GO ON THE RADIO AND SAY HIS NAME IN A MOCKING TONE OF VOICE!

This was a huge improvement on listening to political speeches and understanding them.

Well, fair's fair, so I went to a Rodríguez rally, too. Colorado is the real name of Rodríguez's party and the Colorados have functioned for the past forty-two years pretty much the way Italy's Fascist party used to. All public employees and military men are required to belong and dues are withheld from their paychecks. And there's an election law, cribbed from one written by Mussolini in 1923, that automatically gives a two-thirds congressional majority to the party that steals the most votes.

The Laino speech had been given in a public park and attracted five or six thousand people. They were a seemly, middle-class bunch who walked away at the end talking enthusiastically among themselves like tennis fans after a well-played match. 'What a prepositional phrase he has!' 'Those adjectives – incredibly precise!'

The Rodríguez stumper was more for the José six-pack crowd. It was held in the municipal soccer stadium with the police and the army cordoning off surrounding streets and scores of charter buses bringing in the party faithful. There were packs of food vendors and yards of banners and bushels of fireworks and two *polca* bands (not to be confused with polka bands, which are more melodious entirely). However, the turnout was not extra-ordinary, only about twice the Laino draw.

Rodríguez spoke from the top of the stands, where he was almost obscured by his overfed coterie. They looked like sausages in suits, cooking in the TV lights and about to split their polyester-blend skins. All I could see of the big man himself was a slice of plump forehead. Though, if a forehead can smile, his was doing it. Rodríguez has been all smiles ever since the coup.

The speech itself was a dull, pleasant thing. I kept hearing the words *'democracia'* and *'patria'* and *'necesario'*. I suppose Rodríguez was saying, 'Democracy is necessary for the country and the country is necessarily for democracy and with country and democracy together we can build the democracy that's necessary for the country,' with the soldiers and the police providing the unspoken subtext, 'Vote for me and goons won't come to your house and hit you in the head with a board.'

Whenever Rodríguez said anything particularly pleasant the stadium crowd would break into the same 'People United' chant that the Laino supporters used. Despite this evidence of double-barreled Jesse Jackson influence, no anti-Americanism was heard from either party. Maybe that's a testimony to Ambassador Towell's diplomatic evenhandedness. Or maybe that shows how completely out-of-it Paraguay really is.

The stadium infield was filled with the Colorado Party's most fervid supporters getting more fervid all the time on sugar-cane rum. They were operating noisemakers and compressed air sirens and were snake-dancing and waving huge Paraguayan flags, and sometimes they were just cutting loose and running in all directions like zanies. Hundreds of Colorado Party trademark red neckerchiefs made the scene look like a scout jamboree gone amuck.

I went out on the field and was quickly accosted by a group of Rodríguez supporters so fervid they could barely walk. Laino proponents had been thrilled by the sight of press credentials. Liberals have a quaint and touching faith that truth is on their side and an even quainter faith that journalists are on the side of truth. Not these stewed conservatives. There were five of them at the violently amiable stage of inebriation. They spoke a kind of collective English where one of them could pronounce a few words and a second understood a few words and a third explained to the first pair what they'd said and heard. A fourth began a performance in mime concerning the depth of his devotion to the pudgy general, falling at last to his knees and praying in the direction of Avoirdupois André. The five of them pushed me around for a bit, reading my credentials aloud and saying 'Rolling Stone', that is, 'Roy-ee-guh Stow-nay' over and over. After which the prayerful fellow insisted I write down his official title in some sublocal Colorado Party organization. (It is the beauty of well-designed fascism that it gives every piss-ant an ant hill to piss from.) Then the fifth and largest and homeliest of the group grabbed my notebook and pen and scribbled laboriously for ten minutes. I had this screed translated later and it turned out to be something that could have come from the opposition press editorial pages. It was a demand for 'absolute democracy' and for an end to mandatory party membership and for academic and religious freedom. And it came complete with my bully's signature and his government-identity-card number.

The prayerful guy took off his red neckerchief and shook it in my face. 'Colorado – no comunista! Colorado – no comunista!' he yelled, meaning that he wore red not because he was a Communist but because he was a member of the Colorado party. (Colorado, of course, means 'red' in Spanish, not 'overpriced ski resorts and dingbats who live in Boulder and teach feminist dance therapy'.) The five of them helped one another tie the material around my head Rambo-style, except most of it wound up hanging down in front of my face so I couldn't see anything. Then they all pumped my hand and shouted adiós.

Not everybody at the Colorado rally was quite this enthusiastic. I noticed later, in the stadium men's room, that somebody had used a red neckerchief to wipe his ass.

*

28

I spent election day itself in a little town called Tobatí, fifty miles east of Asunción. This was the first even slightly honest election in the history of Paraguay, and there was some confusion about the mechanics of voting. No one under the age of sixty had ever voted for anyone but Stroessner. I watched a peasant girl arrive at one of the polling places. She was checked off on the voter registration list and had her index finger dipped in ink so she couldn't vote again until she'd washed really well. She went into the *puerta obscura*, as the Paraguayans quite appropriately call a voting booth, came back out and asked the election officials something – who to vote for, I think. They made a little speech about *democracia*. The peasant girl went inside again and returned with a Colorado ballot and a quizzical expression, 'would this be good?' The election officials waved their arms and turned their heads away. This was supposed to be a *secret* ballot. One of the officials covered his eyes and held up an envelope. The girl came out of the booth the third time with envelope and ballot folded and refolded like a love note passed in a high-school class. She and the officials together couldn't get this wad through the slot in the ballot-box lid.

Rodríguez won the election, by the way.

I guess it's like love and marriage, political freedom being so poetic and noble when people are trying to achieve it and so boring and silly in practice. Well, something poetic and noble – and thoroughly awful – will happen soon in Paraguay if the past is anything to go by. In the meanwhile – *tranquilo*.

RETURN

OF THE

DEATH OF

COMMUNISM

On the morning of the twenty-sixth, the day after Violeta Chamorro's victory over Danny Ortega, I walked into the Inter-Continental hotel in Managua and Bianca Jagger was sitting alone in the lobby. Bianca had been ubiquitous during the election campaign: there was Bianca looking smart in an unconstructed linen jacket and yellow socks to match, Bianca looking serious with press pass and camera, Bianca looking thoughtful listening to Jimmy Carter, Bianca looking concerned conferring with Senator Christopher Dodd, Bianca looking committed in simple tennis shoes and neatly mussed hair, Bianca looking important wearing sunglasses after dark. But this morning Bianca looked . . . her age. Here we had a not very bright, fortyish, discarded rock-star wife, trapped in the lonely hell of the formerly cute – one bummed-out show-biz lefty.

I was feeling great myself, ready to turn somersaults over the Ortega defeat, full of good cheer and pleased with all the world. But then the forlorn, sagging little shape of Bianca caught my eye and, all of a sudden, I felt EVEN BETTER.

I hadn't come to Nicaragua prepared for such joy. Like most readers of papers and watchers of newscasts, I thought the Sandinistas were supposed to win this one. I'm a member of the working press; you'd think I'd know better than to listen to journalists. But there's a little bit of the pigeon in every good confidence man. I even believed the 21 February ABC-*Washington Post* poll that had Ortega leading Chamorro by sixteen percentage points. That is – I blush to admit this – I accepted the results of an opinion poll taken in a country where it was illegal to hold certain opinions. You can imagine the poll-taking process: 'Hello, Mr Peasant, I'm an inquisitive and frightening stranger. God knows who I work for. Would you care to ostensibly support the dictatorship which controls every facet of your existence, or shall we put you down as in favor of the UNO opposition and just tear up your ration card here and now?'

Furthermore, when I arrived in Nicaragua I found an Ortega political machine that was positively Bushian in its relentless drumming on the issue-free upbeat. Danny's smiling (I presume they used a photo retoucher) face and Danny's heartthrob-of-the-poli-sci-department moustache were everywhere to be seen. As was Danny – pestering babies, attempting dance steps, wearing Ed Begley, Jr, the-dog-was-sick-on-the-carpet shirts and tossing free baseballs into crowds of squealing totalitarianism fans. The Sandinistas' black and red, Doberman-mouth party colors were painted anyplace paint could stick. Sandinista songs played from every radio. The Danny for President slogan *todo sera mejor* (meaning 'everything will be better' and not, as I momentarily thought, 'major dried toads') was as perfect an all-purpose campaign promise as I have ever heard. There were Sandinista music videos with singing and dancing that could send Paula Abdul back to wagging pom-poms for the LA Lakers. And there were Sandinista ad campaigns tailored to every segment of the electorate. A billboard for city youth (the voting age is sixteen in Nicaragua) showed a moonstruck couple in Ortega T-shirts walking hand-in-hand toward a voting booth beneath the headline 'When you do it for the first time, do it for love.' Banners for the countryside showed a fierce portrait of Ortega with the motto *Daniel Es Mi Gallo*, 'Daniel Is My Fighting Cock'. (These can now be profitably recycled by the Kentucky Fried Chicken franchise outlets soon to open in Nicaragua.)

I confess I believed the Sandys had all the corners nailed down, and I spent the last couple of days before the election committing that original sin of journalism, 'writing the lead on the way to the ballpark'. What was I going to say about a loathsome Sandinista victory? I supposed I'd have to natter on about the unfair advantages of using state resources for party ends, about how Sandinista control of the transit system prevented UNO supporters from attending rallies, how Sandinista domination of the army forced soldiers to vote for Ortega and how Sandinista bureaucracy kept $3.3 million of US campaign aid from getting to UNO while Danny spent three million donated by overseas pinks and millions and millions more from the Nicaraguan treasury, etc.

But this seemed like weak-tea, crybaby stuff. No, I thought, I'll have to go shoveling in the manure pile of political science, trying to uncover the appeal that Marxism and other infantile world views still hold for people. One nice thing about being a conservative, at least I wouldn't feel betrayed by the masses. Democracy is only one of human liberty's safeguards and not always the most effective one. Back in the US we've got a House of Representatives full of bed-wetting liberals to prove it.

THE DOG IS DEAD BUT THE TAIL STILL WAGS.

That was what I planned to call this piece. (It's still a good title – I'll save it for my review of Christopher Hitchens' next book.)

Thus I was in a grim frame of mind when I went to the press conference held by that most ex- of America's ex-presidents, Jimmy Carter. The press conference was at the Sandinista's imposing media complex, one of the few buildings in Managua that won't fall down if you piss against the side of it. This propaganda palace was built with money donated by patsy Swedes, named after their bumped-off prime minister, Olof Palme, and hence called, by the small contingent of conservatives present, the 'Good Socialist Press Center'.

Carter was the head of one of the three principal international election-monitoring groups which were fluttering around Nicaragua pronouncing everything they saw fair and equitable. There was the United Nations ('the turkeys'), the Organization of American States ('the chickens') and Carter's group, the Council of Freely Elected Heads of Government ('the geese').

What Carter thought he was doing, besides proving there are worse things than Marines that the US can send to Nicaragua, I don't know. But there he was, the man who gave the store away in the first place, still grinning like a raccoon eating fish guts out of a wire brush and still talking in that prissy, nose-first, goober-grabber accent, except this time in Spanish: ' . . . new-WAY-vuh Knicker-RAH-wuh deh-muh-crat-TICK-uh . . . '

Carter oozed moral equivalence. 'There have been serious problems in the campaign process on both sides,' said Carter. 'We have to give credit to the Nicaraguan people for establishing an excellent electoral process,' said Carter. 'If the election is certified as honest and fair, the United States should lift sanctions,' said Carter. It's a shame Jimmy was too young to be an international observer at Germany's elections in 1932. 'We have to give credit to the German people for establishing an excellent electoral process.' Maybe he could have given Hitler some help rearming.

The 'press' at the press conference was a dirty and confused bunch, even by press corps standards. Inspection of credentials showed most of them to be correspondents for the Xeroxed newsletter of the Berkeley High-Colonic Liberation Front or television reporters from the Ann Arbor Reincarnation for Peace Coalition's public-access cable program. When a genuine newsman asked Carter about a report of UNO poll-watchers being arrested, the backpack journalists hissed.

A number of celebrity fellow travelers were in Nicaragua for the vote-off – Jackson Browne, Jimmy Cliff, the Sandinistas' Washington lawyer Paul (where's-the-Smith-Act-when-we-need-it) Reichler and Ed Asner, who didn't look like he'd missed any meals due to the injustice of the capitalist economic system. But the real show was the *sandalistas*, prosperous, educated lefties from the United States who've flocked to Nicaragua for a decade to . . . well, to *help*. Although it's something of a puzzle why rebellious middle-class Americans went to Nicaragua to help Sandinistas wreck Central America, instead of, say, going to South Africa to help Boers chase schoolchildren with whips, or to Uganda to help Idi Amin eat people.

Some say the *sandalistas* are just young and dumb. But those folks are only half right. At first glance the Birkenstock Bolshies seem young. They wear 'youth' clothes and have adolescent body language – constantly distributing hugs and touches and squirming with emotion rather than sitting still in thought. But, looking closely at the uniform ponytails and earrings (many of the women wear them too), I noticed the tresses that were still long in back were oft-times gone on top, and the lady *sandalistas*, their underarm hair was streaked with gray.

A number of college-age kids were present, too – earnest and homely and not at all the type who would have been lefties in my day of high-fashion revolt. In 1968 these kids would have been in the ham radio club or Future Stenographers of America.

The Ortega-snugglers were dressed as though they were going to a Weather Underground Days of Rage costume party. They were all in jean skirts and drawstring pants, clogs, folk-art jewelry and tie-dyed tank tops – fashions fully twenty years out of style. I wonder what my hip friends and I in the summer of love would have thought about people wearing zoot suit jackets and reat pleat pants with key chains dangling to the ground.

The Carter press conference was on Saturday morning, the day before the election. That afternoon I attended a less complacent press conference given by the Center for Democracy at the Inter-Continental Hotel. The same bunch of backpack journalists were here, too, hissing even before anybody asked a question. Some of these life-style leftovers had gone so far as to don the red and black Sandinista neckerchief, which, like the neckerchief of Paraguay's fascist Colorado Party, is an item of apparel identical to that worn by the Boy Scouts of America. In Nicaragua the effect was of a scout troop gone deeply, seriously wrong, growing

34

older and older but never graduating to Explorer and earning merit badges in 'Lenin', 'marijuana' and 'poor hygiene'.

I hadn't been keeping up to speed on Nicaraguan nonsense and had no idea why the lefties were heckling the Center for Democracy. The Center is one of those painstakingly bipartisan, painfully fair organizations that I usually heckle myself. CFD was the first election-monitoring group invited to Nicaragua. It was invited by both sides and had been observing the election campaign since the spring of last year. But now the CFD's credentials were downgraded so that its observers couldn't enter polling places, and more than fifty CFD observers had been denied Nicaraguan visas at the last minute.

The trouble was, the Center for Democracy had gotten caught telling the truth. CFD observers were at a UNO rally in the town of Masatepe on 10 December 1989, and they saw a Sandinista mob set upon Chamorro supporters with machetes. The mob killed one person and chopped the arms off a couple of others while the Sandinista police stood around like potted palms. Now, it's all right for observer groups to observe such things, that's what they're there for. But if the Sandinistas had wanted truth-telling groups, that's what they would have asked for. The OAS observers at the Masatepe rally obligingly waffled and claimed 'both sides' were to blame. But the CFD delegation – which included such dyed-in-the-hair-shirt liberals as Bob Beckel – was outraged by the Sandinista attack and said so.

Thus the press conference questions directed to Center for Democracy president Allen Weinstein weren't questions at all but diatribes capped with little rhetorical inquisitions such as, 'How are you going to overcome your bias?' and, 'Don't you think it's idiosyncratic that yours is the only observer group complaining about credential problems?' after which half the press conference attendees would clap. One particularly impassioned and bearded fellow named Carlos, a professor at Glendale College in California, where he teaches 'Chicano Studies', explained how the fact that the CFD was an observer group in the first place and came to Nicaragua at all proved its members had no respect for Nicaraguan sovereignty.

*

I'd gone to Nicaragua with the head of the National Forum Foundation, Jim Denton. Forum has been sponsoring interns from newly de-communized Eastern Europe, bringing them to the United States so that they can see how democratic institutions work and can learn to avoid making terrible mistakes like electing Jimmy Carter. Denton took two of these interns, Slawek Gorecki from Poland and Martin Weiss from Czechoslovakia, to Managua. Jim and I thought the *sandalistas* were funny. Martin and Slawek did not. They were sickened and enraged that citizens of a free nation would go somewhere to promote dictatorship. Even more than disgusted, they were mystified. Trying to explain American lefties to Martin and Slawek was like – simile fails me – trying to explain American lefties to two reasonable and intelligent people who'd never seen any.

Martin and Slawek – and Jim and I too, for that matter – preferred meeting with Commandante Raphael Solis, President of the Sandinista National Assembly. Here was a comprehensible scum bag, somebody who was making a buck off the evil he espoused.

Solis was master of the world-weary idealist act – lots of rueful smiles and care-laden brow rubs. His manners were gracious and welcoming, his grin warm and genuine. He was the kind of Commie who'd never ship anyone to a concentration camp in a boxcar; he'd send them in a taxi.

Solis said he was confident of an Ortega victory and of a large majority in the new National Assembly. But was he? With the improved sensitivity and increased intelligence that hindsight brings, I detect some loyal-opposition bullpen warm-up from Solis. He claimed he was looking forward to national reconciliation and hoped the UNO parties would play a part in it. He dismissed the statement by Interior Minister (and head of the secret police) Tomas Borge that the Sandinistas were 'prepared to lose the election but not to lose power'.

'That is,' said Solis with the aplomb of a born politician, 'campaign rhetoric'. He touted a '*perestroika* atmosphere' in Nicaragua, predicted 'foreign-policy compromises' and, in response to needling from Slawek he said, 'As to the changes in Eastern

Europe, I haven't heard any criticism from the Sandinista leadership. We think these changes are positive, democratic.' And he went on to claim that Nicaragua would be making the same changes soon and, also, had made them already.

At sunrise on election morning we headed around Lake Managua and north into the mountains, visiting polling places in Sebaco and Matagalpa and little villages in between. Then we drove further north to Jinotega in what had been Contra territory. Everywhere we went it was the same: awful roads through beautiful scenery to lousy towns. The whole country is cracked, shattered, dirty, worn-out. Everything dates from the Somoza era or before. Ten years of revolution have produced nothing but the Olof Palme Press Center. Even the lamest People's Republic cosmetic touches were missing. Sandinista graffiti is the only fresh paint in Nicaragua. The nation looks – and smells – like that paradigm of socialism, a public restroom.

The voting was done in dingy schoolrooms with all the window glass broken or missing and bare wires running across the ceiling to fifteen-watt light bulbs. Every voter had the ballot-marking process explained to him personally so that the election went forward at the speed of mammal evolution. People were waiting in line by the hundreds to vote.

Each polling place was run by a brisk, snippy, managing Sandinista woman of middle age, the kind of woman who, in a free society, is known as 'my first wife'. Denton, Martin, Slawek and I didn't have the proper credentials to enter polling places, but we did anyway and, for the most part, got away with it – though at the price of being treated like ex-husbands.

The UN, the OAS and the Carter group were all going around doing about the same thing we were in the way of checking for vote fraud. That is, they popped their heads in and made sure there was no Sandinista with a pistol in a toddler's ear saying, 'Vote for Danny or the rug monkey gets it.' We didn't see any cheating like that, and the UN, the OAS and the Carter group said they didn't either.

We did see a truckload of soldiers being hauled around to vote. 'Who are you for?' we yelled. '*Cinco*! *Cinco*!' they shouted, holding up five fingers to indicate they were voting for the fifth line on the ballot, the Sandinistas. 'Uno', said one little fellow in the back, and they all giggled and made as if to pummel him.

In the village of San Ramón we saw some horseplay. The men and women had decided to get in separate lines. Then the line of men shoved the line of women off the school porch and into the rain. The women confided to us that the men were going to vote for Ortega.

And we saw former Democratic presidential hopeful Bruce Babbitt standing around at one polling place, looking clueless. Jim Denton said, 'That's Bruce Babbitt,' but for the life of me I couldn't remember who Bruce Babbitt was. I guess this tells us all we need to know about Bruce's political future.

The only Nicaraguan we heard complain was a guy who wasn't allowed to vote because he was drunk. 'He admits that he's drunk,' the Sandinista policeman told us. 'Everybody makes mistakes,' the drunk told us. And we told the policeman, 'They let Teddy Kennedy vote in the Senate.'

When we came back through Sebaco late in the afternoon, some of the same people who'd been standing in line to vote at seven that morning were still waiting. 'We've been in line since four in the morning, since three in the morning, since two in the morning,' one person told us with cheerful rural vagueness about time. 'And if it is necessary we will stay here until . . . *ten*!' said another man, naming the latest hour of the evening he could think of offhand.

Of course people don't stand in line for twelve hours in drizzly weather at the ass end of nowhere to vote for the status quo. So there were three hints I'd been given that Ortega might lose. But there's no getting through to the highly perceptive. It wasn't until another journalist told me the Sandinistas were in trouble that I believed it.

We'd gone back to the Olof Palme Center to wait for returns.

Around 11:00 p.m. a network television newsman with (don't be shocked) left-wing connections came by looking agitated. 'P.J., I was just over at Sandy headquarters and something's gone seriously wrong,' he said, meaning the opposite. 'All of Ortega's people are really upset. The early returns show them getting . . .' Getting what the billboard said when you do for the first time, you should do for love.

The UNO people had heard the same buzz and were in a mood of contained but swollen hope. Chamorro's coalition was holding its election-night party at a restaurant in one of Managua's few remaining middle-class enclaves. The crowd was a model of bourgeois propriety. Occasionally someone would stand on a chair and say, *'Viva UNO'* in a loud voice, but that was about it. The place was all clean shirts, hearty handshakes, polite honorifics and, 'How's your brother in Miami?' It was difficult to picture these decent, hard-working, prosperous, commonsensical people overthrowing a government. Sometimes it's hard to remember that bourgeois propriety is the real revolutionary force these days. All over the world we're bringing down dictatorships – or at least forcing them to go condo.

The Sandinista 'victory party' was, on the other hand, a massive street disco populated by kids who in the US would have been selling crack, getting the name of their favorite heavy metal band tattooed on their butts or planning a drive-by shooting. These are the last people on earth that *sandalista* types would consort with back home. But all sorts of big, homely dirty-haired American girls in stained T-shirts and dweeby little chicken-necked American boys in ripped jeans were fraternizing the hell out of the lumpen Nicaraguans (who were dressed in their Sunday best, by the way).

There was no evidence of Danny difficulties at the street dance, really no trace of politics except the general air of thuggishness that hangs over all 'mass' political movements. Lots of beer and cane liquor was being consumed and much smooching in the shadows was being done and fistfights and lunch-blowings were beginning to dot the crowd. After half an hour of walking around with our hands over our wallet pockets, we decided our little group of *wing-tipistas* belonged back at the Chamorro party or – even better by the standards of the bourgeois propriety revolution now afoot – asleep in our beds.

I awoke to the sound of lugubrious Spanish on the television. It was Danny Boy giving his concession speech, old Landslide Daniel. I understand Jimmy Carter had tracked Danny down in the middle of the night and told him – loser-to-loser – the jig was up. The Sandinistas had done everything they could to ensure the validity of this election in the eyes of the world. Now they had to eat what they had cooked. Quite a bit of 'crow in red sauce' was served around the globe in 1989 and '90.

Danny's speech was a long one. There are no brief excuses for communism. And it was punctuated with more pauses for dramatic effect than a high school production of *Macbeth*. Lined up behind Daniel was most of the Sandinista *nomenklatura*, pouting and sniffling and generally looking like dear Uncle Bill had died and left his fortune to the cat. At the end of Danny's speech, he and his pals raised their fists in the air and warbled the Sandinista battle anthem, the one with the last line about Yankees being 'the enemies of all humankind', singing us farewell in the manner of the Mickey Mouse Club, except this crowd couldn't carry a tune on a shovel. The TV cameras pulled back to show the Olof Palme press corps singing along through their tears.

Me, I was singing myself, making up little tunes and dancing and capering around:

> *Benjamin Linder was blown to a flinder,*
> *Dennis Wilson run o'er by a train,*
> *Now it's hasta luego to Danny Ortega,*
> *And United Fruit's come back again!*

I rushed out to gloat. I especially wanted to gloat over the Americans – the ripe-suck liberals and MasterCard Marxists – see them backing and filling and blowing smoke out their pants cuffs. At the Inter-Continental, across the lobby from Bianca, Paul Reichler was excusing the Nicaraguan people to the news media, saying they had 'voted with their stomach'. The poor misguided fools. I suppose they should have voted with their ____hole, Paul Reichler. A few yards away that human rum-blossom Senator Chris Dodd was telling reporters the election 'wasn't a victory for UNO. The Nicaraguan people just wanted change.' Yes, yes. And the 1988 presidential race wasn't a victory for Republicans either. The American people just wanted Michael Dukakis ground into a heap and sold as fiber supplement.

Driving through the streets of Managua, seeing American hippy-dips all fiddle-faced and dejected, it was hard to resist the temptation to yell things out the car window. 'Get a job!' Or, 'What's the matter with your legs, toots, don't you know "Fur is dead"?' In fact I couldn't resist it. My favorite thing to do was just make a little pistol motion with my hand and shout, 'Nicolae Ceausescu!!!'

I headed for the Olof Palme Center to rank on the backpack journalists. Oh, it was almost too sweet for telling, how they bellyached and sourpussed and went around in sulks. Carlos, the professor of 'Chicano Studies', tried to look on the sunny side. 'We can't abandon the people of Nicaragua,' he said with a straight face, and, 'The struggle will continue. People will be even more committed.' But in the end, Carlos was reduced to racism in his attempt to explain why the polls said Danny would win but the voters said otherwise. 'It's the Latino culture,' said Carlos. 'People love to say one thing and do another.'

The younger *sandalistas* looked like they'd just seen Lee Atwater open for the Grateful Dead. They weren't angry, really, just deeply, deeply disappointed. Here they'd blown their semester break and Mom was going to have a cow when she got the VISA bill for the plane ticket, and then the Nicaraguan people went and let them down like this. But the old *sandalistas*, the New Left geezers, they looked like they'd gone to hell in a bong. It's into the trash can with this sixties litter, and you could see they knew it. They looked like Abbie Hoffman was looking the last couple of years of his life, as though every night when they go to sleep a BMW chases them through their dreams.

*

41

And in that BMW, or hoping to be there soon, were all the regular Nicaraguans down at the Eastern Market.

Were they surprised that UNO won? They laughed. 'We expected victory, especially the mothers,' said a mother.

'All the mothers are happy,' said another mom.

'We hope Violeta fulfills her promises,' said the proprietess of a shoe store. 'Or we'll get rid of her too,' she added in the tone of an experienced democrat.

'If Ortega doesn't give in, the people will rise up,' said a cobbler. 'We have *other countries* that will help us.' And he nodded toward the Congressional Press Gallery ID I was wearing around my neck.

'What about the polls?' I asked. 'Why were they so wrong?'

'People were afraid,' said a man in a barbershop.

'The same old experts who always come here came here and gave us the same old results they always give,' said the barber.

Another customer began yelling, 'All we had to eat was old lard and the kind of sugar they feed to cattle!'

And that set off a passing drunk who may have been confused about geopolitics – or maybe not – but, anyway, had the right attitude. 'Tomorrow, Japan!' he shouted.

RETURN OF THE DEATH OF COMMUNISM, PART III — THE SAGA CONTINUES

Kiev and Tibilisi,

September 1991

'Do they remember the good times? "Yes, under Stalin in the early 1950s. There was enough food and there was order." What do they want for their grandchildren? "Lots of food and order."'
—NATALYA KRAMINOVA, INTERVIEWING RUSSIAN VILLAGERS FOR
THE MOSCOW NEWS, 22 SEPTEMBER 1991

Kiev

It's impossible to get decent Chinese takeout in China, Cuban cigars are rationed in Cuba, and that's all you need to know about communism. But communism is illegal in the USSR or the Soviet Union or the Union of Sovereign So-and-So Republics or whatever they're calling themselves, so when you order Chicken Kiev in Kiev . . . 'Chicken is finish,' said the large, mopey waiter, making two fists and banging his forearms together in the national signal for 'we're out of it or we're closed or anyway the hell with you.'

I never did get to place an order. 'Is beefsteak,' the waiter explained when he'd returned from the hour-long hourly break which is the customary right of all Soviet food-service employees.

43

A plate full of something and cabbage was deposited in front of me. It was, in fact, beef, though not the steak kind. It tasted all right, but this was Monday. I would get 'beefsteak' for lunch every day that week. I would order veal, pork, fish and something I couldn't pronounce, and I would get beefsteak. Monday's beef was, as I said, fine. Tuesday's was middling. Wednesday's wasn't very good. Thursday's was pretty bad. And Friday's was the color of gunmetal and smelled. That was when I realized that all my beefsteaks had been cut from the same large and increasingly elderly piece of beef.

Marina, my Intourist guide, said this was the best restaurant in Kiev. At the table next to mine another smaller, more dandruffy waiter was chatting up a customer's date. The little waiter filled her wineglass, managing to dribble some of the wine on himself. Then he grabbed the skirt of the tablecloth and wiped his hands. Over by the kitchen door the restaurant's busboy was drinking the dregs out of mineral-water bottles. In the kitchen itself three or four people were conducting a loud quarrel punctuated with thrown pans. And a total of seven restaurant employees were operating the cash register. They passed my lunch tab around among themselves for almost half an hour before I was allowed to pay the bill, which amounted to 16 rubles, 53 cents.

But you couldn't blame communism. Communism was illegal. And communism was extra-specially double-illegal in Kiev – Kiev being the free and democratic capital of the entirely and completely, you-bet independent republic of the Ukraine. On 15 September, the day I arrived, there was a huge rally downtown where thousands of citizens cheered as members of the Ukraine Parliament officially declared the Ukraine independent. 'This is the fourth time they have officially declared this,' said Marina. So I guess independence in these parts works the same way the restaurants do. Anyway, the Ukraine was independent, and the only reason it didn't have borders and money and an army and a post office was that the people in charge of those things were waiting for somebody to add up their lunch checks.

You could tell for sure that there was no more communism

in the Ukraine because all the giant statues of Communists had been hit in the face with paint bombs. Every bronze, concrete and marble Communist had a big white paint splash across the kisser, making the Ukraine look like a country that acquired its national heros in a custard-pie fight. In the main square a particularly huge statue of Lenin – which, besides paint-bomb disfigurement, had KILLER and FASCIST graffitied on its base – was being torn down (or would have been if anyone could have found the crane operator). All the avenues, plazas and thoroughfares commemorating Bolshevism were getting 'Oak Street'-type monikers. And the most popular piece of wearing apparel was a stone-washed denim shirt with a label over the breast pocket reading 'US Army'.

Private enterprise had appeared in Kiev, at least a larval stage of it. Street vendors didn't exactly hawk their wares but they did sit behind tables and impassively offer for purchase books, flowers and clothes. Almost every neighborhood had a private market selling food – good food. There were big, fat potatoes in Coppertone skins; turnips the size of artillery shells; beets with a *grand cru* tint; noble, leonine heads of cabbage; pot cheese with curds in folds as white as tuxedo shirts; and melons as big and fresh as diaper-commercial babies. The meat counters were impressive, too, though not someplace you'd take k.d. lang on a date. Massive chunks of animals were being heaved around and chopped to pieces. Tongues, brains, hooves, feet and personal, private parts decorated the cutting boards. The tile floor was sloppy with blood puddles. But the meat was good-looking if you could bear to look: pink-champagne-colored pork, beef red like valentines and crocheted with savory fat, good teeth in the sheep skulls and clear eyes staring from the future-soup-stock cow heads.

They were fabulous markets. They'd do any nation proud. Except for one little problem – no customers. Some people were wandering around but it was the kind of wandering that Americans do in Porsche showrooms. Prices in the private markets were high. Meat was selling for 25 rubles a kilo. That's 38 cents a pound, but the average Ukrainian makes 250 rubles a month.

So 38 cents a pound is like going to the Safeway and getting 16 ounces of London broil for a hundred bucks. But it wasn't poverty alone that made the private markets such dysfunctional and unbustling places. Prices weren't just high, they were bizarre. For one thing, they were all the same. Each babushkaed grandmother selling lentils was selling lentils for the same price as every other grandmother – no premium for quality, no discount for quantity and no haggling.

I asked Marina about the beef. I said, 'Isn't beef cheaper this time of year? I mean, if you don't slaughter cattle in the fall, then you have to feed them in the barn all winter, and, especially in a country with a grain shortage, I'd expect lots of people would be bringing cattle to market right now, increasing supply and driving down prices.'

'No,' said Marina.

'Now pigs, on the other hand,' I said, 'are raised on slops, and people are going to be tossing out food scraps year 'round, so the price of pork would tend to remain constant.'

'Meat,' said Marina, 'sells for twenty-five rubles a kilo.'

'Beef and pork, they both sell for the same price?'

'Meat,' said Marina, 'sells for twenty-five rubles a kilo.'

'Fresh spring lamb?'

'Twenty-five rubles a kilo.'

'Stringy old mutton?'

'Twenty-five rubles a kilo. Meat,' said Marina, 'sells for twenty-five rubles a kilo.'

There was another way to buy food in Kiev, at the state food stores with their long, scuffling lines at the head of which was nothing, just about nothing at all. There was bread, sometimes, that you could use as a medicine ball or a boat anchor. There were ten or a dozen five-gallon jars full of murky liquid with a few unidentifiable pickled things resting in the bottoms and other jars of the same kind which contained plain water. The sausages, when there were any to see, were a shock and a horror, looking like nothing but discarded sex toys. The produce was appalling. The potatoes resembled gray prunes and no other vegetable was distinguishable from compost.

But the prices were right. The state store's carrots – which could have passed as criminal evidence, wizened remains of a kidnap victim's severed fingers maybe – cost 50 kopecks. And a kopeck is three-thousandths of a penny. The carrots in the private markets cost six times as much. Thus the Soviet economy is undermined by a kind of reverse black market from an anti-matter universe, a black market where it is legal to buy things you don't want too cheaply.

Every aspect of material life in the Soviet Union works this way. If you stand in line long enough the state provides goods and services. The services are out of service and the goods are no good, but food, clothing, shelter and medical care are – just barely – available. And they are hilariously inexpensive. The babushkas in the private markets don't really have to sell you anything. They're there to make money, not a living. If you don't buy the food, well, then . . . fist/fist, forearm/forearm . . . they'll take it home and eat it themselves, and you can stand in line for mummified carrots.

Marina, eyeing a selection of lard in a broken dairy cooler at the state food store, said, 'The two most difficult things in the Soviet Union are getting enough food and losing weight.'

An American's first reaction to the Soviet Union is to roll up his sleeves. There is so much to be done. Of course, that's true in any poor country, but in the Soviet Union there is the what with which to do it. Give an American a couple of gallons of paint, some Murphy's oil soap, a mop and a can of Lysol spray disinfectant and the private food markets would look like Balducci's. The beefsteak restaurant could be fixed in an afternoon, just turn anybody's grandmother loose in there' with a Fannie Farmer cookbook, a copy of *Emily Post's Etiquette* and a .38 revolver. Something could even be done with the lurching, squealing, backfiring, oil-dribbling Volga sedan in which I was being driven around town. Two cans of Bondo and it's a 1956 Studebaker President – a real collector's item on the classic-car market.

Not that the Soviets are incapable of helping themselves.

Marina described how her friends take local goods to Poland to sell them for hard currency (it says something that Soviets consider the zloty a hard currency) then fly to Turkey because that's the cheapest Western country (it says more that Soviets consider Turkey a Western country). In Turkey they buy clothes and dry goods and bring these back and sell them for a sizable profit in consignment stores. But Marina was embarrassed by this. 'We hate to be seen trading,' she said. 'It makes us feel almost like Negroes.'

Out in the country north of Kiev the topsoil was turned up in lustrous brunet furrows and smelled so rich it seemed like you wouldn't need to grow food, you could just cook soup from the loam itself (the beefsteak restaurant tried this). The peasant houses were big and well-proportioned, made of clay-tile bricks with hipped roofs of tin sheeting. Doors and windows were deep-set in elaborately carved wooden frames. On the second story of most houses was a large glassed-in porch, the Ukrainian equivalent of a Florida room, a Siberia salon perhaps. The homes all had generous yards surrounded by Tom Sawyer board fences, many with the palings painted alternately blue and yellow, the Ukrainian national colors. These quaint but substantial homes could be sold by the thousands as vacation getaways for two-income urban professional families if only the Ukraine could be made trendy. And who knows? Fashion is an odd thing. Collective farming may replace skiing or tennis as the thing to do. Hollywood executives could start driving wheat combines to work. And Ralph Lauren might bring out a Potato Digger line of leisure clothes. This would be a great relief to the Ukrainian peasants, who would then be able to move somewhere – anywhere – besides these handsome villages surrounded by the best farm land in the world.

Because there was nothing in those villages. There were no stores except the state food stores and no food in these. Out in the fields men and women were using the kind of wooden farm implements which decorate walls in the United States. There were no roads, just mud spaces impassable for half the year. 'At least the highway to Kiev is well-paved,' I said to Marina. She

48

laughed. The highway was paved because this was the highway to the dachas belonging to high officials in the Ukrainian Communist Party. (Not that they're high officials in the Ukrainian Communist Party anymore, now they're high officials in the National Government of the Ukraine.) The peasant's houses all had wells outside, with cranks and buckets and little roofs over them. I thought they were lawn ornaments. They were the only source of water. The wells were shallow and there were no sewers, only cesspits even shallower than the wells. If any of these had really been wishing wells, what the peasants would have wished for was clean water. And it was all so easily put right – one day with a drilling rig and a pick-up truck full of cheap pipe would do it. Even Soweto has indoor plumbing. A septic tank is nothing but a concrete box, and, to judge by Soviet architecture, the locals were plenty capable of making one. The Dnieper river was only a few miles away. A couple of cartloads of riverbed gravel, some shovel work and a tractor or an ox or the kids pulling a log drag would make for weatherproof roads.

'We need some economist to give us a plan,' said Marina.

'You had that already,' I said.

We drove about fifty miles north on the dacha highway to the edge of the 'closed zone' around Chernobyl. The zone has a radius of just eighteen miles. Right outside, food crops were still growing, dairy cows were still grazing and people were still living – sick, maybe, but still living. The irradiated ground did not glow or make drive-in-movie noises. No giant mutant predators or revivified lizard monsters stalked across it. I would have felt better if I'd seen one. A cicada the size of Space Mountain would have gotten somebody's attention, even in the Soviet Union. But radiation doesn't have very immediate or clearly visible effects, so nothing very immediate or clearly visible was being done about it. The border of the closed zone was one strand of barbed wire. There was a checkpoint on the road with a sign reading, 'Citizen, attention. You enter a place of special regime.' Another sign warned visitors not to hunt, fish, swim, camp, pick mush-rooms or drink water.

Three atomic reactors (one of which has since caught fire) were still operating at Chernobyl. A busload of men and women coming home from work stopped on the other side of the check-point. None wore protective clothing. The bus was given a cur-sory check with a Geiger counter. The workers passed in one door of a little shed and out another faster than passengers go through an airport metal detector. They looked depressed, but, then again, everybody in the Soviet Union looked depressed.

'Do you want to interview them?' said Marina.

'I want to know why they're still working there.'

'For pay,' said Marina. And I couldn't think of anything else to ask.

On our way back we stopped to look at a hydroelectric dam with rusty sluice gates and unkempt high-tension wires. It was immediately upriver from the city. Thirty-three feet of water loomed above downtown Kiev – a Super-Soaker of Damocles held in place by the same quality of materials and engineering that went into the Chernobyl reactors.

Marina was pessimistic about the dam. 'One day – woosh.' Marina was pessimistic about everything. She explained how it was now legal for Soviet citizens to buy Western goods in the special hard-currency shops but still illegal for them to own hard currency. 'We visit these stores like you would visit a museum,' she said. (She meant Porsche dealership.) Nothing had happened with land reform. 'It's like knocking on a door that isn't there,' said Marina. And, although all the property of the Communist Party had been confiscated, it had been confiscated by the state that was created by this Party. 'So, what,' I said, 'does that mean?' Marina shrugged.

Marina's grandfather had been a government official in the Ukraine when Stalin was in power, and, like many government officials then, he'd been sent to a prison camp. He got out only because Stalin died. None the less, Marina grew up with a certain faith in the Soviet system. Then when she was in high school in the 1970s she heard Alexander Solzhenitsyn's *Gulag Archipelago* being read on Radio Liberty broadcasts from the West. 'This upset me terribly,' she said. In 1979 she was allowed, as an Intourist guide, to travel to Western Europe. She spent the first hard currency she ever possessed on Solzhenitsyn books, which she could only find in English. She hid them carefully in her luggage because she knew that if they were found, she wouldn't be traveling to Western Europe again.

Marina read these books aloud to her family. They sat every night around the kitchen table with Marina translating, a Russian–English dictionary by her side for words she didn't recognize. 'Too many intellectuals were killed, imprisoned,' said Marina. 'No one wants to be an intellectual here. In America you call somebody a fool, we call them an intellectual.'

Tibilisi

There was no shortage of foolish intellectuals in the Republic of Georgia. And they all had guns.

Georgia is, of course, claiming independence from the Soviet Union. The whole Soviet Union is claiming independence from the Soviet Union. And all the independent places have places claiming independence from them. Something called South Ossetia is trying to secede from Georgia. I'll bet South Ossetia starts having trouble with South-Central Ossetia soon. And what was once the second most powerful nation in the world is becoming a collection of countries with names like 'The Republic of Me and You and I'm Not Sure About Me'.

But that's not why the intellectuals had guns in Georgia. They weren't rebelling against somebody else's government. They were rebelling against their own.

Last May Georgia held its first free elections since the Neo-lithic Age and elected one Zvaid K. Gamsakhurdia president. Gamsakhurdia (pronounced sort of like 'Gram's accordion' but not really) is a distinguished-looking, hammy-acting university professor and a prominent Georgian nationalist. He helped found the local Helsinki Watch civil-liberties monitoring group, was convicted by the Brezhnev government of monitoring civil liberties and was sent to jail for it. Gamsakhurdia was quite the local hero and was elected by an 87 per cent margin.

Once in office, however, Gamsakhurdia began acting like a butt-head. He closed newspapers, arrested opposition leaders, fired everybody in the government who didn't agree with him, spent $460,000 on bullet-proof Mercedes limousines, forbade Georgians to sell meat, vegetables or building materials anywhere except Georgia, blocked business privatization and land-reform programs and accused the United States of conspiring with Moscow to prevent Georgia from becoming independent.

So Georgians began to demonstrate. Thousands of them marched up and down Rustaveli Prospect, Tibilisi's main street. The anti-Gamsakhurdia protesters occupied their own opposition-party headquarters, but that seemed inadequate, somehow, so they took over the National Congress Building and swore to stay there until . . . I'm not sure until what. The government responded, not by attacking the protesters but by calling on protesters of its own to protest in favor of itself. Gamsakhurdia went on national television and asked people from all the little towns and villages of Georgia to come to the capital and protect him. And come they did, in scores of flag-decked buses. Thousands more Georgians marched up and down Rustaveli Prospect. Police used the village buses to build barricades around the National Government Building, down the street from the National Congress Building, and the pro-Gamsakhurdia protesters swore to stay there until whatever, too.

Actually, the government did attack the opposition a little bit. On 2 September, Georgian Special Security Forces (which may not have been very special because up until 2 September Georgia hadn't had any Special Security Forces) shot at some demonstrators. But, despite a lot of impassioned rhetoric, no one managed to die until 21 September, when a thirty-five-year-old cardiologist set himself on fire in front of the National Opera

Building, on Rustaveli between the National Congress Building and the National Government Building, leaving a note saying, 'If Georgia needs blood to settle the conflict then take mine.' Although, up until then, Georgia hadn't.

Meanwhile Georgia's National Guard – which is commanded by a sculptor and looks about as professional as a group of middle-aged duck hunters – split into two groups professing neutrality. One group was neutral and prepared to defend the nation against opposition lawlessness, and one group was neutral and prepared to defend the nation against government oppression.

The anti-Gamsakhurdia protesters and the part of the National Guard that was neutrally on their side then took over the national television station, but, since this is a very bureaucratic society, they stormed the offices of the television station's bureaucracy, leaving the government with the actual broadcast facilities.

If none of this makes sense it's because – believe me, I was there – none of this makes sense.

Georgia was less perfectly depressing than the Ukraine. The food was better. The weather was cute. The Caucasus Mountains are – I don't think I'm saying this just because I'm Caucasian – really beautiful. Tibilisi, the capital of Georgia, squats prettily in the Kura River valley about 160 miles inland from the Black Sea at what was once the extreme southeast corner of Hellenic civilization. Medea, of Golden Fleece fame, was from Georgia. After Medea got divorced by her Argonaut husband, Jason, she murdered Jason's second wife, tore her own sons limb from limb and ran off to Athens in a chariot pulled by dragons. I'm told that this, except for the dragons, is not untypical Georgian behavior. Stalin was from Georgia, too.

Anyway, Tibilisi is sort of charming and old. There are little, crimped streets overhung with New Orleans-style balconies, some Constantinople Jr churches, lots of midget stucco houses with grape vines tangling their patios and only a large – rather than an infinite – number of horrible communist cement apartment houses. The city has been destroyed forty times in Georgia's quarrelsome fifteen-hundred-year history, but not lately. In 1801 the last king of Georgia – named, as you might have guessed, George – turned the whole country over to Russia. If Stalin, Medea and the protesters on Rustaveli Prospect are anything to go by, who can blame him?

There were huge demonstrations the night I arrived. I wasn't scheduled to meet my Intourist guide until the next morning. I don't speak a word of Georgian and the only word of Russian I speak – *tovarish*, 'comrade' – is a word you don't say anymore. So I didn't have any idea who was demonstrating against what. I knew the opposition was made up of intellectual urban elites, and I knew the pro-government people were peasants and factory workers, but everybody dresses so badly in the Soviet Union that it was impossible to tell which was which. All of them, including some members of the National Guard, were wearing those stone-washed denim shirts with 'US Army' on the pocket.

Sometimes the two sides marched around ignoring each other and sometimes the two sides argued with each other and sometimes I couldn't tell for sure if there really were two sides. I gave up and went to my hotel, where I found the restaurant closed because – as best I understood – 'it was dinner time'.

This hotel was just off Rustaveli, around the corner from the occupied National Congress Building (though I didn't know that was what it was). I left the door to my balcony open so I could hear if whoever started fighting with whomever else. Which, at three in the morning, they did, but I slept through it.

When I woke up everybody was really mad. Barricades and sitters-in had been forcibly removed from the Congress Building. My Intourist guide, Nina, and I drove to the TV station, where Nina went looking for people for me to interview. She produced a large, bearded fellow still blood-splattered from being whacked on the head early that morning. 'I will never move from here! I will defend democracy! I want the world to know!' he said, although what he wanted the world to know I had a hard time getting him to tell me. Not that I understood when he finally did. According to my notes, pro-Gamsakhurdia protesters approached the barricades at the Congress Building in a friendly manner so that the bearded man thought they were coming for a reconciliation. But then they attacked the barricades with a crane. Three a.m. seems an odd time to be reconciled and a crane an unlikely item to bring on the errand, but never mind. 'Stones were thrown.' The bearded man got hit by one 'the size of a cabbage'. Pro-Gamsakhurdia protesters further attacked him, pushing him into a building, but then, when these attackers saw that he was covered in blood, they helped him out of the building and tried to get him to an ambulance. However, he was attacked by other pro-Gamsakhurdia protesters, but the pro-Gamsakhurdia protesters who'd attacked him first attacked the attackers, drove them back and got him medical treatment after all. 'I really felt the support of those people who attacked us,' said the bearded man.

Several thousand people were gathered at the TV station, most of them infected with that happy sense of purpose people have when they are standing up for a principle they haven't really been knocked down for yet. People who direct mob scenes in movies have obviously never seen a mob. Movie mobs are decided and purposeful and achieve instant internal government by means of one guy who stands on a chair and yells, 'hanging's too good for 'em'. Then off the mob goes to lynch Sidney Poitier. Real mobs just mill around acting pointlessly upset while being addressed by a series of half-important people speaking into PA systems that turn all human speech into car-theft-alarm noises. Nobody knew what was going on, which made everybody talk loudly about what was happening, and it was embarrassing if you talked too loudly because then everyone in the mob would come cluster around you hoping to hear some bewilderment more illuminating than their own.

Nina took me to talk with the leaders of the TV-station protest. This was one of five or six political interviews that I did while I was in the Soviet Union – with Ukrainian Nationalists, Ukrainian non-Nationalists, a member of the Ukrainian Parlia-

55

ment, anti-Gamsakhurdian Georgians, pro-Gamsakhurdian Georgians and some people I don't know who they were.

I can tell you what they all had to say, if you like, I mean if you're having trouble getting to sleep or something. I would ask them what their group advocated, and they would say, 'Democracy must be defended.' I would ask, 'How do you propose to do this?' They would say, 'There must be a structure of democracy in our society.' I would ask, 'What are your specific proposals?' They would say, 'We must build democratic institutions.' I would ask, 'By what means?' They would say, 'Building democratic institutions is necessary so that there is a structure of democracy in our society at all levels.' And by this time I'd be yelling, 'BUT WHAT ARE YOU GOING TO DO??!!' And they would say, 'Democracy must be defended.'

The Soviets were firmly rooted in the abstract, had both their feet planted in the air. It was impossible to get them to understand that government isn't a philosophical concept, it's a utility, a service industry – a way to get roads built and have Iraqis killed. Talking politics to Soviets gave me the same dull headache that I'd had, back in college, reading *Anna Karenina*. There was Tolstoi gibbering for pages about the Russian peasant's spiritual relationship to yackitty-yackitty-yack and me going, 'Leo, why'd she fuck the guy?'

By the time I got done with the interview at the TV station, I was surrounded by two or three hundred pushing, crowding eavesdroppers. The men and boys were armed. I thought civilians didn't have guns in the Soviet Union, but I was wrong. There are liberals who have nightmares about the NRA, and those nightmares look like this crowd. Every kind of firearm imaginable was being waved around with brainless gusto. There were ancient shotguns and decrepit hunting rifles, rusty burp guns from World War II and broom-handle Mauser pistols that looked like they'd been buried in the yard since the revolution. There were scatterguns and target rifles and air pistols and hundreds of AK-47s. I saw a twelve-year-old carrying one of these. He was guarding the place where the mob had parked its cars. (Remember, this was a mob of urban elites.) I'm actually a member of the NRA and it was still a nightmare. The Second Amendment says the people have a right to 'keep and bear arms' not a right to wildly swing, waggle in your face, mispoint, stare down the barrel of and accidentally discharge the things. (Somebody did do that, fortunately into a flower bed.)

'Just what,' I said to Nina, 'is going on here? What are you people trying to accomplish? What gives?'

Nina, who was very pro-anti-Gamsakhurdia, repeated all the complaints against the man. 'But,' she said, 'in reality the problem is our president is not acting rationally. He behaves in a hysterical manner. He is crazy.'

'Crazy?' I said. 'Is that all? Nina, in the United States we elect crazy presidents all the time. You people really *don't* understand democracy, do you?'

The pro-Gamsakhurdia protesters, gathered in their own mob in front of the National Government Building, had fewer guns but seemed more dangerous – that is, more likely to beat you up instead of talk you to death.

The peasants and factory workers who supported the government were angry rather than indignant. And they'd come a long way for the purpose of being angry. On close inspection they were easy enough to distinguish from the urban elites. The pro-Gamsakhurdia protesters were older, thicker-limbed and fewer-toothed. Their clothes were the same but smellier. They were sleeping on their buses or the street and being fed free bread and pieces of dense, salty goat cheese. A movie theater had been requisitioned so they could use the rest rooms as wash stalls.

The Gamsakhurdia supporters looked satisfied enough with their accommodation. The lines for food and toilets were shorter than most lines in the Soviet Union. I watched one magnificent old man snoring on the neoclassical portico of the Government Building. He was dressed in a wrinkled suit with World War II campaign ribbons on the jacket pocket. He had shoulders as wide as a wingback chair, hands like Kool-Aid pitchers and his huge head of white hair was pillowed on a four-foot cudgel.

These were the same kind of poor, benighted slobs who supported Noriega in Panama, Pinochet in Chile, Marcos in the Philippines and Nixon during Watergate. They were mindlessly patriotic and full of ignorance and prejudices. The people at the TV station were much more like us. They really cared about human rights and social justice and even ecology, too. They were hip. They were smart. And they were wrong. The president had been duly elected. He hadn't done anything terribly unconstitutional. In fact, by the standards of the Soviet Union, he hadn't done anything worth mentioning. When, at the TV station, I'd interviewed Nodar Notadze, leader of the anti-Gamsakhurdia opposition in the Georgian Parliament, Notadze had said, 'There is no legal ground to demand his resignation. But there is moral ground.' The anti-Gamsakhurdia protesters were so smart, so hip and so much like us that you just knew, as soon as freedom and democratic government really were established in Georgia, they'd be voting for Jerry Brown.

Not that the anti-Gamsakhurdia protesters were as wimpy as Jerry Brown voters yet. Wednesday morning, 25 September, at 3 a.m. again, they tried to destroy the Tibilisi electric-power system, killing three pro-Gamsakhurdia National Guardsmen and getting two of themselves killed in the attack.

I could hear it happening – the unmistakable 'Buddha-Buddha' of AK-47 fire. I got out of bed and went rushing around the empty streets of Tibilisi looking for some sign of panic or alarm. Then I tried to call the other foreign reporters in the city, but the phone in my hotel room had a large label reading:

You are being served by Kvazy-Electronic telephone station 'KVANT'.
– Do not lift the receiver while it rings!
– Do not delay dialing!
– Do not depress the lever on the phone!

And so forth. I gave up.

It wasn't until ten in the morning that I found the site of the shooting. It was on a suburban side street, an unprepossessing structure with bullet holes and lots of shattered glass. A very rattled night manager named Jemal Bibileishvili was still behind his desk. 'I do not understand what they wanted,' he said. 'We do not control anything here.'

It turned out the anti-Gamsakhurdia protesters had attacked the office of the electric company's maintenance dispatcher. 'There is nothing here but a telephone,' said the night manager. I asked him if he could think of any possible reason for the protesters to attack this particular building. 'No,' he said, 'only, when power goes out, this is the place everyone comes to protest.'

There's a joke people tell in the Soviet Union: Mitterand, Bush and Gorbachev have a meeting with God. Mitterand says, 'My country faces many difficult problems – lagging exports, Muslim minorities, European unification. How long will it be before France's problems are solved?' God says, 'Fifteen years.' Mitterand begins to cry. 'I'm an old man,' says Mitterand. 'I'll be dead by then. I'll never see France's problems solved.' Then Bush says, 'My country faces many difficult problems – recession, crime, racial prejudice. How long will it be before America's problems are solved?' God says, 'Ten years.' Bush begins to cry. 'I'm an old man,' says Bush. 'I'll be out of office by then. I won't get any credit for solving America's problems.' Then Gorbachev says, 'My country faces many, many difficult problems. How long will it be before the Soviet Union's problems are solved?' *God begins to cry.*

IT'S THE END OF HISTORY, AND POLY SCI ISN'T EXPECTED TO RECOVER EITHER

Vietnam,
February 1992

Hearts and Minds

Shhh, they think they won the war.

The old communists who run Vietnam believe they defeated imperialism, colonialism and decadent western capitalism. So where did the little girl in Hoan Kiem park, in the middle of downtown Hanoi, get a hula hoop? Why does every house in the city have a workshop, store or tea parlor in the front room? Whence the hundreds of tiny factories? Wherefore the hawkers, barkers, jobbers and drummers shouting their wares in the street? How come foreign investors pack the haute cuisine restaurants? How come there's haute cuisine? And what is that eminently imperialist corporation, British Petroleum, doing signing a co-venture agreement with the state-owned Vietnamese oil company in the lobby of my hotel? With an open bar?

After the signing, pyrotechnics were ignited to drive away evil spirits. Twenty-foot strings of firecrackers hung from the hotel balcony. The explosions were forceful. I kept thinking about all the effort I put into dodging the draft. Now I was going to

60

die in Vietnam anyway, twenty years late, from a stray cherry bomb.

When that famous last helicopter left the roof of the American embassy in Saigon in 1975, we were – imperially, colonially and capitalistically speaking – just going out for a beer. Now we're back. Actually *we're* not back. The United States still has some snit-induced total embargo on trade with Vietnam. But everybody else is back – French, British, Japanese, Taiwanese, Hong Kong Chinese, Mainland Chinese, overseas Vietnamese and smelly Scandinavian backpackers. Meanwhile the locals have let go of Karl Marx with both hands.

I'd come to Vietnam with photographer John Giannini who speaks Vietnamese and has been in and out of the country for most of a generation. He served two combat tours with the US Army, returned as a journalist, lived in pre-communist Saigon, got wounded during the Khmer Rouge take-over of Cambodia and – John being as persistent as Rambo sequels – came back to Vietnam again after the fall of the South. He'd been in Hanoi, last, in 1990 and warned me that, although so-called Ho Chi Minh City was coming to life, the North remained a typical People's Republic locale – short on everything except lines to stand in, dull, gray, glum, 'a big slab of drab'.

But Hanoi had definitely changed. On first impression it seemed like 1960s America – not pot, war and hirsute aggravation 60s America, but the madras-clad, record hop, beach-bunny nation of my high school days. Of course Hanoi, with its crumbling tropical seventh *arrondissement* architecture and dilapidated boulevards shaded by enormous tamarind trees, couldn't look less like midwestern suburbia. And everyone was working instead of doing the hully-gully. Nevertheless there was a doo-ron-ron in the air. Hanoi is a young city. More than half the people in Vietnam are under twenty and cheerful with the infinite possibilities of baby-boom cheer. These kids wear jeans. They wear T-shirts with catch phrases in English (sort of in English –

'Darling Pigeon/My Peaceful Mind' and 'A Life's Beach'). And they ride Honda 50s just like we did. The coffee-can exhaust note, the 2-cycle gas smell, the wind-up-toy gear racket are exactly the same as they were in Ohio the summer 'Little Honda' was a top forty hit.

The streets of Hanoi are thronged with hundreds of these motor bikes and thousands of pedal-operated *cyclo* rickshaws and tens of thousands of bicycles. All are preposterously overloaded. I saw four schoolgirls on one Honda seat, a hundred cartons of something lashed to a single bicycle and ten adults and children – I counted twice – packed into and hanging off a *cyclo*.

Everyone seems to be making, selling or accomplishing something or hurrying someplace to do so. The most modest resources suffice to start a business. At every intersection old ladies hunker next to bicycle pumps, selling tire air. There aren't many black pajamas to be seen and some that I did see I suspect were Armanis. There are no long Bolshevik files of people either. The only lines I saw were lines of *cyclo* drivers waiting for fares outside restaurants and hotels. Gasoline itself is readily available – this unheard of in a Marxist country; 93 octane unleaded sells for $1.04 a gallon. It even seemed to be a buyer's market at the Ho Chi Minh Mausoleum with short, fast-moving queues to see the dead guy.

A wealth of construction is underway, mostly private houses. These are only one room wide but as much as sixty feet deep and three or four stories high. They're built of fired clay blocks or of rubble framed between poured concrete uprights. Exteriors are bright-painted stucco with mozaic decorations. Porticos, balusters, cornices and roof crestings are given shapes as fantastic and modern as the simple building materials allow. The effect is Frank Lloyd Wright in Lego blocks.

Our government translator and guide, a young foreign service officer I'll call Pham, said property is expensive in central Hanoi. Pham had no idea what the city's many 'Heroic Workers' and

'People's Victory' monuments commemorate. He had to go up and read the plaques like anyone else. But he knew to the penny – or, rather, to the karat – what real estate costs: one ounce of gold per square meter, payment in bullion only.

A government department store, the Universal State Shop, still exists, but 'steerers' hover at every counter. These are young men who tell you how you can find better, cheaper merchandise in the private shops which pay them to stand there. The steerer in the bicycle department said, quite loudly, that bikes made by the Vietnamese state monopoly cost too much, $30 to $35. He could get us a smuggled Chinese bicycle for half that price.

The private vendors in the vast, glazed-roof, trainless train-station central market have spices, vegetables, fruits, poultry and fish in profusion. I stumbled over a yard-wide wire basket filled with a python. 'God, what's that,' I said.

'Food,' said Pham.

But a large part of the Hanoi market – and of every other market in Vietnam – is given over to tools. Pipe threaders, die cutters, soldering irons, calipers and micrometers are for sale along with the usual third world hoe blades and axe heads. Plus there are all kinds of motor parts and bits of electrical and even electronic hardware. The marketplace is devoted not just to things but to things that make things. It's an industrial revolution in its nonage – like seeing young Thomas Watt stare at a boiling kettle or watching a callow Thomas Alva Edison get a shock after petting the cat.

Plenty of consumer goods are sold, too – clothes, shoes, clocks, thermos bottles, dishes, kitchen utensils – cheap but serviceable products of mainland China. Giannini said the pots and pans used to be made by hand in Hanoi. He wondered if Chinese imports had put people out of work. We drove a few blocks to Hang Thiec, 'Tin Street', but found everyone fully employed. The tinsmiths were spread out across the sidewalks and had laid sheets of corrugated metal in the road to be flattened by passing cars and trucks. Men banged on various objects with a noise like a thousand skateboarders on the roof of a quonset hut. One fellow was hammering out a medium-sized rectangular thing

the purpose of which escaped us. 'What's that?' asked Giannini.
  'Ice cube tray!' said the artisan.

Of course the place is a dictatorship. You can do what you want,
but you can't have opinions. Vietnam is still a very poor country,
however. Most Vietnamese can't afford a subscription to *The New
Republic* and are too busy working to watch 'Crossfire'. So there
aren't that many opinions around.

  It's too late for opinions anyway. The night after the British
Petroleum signing, John and I were leaving our hotel when the
foreign minister of China walked into the lobby. He was fresh
from a first-ever meeting with his Vietnamese counterpart, and
the two were giving a press conference in the banquet room. We
peeked through the doorway. Everybody in there was Chinese
or Vietnamese, but the press conference was being translated
into English. That night, listening to the BBC World Service on
shortwave, we heard Vietnam is sending food aid to the former
Soviet Union. And two weeks later in Saigon – which no one
pretends to call Ho Chi Minh City – I watched a young man
make model airplanes out of beer cans. He folded the aluminum
into carefully detailed bar room origami – C-130 transports, F-4
Phantoms, Huey and Cobra helicopters and one triangle-shaped
jet with a star embossed on each wing. 'Soviet?' I said.

  'No, no Soviet,' he said. But it looked like a Mig-21.

  'Soviet?' I repeated.

  And he pulled out a much-fingered US military plane spot-
ter's-guide, older than he was, and pointed to a picture of this
plane, a General Dynamic F-106 Delta Dagger. 'No Soviet,' he
said. 'All American. Soviet no good.'

The North

A pleasant flurry of economics
spreads from town all through the fields of the Hong River valley.
Every garden plot is tended with the kind of care westerners

wouldn't give a bonsai tree. This pays, to judge by the Hondas in the farm yards. And the same gaudy, perpendicular Hanoi houses rise from the middle of rice paddies like misplaced cubism exhibits.

We drove east to Ha Long Bay on the Tongkin Gulf. The Hong River delta has only a few bridges. The Soviets and the Chinese collaborated to build an enormous one, but they built it where there isn't any traffic. We crossed a Hong tributary, the Peaceful Time River, on a listing barge. Our car was surrounded with peasants, all of them spitting something – sugar cane pulp, sunflower seed hulls, betel nut juice – like 200 high-school juniors making their first try at dipping snuff. The barge was nudged across by a Chinese tugboat. The tug looked to have been sunk and raised several times. Running it was a position of social consequence. The captain was dressed in a three-piece suit and fedora and flew a large red flag made of painted burlap.

At Bai Chay Town on Ha Long Bay the mountains rise immediately from the riverine plain the way papier mâché tunnels used to on O-gauge train layouts. These dolomite and limestone promontories are eroded into whimsical towers, looking like the mountains on Chinese scroll paintings, as well they might since they served as models for many of those paintings.

The mountains continue directly into the sea giving Ha Long Bay some 3000 islands which are in fact the tips of mountain peaks. Waves have further eroded the limestone so that each island is wider above the high tide mark than it is at water level. Many of the islands are named after the strange resulting shapes – Teapot Island, Head Island, Turtle Island. And you can go on naming them yourself – Large Order of Fries with a Big Mac Island, Overturned Car Island, Tip of My Dick in the Bathtub Island, etc.

We hired a wooden boat, some thirty feet long and powered by a Chinese diesel engine with a single cylinder the size of a waste paper basket and r.p.m.'s so low that you could hear each stinking detonation in the combustion chamber. We motored at dog-walking speed into a flat and misty ocean. Wooden junks with their fish fin sails were becalmed in the distance, and all around us were woven basket boats or coracles hardly bigger than front hall rugs. Fishing families live in these year-round, going to bed under a roof of bowed matting and coming ashore only to sell their catch and get fresh water.

'They have lots of children,' said Pham. 'Not much else to do.' But I didn't see more than two children in any basket boat so maybe they lose a lot of children overboard, too.

The little islands, few of them more than ten acres, were covered in gnarls of vegetation. Every island seemed to have a cove and a sea arch, a little beach and a cave. One cave opened at the water line like a whale sneer, stalactite-toothed and deep enough to hide everybody in a Scout troop who wanted to sneak a smoke.

Three thousand oriental Neverlands. It was a scene of incredible beauty and hence annoyance to a journalist. Journalists aren't much good with scenic beauty. The scenic beauty story has too many unattributed sources and is short on sexual scandal. Besides, Americans have lots of questions about Vietnam and two of those questions aren't 'Is it pretty?' and 'Did you have fun?'

It is. I did. An old woman skulling a coracle came alongside and sold us ten quarts of Chinese beer. We puttered for hours, wholly content, returning to shore only in the last moments of an immense red-gold sunset so beautiful that it reduced journalists to total silence. Temporarily.

Back in Hanoi, Pham dutifully took us to Ho Chi Minh's home, a simple, open, tile-roof affair built in the Thai mountain tribesman style. It's little more than a gazebo, really, with two small rooms surrounded by a veranda upstairs and with nothing but a patio underneath. On the patio is a conference table with three telephones, and here Ho used to sit and run the whole Vietnam war. Ho Chi Minh adopted this spartan style of life in order to devote all his energy to Marxist/Leninist revolution. It makes you think better of Imelda Marcos.

Ho's house, Ho's tomb and a Ho Museum are all contained in a large park, a sort of Six Flags Over Ho with several nice ponds but no water slides into them.

The museum is supposed to be a monument to world social- ism. It was designed by an unperestroikaed Czech architect work- ing with ferroconcrete in the pre-post-modernist style – all needless parabolas, ramps to nowhere and soaring spaces that don't contain anything.

The gift shop had a display of stuffed carcasses of various animals which are nearing extinction in Vietnam. These were 'for sale to benefit endangered species'.

The exhibits were confusing. One seemed to detail the history of man from the neolithic age until the time when countries all over the world – Albania, Cuba, Laos, Mongolia, Peru and Ceylon – sent souvenir gifts to Ho Chi Minh.

The American Communist Party had sent Ho a wristwatch, a gold 'Jules Jurgensen' on a leather strap. Back in the States I asked a jeweller about this brand. He said, 'It's the kind of thing you see in a catalogue. You know – "$795 List Price. Discount Price $395. This week only, $259."'

Another exhibit contained a Coca-Cola sign, a blow-up photo- graph of a dead US Marine, a Marilyn Monroe poster and a plaster sculpture of an Edsel grille. This was, I think, supposed to be a mixed media presentation about the failure of bourgeois materialism, but I couldn't tell for sure because the lights and sound system were broken.

No bourgeois materialism was evident at our hotel – a govern- ment guest house, actually. The place had been built and decor- ated in a purely Soviet spirit. The exterior walls were made of pre-formed concrete. The interior walls were painted a Bulgarian green, and each room was lit by a single six-foot fluorescent tube so that you felt like cheap merchandise in a display case, a Jules Jergensen wristwatch perhaps. But there were non-communist touches – hot water, a new bar of soap, *two* towels. And when Giannini came down with some kind of malarial frisson the room boy gave him a massage and rubbed Tiger Balm on his eyelids.

Meals were served in traditional socialist fashion – very slowly, with the courses out of order so that the jam arrived half an hour after the toast and the coffee didn't come until you'd called for the check. However, it's hard to be angry at a place that has ice-cream, beer and cigarettes on its breakfast menu. And the cooking was good.

Everywhere else in Hanoi the cooking was even better. Also, cheap. Dinner for two at the best restaurant was $6. Vietnamese food is like Chinese food prepared by a great French chef. No. That would mean frog fried rice and trying to get snails out of their shells with chopsticks. Vietnamese food is like French food with wonderful Chinese . . . That isn't it either. There's no mu shu pork in sauce *Béchamel*. Though some odd things do turn up on the bill of fare:

Vaporize Sea Fish
Volcano in Raw Mixture
Fried Beep in Minute
Fish-Sound with Chicken
Tortle in Rose Souse
Creamable Eggs
Spaghetti Soup with Chicken

The last being an accurate description of the dish. But it's delicious. It's all delicious. And every meal comes with perfectly baked baguettes, the only decent bread in Asia, and cups of *café filtre*, the only drinkable coffee east of Peshawar.

Not that Giannini and I were drinking much coffee, not with Johnny Walker Red (listed on the menu as 'Scotland Whiskey Wine') available at $17 a quart and 750 ml bottles of Stolicnaya for only $1.75. After plenty of that and some surprisingly drinkable Singapore cognac, we would be pedaled to the guest house in a pair of *cyclos*, rolling through the pitch dark but still bustling streets of Hanoi, lolling around in our chairs like participants in an Alzheimer's Olympics.

We drove out of Hanoi again, heading south on Highway 1, the old colonial road to Saigon. Every bridgehead, rail crossing and flood dyke is marked by a squat, crumbling, mold-blackened

French pillbox. In the Indo-Chinese War the French managed, by means of these pillboxes, to control all the pillboxes in the Indo-Chinese War. Sometimes.

In Japan people drive on the left. In China people drive on the right. In Vietnam they drive on both sides. Not that it matters since Highway 1 is a no-lane road. Vietnam seems to have abandoned not only the idea of communism but the idea of commonweal. There is no infrastructure. There are no sewers. Electricity is a sometimes thing. The tap water is an instant weight loss plan – one tablespoon with every meal and eat what you want. The pavement on Highway 1 is so bad that you'd make better time if you drove off it and sunk to your hubs in the rice paddies. But Vietnam has private property now and you can't do that.

We were traveling in an old Toyota Land Cruiser wagon with solid axles and a leaf spring front end – a vehicle designed to dispel any notion of the Japanese as automotive geniuses.

Our driver, whom I'll call Vo, had been a convoy trucker on the Ho Chi Minh Trail during the war. And we could have used some US air strikes on Highway 1's bicycles, water buffalos, motor cycles, jeepny buses, tractors, goats, dogs, children, ox carts, flocks of ducks, private automobiles and genuine Vietnamese pot-bellied pigs, the kind fashionable Americans have for pets and we had for dinner. Vo was good – able to drive around (or over) all these at 40 m.p.h. on road surfaces barely fit for walking. But an hour out of Hanoi he suddenly pulled to the side. 'We have a serious problem,' he said. 'We can go no further.'

'What?' we said.

'The horn is broken.'

Vo sorted through scavenged car parts at a roadside repair shed while farmers tried to sell wives to Giannini and me. Used wives. A crowd of children collected around us.

'Lien Xo! Lien Xo!' ('Soviet'), the children said.

'Ngoni My! Ngoni My!' ('American'), said John.

The children pondered that. We looked pretty scruffy. John was obviously wrong. 'Lien Xo! Lien Xo! Lien Xo!'

This plus a couple of Moscow businessmen wearing bowling-shirt-type sport clothes and one souvenir store at China Beach with a faded sign in Russian were all that remained of Soviet presence.

Vo jury-rigged something that made enough noise to get us south. Away from Hanoi, the farms are still rich but the farmers not so much so. Houses are made of straw thatch or woven sticks or, sometimes, brick. It looks like the three little pigs are the local architects. Except for traffic it could be any century you like, though here and there tall bamboo poles rise with television antennas lashed to the tops.

As we neared the coast the land became hilly and dotted with limestone formations, chimney-like cousins of the towers in Ha Long Bay. The locals are breaking these up with picks and shovels – chipping away at the sights to make gravel for roads; but anyone who's been on the roads in Vietnam would rather have pavement than scenery.

The country people really do wear conical hats, called *non la*. Peering down from the highway at the open-air markets in the villages, all you can see are hundreds of these bobbing, weaving, swaying bonnets – the dancing mushrooms from *Fantasia*. Once that thought enters your head, you can never look out the car window in Vietnam again without hearing Tchaikovsky's *Nutcracker Suite*.

We reached Vinh, about 170 miles from Hanoi, after ten hours of travel. We checked into another government rest house, like the last one but with cockroaches the size of bronzed baby shoes. 'Guests are requested to dress in a regular way in hotel restaurant and bar', read a sign in English over my bed. Vinh had been the great staging point for the Ho Chi Minh Trail supplying the guerrillas and NVR regulars fighting in the south. But the only evidence of that was a weed-grown freightyard where a single watchman was keeping an eye on abandoned railcar undercarriages.

Below Vinh is the neck of Vietnam where the Indochinese cordillera, the *Chaine Annamitique*, runs in close parallel to the sea. At its narrowest point, the country is only thirty miles wide.

The Ho Chi Minh trail wasn't a sneaky communist invention. It's the old trade route through Laos and Cambodia to Saigon. The North Vietnamese had to either use this or come down the middle of Highway 1 like a St Patrick's Day parade.

This has always been the poorest part of Vietnam and, as the poorest parts of so many places do, it has the best views. At one spot near the Giang River the landscape fell in multicolored bands like a fancy after-dinner drink – a layer of sea, a layer of dunes, a layer each of grass shacks and gardens, a layer of bamboo-shaded road, another of rice paddies and a final layer of thick, dark mountains – a *pousse-café* of beauty.

The mountains are covered in enormous growths of tropical hardwoods. Though not for long, to judge by the number of trucks we saw carrying logs the size of trailer homes. This is all government timbering, done to get hard currency exports.

A high lump in the coastal plain marks the DMZ, the 'Demilitarized Zone' that used to exist between North and South Vietnam. A cow was scratching herself against a barely legible sign commemorating the 'Vietnamese people's victory over the Mac-Namara Line'. This, if anyone remembers, was a system of highly sophisticated electronic sensors devised by JFK's Secretary of Defense and planted in the DMZ to detect North Vietnamese infiltration – infiltration which would have been as hard to miss as 10,000 Irishmen with bagpipes and the mayor.

The food stayed good or even got better, improving in proportion to the filth of the restaurants along the road. Maybe the best meal we had in Vietnam was in a sagging, cobwebbed, three-walled shack in Dong Hoi where rats were running along the rafters and I had to step over a pig to get to the bathroom. Not that there was anything on the other side of the pig except a hole in the dirt floor.

Here they brought us *cha gio*, miniature spring rolls, chicken *pho*, the 'spaghetti soup' that was on the menu in Hanoi; another soup called *bun bo hue*, made from beef and noodles and, I think, 500 chili peppers; still another soup, *chanh chua dau ca*, 'sour fish soup' (the Vietnamese will turn anything into a soup, just as the Germans will turn anything into a sausage); plus pork balls and grilled shrimp and sticky rice and regular rice and beer and tea and mineral water, all for a buck apiece.

Food is eaten by holding a bowl under your nose and pretending to use chopsticks while sucking food into your mouth with loud slurping noises. Holding your chopsticks too close to the tips is considered uncouth but belching, smoking, picking the teeth and spitting on the floor are fine. It takes a while for table manners to return to normal after a visit to Vietnam. As my wife pointed out.

Most of the food is dipped in, and all of the food is flavored with, *nuoc mam*. *Nuoc mam* is made by squeezing the juice out of fish and letting it rot in a large clay vat. The resulting liqueur is diluted with water and vinegar and set in a shallow dish on every table – the salt, pepper, mustard, ketchup and A-1 Sauce of Vietnam. *Nuoc mam* is an acquired taste, a taste you'd better acquire quickly if you don't want to do a lot of gagging.

We did not have – so far as I know – any of the other local delicacy which is dog. It is disturbing to western sensibilities to see a wire cage full of puppies on the way to the abattoir or, in the market, to brush against a hanging hindquarter of Rover. There is that little tail which did so lately wag at master. 'Sit!' 'Fetch!' 'Shake hands!' 'Now jump in the frying pan!' 'Good dog!'

We arrived in Hue, on the Perfume River, at sunset. Hue was the imperial capital of Vietnam, famous for its two-square-mile fortress, the Citadel. This was built by the Emperor Gai Long in 1804 but never saw any actual fortress use until the 1968 Tet offensive and then the Viet Cong attackers got on the wrong side of the walls and held out in there for twenty-four days.

Inside the Citadel is the impressive Palace of Supreme Harmony. Though what impresses you, really, is the unfamiliarity of the decorations – the dragon tangles carved into the woodwork, ,the Parcheesi board patterns in the screens and railings and the old-shoe-in-the-closet turned-up tips of the roof corners. Once you've looked at it awhile you realize that the Palace of Supreme Harmony is squatty and dank and not a patch on the average Grand Hyatt.

Hue is also famous for beautiful women though all of Vietnam has them and not just singular enchantresses but huge aggregate percentages of sirens and belles. Any random group of thirty Vietnamese women will contain a dozen who make Cindy Crawford look like Ross Perot. In the early evening in Hue the girls from the secondary schools come home from classes, fleets of them bicycling through the streets, all dressed in white *oa dais*, trim shirt dresses worn over loose-fitting trousers. Not for nothing do the remaining Catholic churches ring the *angelus* this time of day. I wonder if it changes the nature of a society for beauty to be so common. Maybe in Vietnam 'she has a wonderful personality' really means something. But I couldn't figure out a polite way to ask.

We left for Da Nang at dawn. Driving in the dark is impossible in Vietnam, so we had reverted to the visceral body clock of the medieval serf – passed out in the vermin by nine and up before five. Thirty-five miles south of Hue we drove up an astounding set of switchbacks, un-guard-railed and rapidly coming unpaved, our precarious roadbed crossing and recrossing the equally precarious roadbed of Vietnam's single railway line.

Then Vo wheeled us down at a startling angle onto a coast of little shining harbors and cheddar-colored beaches arrayed in quarter moons and trefoils between rocky headlands. Thatch villages sat in palm groves between the ocean and the road, emerald gardens opened out to the west. Either Eden looked like this or Eve was right to back the snake.

Now I understand how we got involved in Vietnam. We fell in love. Maybe the grunts didn't. They had to look at too much incoming and too many other grunts. But the big shots we sent here – the suits, the brass hats, the striped pants cookie pushers, the CIA white shoe boys and the special envoy face cards – they swooned for the place. Everybody, from the first advisers Ike sent in 1955 to Henry Kissinger at the Paris Peace talks, had a mad crush on Vietnam. It broke their hearts. They kept calling and sending flowers. They just couldn't believe this was goodbye.

Qua Roi

It's been nineteen years now. US newspapers, magazines and television programs weren't, in 1964, filled with agonizing reappraisals of World War II. I'd like to be the first American to write something about Vietnam without having kittens. I wasn't in the war. I didn't lose my youth and innocence here. (I lost them the regular way, with a calendar.) I don't feel guilty about dodging the draft. Well, maybe a little, but I'm forty-four years old and, by now, I've done a lot of things to feel guilty about. Ducking conscription into a dubious military venture is way down the list. Yes, I had friends who died here. But I had friends who died from cocaine and I don't get all weird every time I see a glass-topped coffee table.

'*Qua roi*', 'past enough', is what the Vietnamese say when you ask them about the war. Our battles in Vietnam are as remote in time for the majority of Vietnamese as our battles in Korea are for me (if Korea had taken place on my block, of course). To look at Vietnam, you'd never know there'd been a war. Giannini said the farmers used to use bomb craters to raise catfish. But since price controls on rice were lifted, the craters have been filled and smoothed into the surrounding paddies. I heard that damage from the defoliant Agent Orange lingers in some places, though how you'd tell it from government lumbering I don't know. US airbases stand fenced-off and unused in Da Nang and Tuy Hoa, the rocket-proof hangars looking like upside-down poker chip trays. The great strategic jackpot of southeast Asia, Cam Ranh Bay, contained exactly one freighter, rusting and locally registered. On a scrap heap south of Hue I saw two empty napalm pods stenciled 'U.S.A.F'. I saw a Mig fighter plane kiddie carrousel in Vinh. In Hai Phong a ruined street has been preserved to commemorate the 1972 'Christmas Bombing' which President Nixon launched to remind the North Vietnamese to pay attention at the negotiating table. But when Pham and Vo asked around in Hai Phong, nobody could recall where the street was.

John and I had gone to the War Museum in Hanoi. Its main

74

courtyard is filled by a ziggurat of American plane wreckage – a Hellcat supplied to the French in the 50s, some kind of pilotless drone from 1965, an F-111 shot down in 1972 and large sections of a B-52 intercepted that same year. Perched on top, all in one piece, is a North Vietnamese Mig-21. This is supposed to be a triumphal display, but it only succeeds in looking like the pile of waste that it is.

Inside the museum just a few of the galleries are dedicated to what we think of as the War in Vietnam. Displays are arranged chronologically. The first exhibit concerns Trung Trac and Trung Nhi, sisters who led a rebellion against Chinese colonists in 40 AD. Thus the Vietnamese had 1,923 more years of experience in guerrilla warfare than the US Army did. The largest exhibit is a scale model of the valley at Dien Bien Phu, a miniature landscape as big as a tennis court showing, in precise detail, just how dumb were the French.

In the room devoted to the American era there are huge photos of US college students protesting the war policies of President 'Gion Xon'. I couldn't actually find my own face in any of the pictures, but close enough. A little embarrassing – it's one thing for me to be nostalgic about hippie days and something else for commie dictators to celebrate my past.

And then the museum just keeps going – fall of the South Vietnamese government in 1975, expulsion of Pol Pot from Phnom Penh in 1978, border clashes with the Chinese in 1979. 'When,' I asked Pham, 'was the last period of sustained peace in Vietnam?'

'Oh, seventeenth, eighteenth century,' he said.

The only thing the Vietnamese seem to have against America now is that we won't do business with them, won't open our markets, won't let them make money off us the way everybody else in Asia does. (Won't, that is, not counting the thousands I was paying the Vietnamese government for this grand tour.)

The problem is, of course, POWs and MIAs. As of 1 July 1991, 2,266 Americans are unaccounted for in Southeast Asia. Of these 650 are believed to have been captured alive. John and I had dinner with one of the people from the US government's Office for POW/MIA Affairs in Hanoi. He believes it's possible that American POWs are still alive in Vietnam. He doesn't think it's likely, but the Vietnamese government is morally capable of a thing like that. 'Live Americans are political chips,' he said. 'Dead Americans are economic chips.'

The sad thing is that political chips aren't worth much now the cold war is gone. It would be embarrassing for a live American to show up in Vietnamese custody at this late date. I personally have a bad feeling that, if any American POWs 'were alive, the Vietnamese government killed them. We're not dealing with Vaclev Havel here.

The dead bodies of Americans, however, are definitely being held in Vietnam. The Vietnamese government may be warehousing remains as some kind of bargaining ploy – nobody knows. But we do know that the peasants and mountain tribesmen in remote parts of Vietnam have some bones and dog-tags. American pilots wore, sewn into their flight suits, something known as a 'blood chit'. It said – in Vietnamese, French, English, Laotian, Kamchukian and other languages – that the US government would reward anyone who returned that pilot. People in rural Vietnam are caught between greed and fear. They believe they will be given money and help in emigrating if they return American remains to Americans (which isn't true). And they believe they will be in trouble if their government catches them trying this (which is true). So the farmers and hill folks hoard these sad and grisly artifacts. And the men from the US Office of POW/MIA Affairs travel all over Vietnam tracking down rumors and leads.

One night at dinner Vo and Giannini discovered they'd been on opposite sides of the same series of battles along the Cambodian border in the early 70s – something they both seemed to think was very amusing. A large number of toasts were drunk. Pham, who was too young to fight Americans, and I, who was a long-haired peace creep, were left out. John and Vo filled their glasses first with beer, then with Scotch, then with a terrifying rice whiskey called *ba xi de*. 'One hundred per cent!' Vo would shout, the Vietnamese call for a chug-a-lug. '*Di di mau*!' John would shout, which means 'get the hell out of here'. And they'd drain their drinks in a gulp. They got quite merry. And so did the restaurant owners, happily totaling the check.

The South

It was the first full moon of the lunar new year, an auspicious day. New fishing boats were being launched into the harbor at Da Nang with so many good luck fireworks that these boats would never sink, they'd blow up. We went down the coast a few miles to the old port town of Hoi An, a center of Vietnam's ethnic Chinese, or Hoa. They number 1.3 million, or did before 1975 when many became 'boat people'. The Hoa were merchants and manufacturers. They were very successful and thus, according to the logic of Marxism, responsible for society's failures. The Hoa suffered the same fate as the pizza parlor owner in Spike Lee's *Do the Right Thing* except at the hands of the world's fourth largest army instead of a small, petulant movie director.

But most Hoa stuck it out. On this day they'd come to Hoi An's pagodas to pay respects to their ancestors. We saw our first civilian Mercedes-Benz here and several Honda Accords. New clothes and big jewelry abounded. We visited a house on the quay along the Thu Bon River, built in the eighteenth century and occupied by the same family of Hoa merchants for seven generations. These tradesmen had survived the radical leveling of the 1771 Tay Son Rebellion (slogan: 'Seize the property of the rich and distribute it to the poor'), the ridiculous taxes of the subsequent Nguyen Dynasty, the thefts and depredations of French colonialism, the worse thefts and greater depredations of Japanese occupation, the amazing corruption of the Ngo Dinh

Diem regime, the drunks and diddlings of American soldiers and the all-of-the-aboves of communism.

The long, dark interior of the house was dense with ornament, its walls carved and lacquered like an inside-out reliquary. The exterior looked – wisely enough – like nothing much.

Vo had to go back to Hanoi. We got a second, and very bad, driver to take us on to Saigon. We went along the coast, past the fabulous expanse of China Beach where there's no trace of Americans, not even actress litter such as wadded-up divorce rulings or left-over nose jobs. A quack doctor was giving a show by the roadside. He held forth with the wide gestures and speedy cadences universal to his type. But humbug is improved by ignorance of the language. ' . . . relieves Marxist/Leninism!' perhaps the quack was saying. 'Purges collectivist thinking! Relieves central planning! An unfailing antidote and panacea – it will even cure socialized medicine!'

South of Da Nang the villages were small – grass shacks on the beaches with terraced fields cut out of the hills on the other side of the highway. Despite the heavy traffic the farmers leave sliced sweet potatoes on the road to dry in the sun – sweet potatoes in a light asphalt sauce finished with truck tire. There's no other place to put the crop. Only 20 per cent of Vietnam's land is flat enough to farm. And that 20 per cent is some of the most densely populated acreage in the world. You're never out of sight of people. And this is a problem if you want privacy for certain body functions.

Traveling in the third world entails an extraordinary amount of having to go to the bathroom. And right now. I've read a lot of travel writing and never seen this mentioned. T.E. Lawrence does touch on bowel movements in *Seven Pillars of Wisdom*, but that's war reporting and, anyway, he was constipated which hardly counts. The irresistible food and unmentionable hygiene of Vietnam make a particularly bad combination. And no amount of Lomotil, Pepto Bismol or quick trips over the top of restaurant pigs seemed to do any good. Between Da Nang and Na Trang I actually found a gas station with a decent john. It was a Turkish, squatter-style toilet in a dark, damp room. But it didn't smell and it had toilet paper instead of the usual small jug of water. I got my jeans around my ankles and was just hunkering down when I spied movement. I stood up and lit a match. The toilet was full to the brim with crawling insects, uncountable numbers of them, each as big as a Bic lighter.

Even when I didn't have to go to the bathroom I felt like I did. My kidneys were swinging around like twin tether balls during the fourteen hours a day of jolting in the Land Cruiser, and my prostate was swollen to the size of a paperback book. Actually this was a welcome distraction from back pain. My spine felt like a stack of broken china. But, since we were getting up at five, no discomfort was too severe to keep me from dozing off. Then the car would drop into an abysmal pot hole and my sleeping face would be sent on a long arc into the dashboard.

Fortunately Giannini and I were adhering to the two key rules of third world travel:

1. Never run out of whiskey.
2. Never run out of whiskey.

We were also calling frequent halts so we could make notes or take pictures. We were willing to do anything, even our jobs, to get out of the car.

We stopped in a village called Xuan Tho where the men were all building a wooden boat like the one we'd used in Ha Long Bay. The timber had been cut locally. The keel, transom, gunwales and other specially named pieces of boat wood were being shaped by hand. One man squatted by a whetstone doing nothing all day but sharpening adzes and chisels. There was one power tool, an electric drill hooked up to the village's small generator. Bolts, washers and nuts were the only machine-made parts in the hull, and there were only a few of these. The rest of the boat was being put together with wedges and pegs. The whole, including cabin and fittings, would cost about $2000, but then they'd have to pay $3500 for a Chinese diesel. It won't be long before they hear about outboards. By the time I get back to Vietnam they'll be skiing behind this boat.

We stopped at another village to watch a fight. The long wooden yokes used to carry coolie baskets turn out to double as quarter staffs – in case anyone wants to do multicultural casting of Little John in the next Robin Hood remake.

And we stopped in yet another village to look at circus posters. Most of the acts seemed to involve severed heads or girls in tight clothing being pierced by knives, plus some levitation and swallowing of razor blades. The circus posters were propped against a wall, obscuring a communist propaganda mural. The figures in the mural – a worker, a peasant, a soldier and so forth – were staring off into the distance. People in communist propaganda art are always staring off into the distance. Did they just cut one?

Giannini tried to talk to everybody we met – so we wouldn't have to get back in the Land Cruiser. But he didn't have much success. John speaks with a Saigon accent and Vietnamese regional pronunciation varies greatly. I had a little book called, tellingly, *Vietnamese So Easy!* I didn't even try. Vietnamese is tonal so that meaning varies not only according to the sound you make but according to whether you make that sound as a tenor or a baritone. *Cho*, *cho* and *cho* mean, with tonal variations of the vowel, 'market', 'dog' and 'to give'. The rest of the language is just as phonetically subtle. *Com* (cooked rice), *khong* (no), *cam* (orange), *ca'm* (not allowed) and *kem* (ice-cream) are all pronounced, to the American ear, 'kum'. Thus you can ask somebody to give you ice-cream and wind up in the market with a forbidden orange dog.

We stayed the night in Na Trang, another of Vietnam's exasperating number of beauty spots. The little harbor here is tucked between mountains. Bright blue fishing boats ride at anchor, gimlet eyes painted on their bows. A miniature shrine to the sea gods sits on the harbor rock. And a seventh-century Cham tower commands the scene, the Cham being an indigenous people of Hindu beliefs who built sandstone monuments in chocolate-dipped Dairy Queen shapes.

It is a photograph damned to endless appearance in tourist brochures. And, indeed, the French are planning a Club Med in Na Trang. The French will then accomplish, with sexually transmitted diseases, what they failed to do with soldiers and rubber plantations.

Rubber plantations were what made the French so intent on keeping Indochina – lest the Michelin Man have to go around in a barrel. Rubber plantations seem like an odd idea. It's hard not to imagine the woods full of tire swings, or worse. In fact they look like any forest except the trees are in perfect rows – as if God had, for one moment during creation, been spelled by a certified public accountant.

In between the rubber plantations were hop yards for Vietnam's excellent beer and vineyards for Vietnam's execrable wine and mango trees smelling like perfume on your high-school girlfriend.

We turned inland at Phan Thiet. The hills here, at the end of the dry season, are sere and almost Mexican looking. Old American and European cars began to appear on the road. The mile markers all read 'Saigon' now instead of being painted over with the abbreviation for Ho Chi Minh City. Buddhist monks wandered around with their begging bowls – almost as many as in Boulder, Colorado. Churches were open and I saw a new Catholic church being built.

Saigon doesn't begin at any particular place. It just oozes out of the surrounding country until you realize the farms are gone and you're circled by industrial litter. Billboards advertise Taiwanese electronics and Japanese cameras. And traffic is heavy enough to bring itself to a halt, something that doesn't happen anywhere else in Vietnam. There are four stoplights in the 1,050 miles between Hanoi and Saigon, and only the one in Saigon is being obeyed and that only because the intersection is blocked. Here, finally, is something other than a beauty spot. Saigon has none of rural poverty's loveliness, none of manual labor's charm. Saigon is like all the other great modern cities of the world. It's the mess left from people getting rich.

Hearts and Minds and Wallets

Never has there been such pure, unconcealed all-hogs-to-the-trough capitalism among the citizens of a supposedly collectivist milieu. (Never, that is, if you don't count the drug and tie-dye bazaars in the parking lots outside Greatful Dead concerts.) The Vietnamese government had been edging towards economic reform since the late 70s. But nothing seemed to work. Whatever the government tried, the country remained a socialist butthole. Then, about a year and a half ago, the commies just gave up. They took the price controls off everything, put privacy back into private property and told everybody to go make a living. Faced with a choice between leading and following, the Vietnamese government got out of the way. And the Vietnamese people aren't Russians. They didn't just stand there with their dong in their hands. (Dong is, no joke, what the money's called. $1 US = 11,500 dong. As Claudia Rosset, editorial page editor of the *Asia Wall Street Journal*, has pointed out, the first thing the Vietnamese have to do, if they're serious about being a credible part of the world economy, is change the name of their currency.)

The economic situation in Vietnam is so interesting that I was almost interested in talking to economists. I interviewed Do Duc Dinh whose business card read, 'Head of Developing Countries Economic Study Department, Institute of World Economy, National Center for Social Sciences of Viet Nam' – a title almost as long as one of those articles in the *New York Review of Books* excusing the failure of Marxism. Speaking of which, Mr Do is firmly against central planning. The people who generate central planning's abstract theories are no longer important, he said. 'You may think of sky,' said Mr Do, 'and not know sky. You may think earth looks like sky.'

Where this left the Institute of World Economy and its Developing Countries Economic Study Department, I didn't ask. But wasn't Mr Do – as a nominal marxist, or employee of nominal marxists, or, anyway, public official in a country with a famous dead marxist stuffed and exhibited for veneration – worried about capitalist exploitation of the masses? 'People were afraid if the window was opened flies and mosquitoes would come in,' said Mr Do. 'But with money we can buy mosquito repellant or screens.'

Le Dang Doanh, Deputy Director of the Central Institute for Economic Management, was even more emphatically against economic management being centralized in things like institutes. He told a story about a fisherman who was a Communist Party member and the head of a local fishing co-operative. The government-set price for fish was less than the cost of catching them. The other fishermen sold their fish on the black market and made a living. But the party member felt the dignity of his office and couldn't bring himself to break the law. He lost money every time he went to sea. Finally he cut off his thumb so he'd never have to fish again.

Mr Le said that in 1989 state-controlled markets were selling rice for 50 dong a kilo. When price restrictions were lifted the price increased by more than 1200 per cent. For a moment I thought Mr Le was describing the other side of the coin, that I was going to hear another story, this time about someone who cut off his thumb for food. But no. 'In one year rice production increased by one million metric tons,' said Mr Le. Vietnam, which had formerly needed to import 500,000 metric tons of rice a year, now exports 1.4 million. 'Production increased and consumption fell,' said Mr Le. But, I asked, does that mean people are going hungry? 'Ha!' said Mr Le. 'They used to stand in line to buy rice for pigs. It was cheaper than pig food.'

Mr Le – who is sometimes called, for his rhetorical style, 'Mr I-would-like-to-say' – then lectured me on the benefits of the free market. Lectured *me* – a New Hampshire tax refugee and unreconstructed country club Republican who twice voted for Ronald Reagan and will vote for him a third time this fall. Le Dang Doanh was educated in East Germany. Le Dang Doanh was an economic adviser to Truong Chinh, the hard-line former Secretary General of the Vietnamese Communist Party. And Le Dang Doanh wanted to make sure I understood economic liberty.

Next some liberal Democrat American presidential candidate will come out for a 15 per cent flat rate income tax.

American presidential candidates – that's about what Le Dang Doanh and Do Duc Dinh are. Their free market gab is all mixed – like Bill Clinton's – with calls for government programs. In fact, they and Bill are calling for government programs from the same government – ours. Le and Do want US aid in the form of IMF and World Bank loans to the Vietnamese state.

Le and Do saw nothing contradictory about pursuing free enterprise while increasing totalitarian wherewithal. Nor did a third economist, Dr Nguyen Xuan Oanh. Dr Nguyen went to Harvard and was once an official in the South Vietnamese government. He was sent to a re-education camp after the fall of Saigon but is now rehabilitated and a member of the People's Assembly. Imagine the coals-to-Newcastle problem of turning a Harvard grad into a socialist. Not that Dr Nguyen is a socialist anymore. 'If you keep on being socialist, the only way you go is down,' he said. None the less he was full of ideas for social engineering. He proposed mandating 'weaker beer' to alleviate the social chaos that might result from capitalism. Isn't it danger-ous, I asked, to mix the unlimited economic power of an unregu-lated market with the infinite political power of an undemocratic state? Isn't this a recipe for corruption on a truly US Con-gressional scale? Dr Nguyen disagreed. 'I don't think it would cost much to corrupt *our* politicians – they wouldn't know what to do with large amounts of money.'

Le Dang Doanh told me that in Vietnam 'the taxation system is quite weak'. He seemed to think this was a problem. 'The state is poor but people are rich,' he said. Consider the glorious prospect of President Bush living in his car. Imagine Senators forced to panhandle for legislation. 'Spare fifty billion for a five-year omnibus farm bill?' Picture the US Attorney General driving a cab at night and the Secretary of Housing and Urban Develop-ment living in the projects. Think about the Drug Czar on drugs and Ted Kennedy trying to cash food stamps at a liquor store. Envision, if you will, 435 congressmen on street corners with hand-lettered cardboard signs: 'Will Work for Votes'.

The Light at the End of the Tunnel Is Neon

Saigon looks like it's governed by bums already. People are sleeping in doorways. Laundry hangs in the guard towers of the former US Embassy. The old architecture has long gone to seed and wasn't much to begin with, a product of 50s aesthetics and 60s communal violence – bunker modern.

Gnat packs of little kids follow you down the sidewalks shouting, 'Where you from ! Hello! You give me money!' The pedlars and shopkeepers shout at you, too, 'You buy here! Where you from! Where you from!' You wave them all away trying to say 'No! No! No!' in Vietnamese and probably saying 'Ice-cream! Cooked rice! Orange!'

Saigon is still a predominantly two-wheeled city, but motorized and not just with little Honda engines. Young idiots hardball down the avenues on 500cc café racers. Even bicycles are ridden with attitude. Traffic is like a bad dog. It isn't important to look both ways when crossing the street. It's important to not show fear.

There are many more cars here than in Hanoi. Some are new and Japanese, but there are also Citroëns and Peugeots from the 50s, Mustangs and Mercedes from the 60s and giant Chevrolets from the early 70s. The older cars are well-preserved. In 1975 the citizens of Saigon drove their automobiles through the french doors into the front parlors of their homes, turned the locks, pulled the blinds and waited until Vietnam got over communism.

John and I visited a little garage the size of the basement at your house and not much better equipped. The mechanics had one drill press, one lathe, a paint sprayer and an acetylene torch. With these, a dozen cars from Saigon's unintentional time capsule were being restored – a 1971 Peugeot 404 convertible, a little A-2 US Army jeep, a 1972 Toyota 800 sports car and so on. They're collectors items now and will all be re-exported to foreign buyers. An exquisite 1958 Citroën Traction – the getaway car of choice in twenty years of French bankrobber movies – had just been sold to someone in Italy for US $6000.

This was one of thousands of plans and schemes, projects and plots. In the rest of Vietnam people are trying to make money. In Saigon they're succeeding. Restaurants are opening by the score, none as good as the Dong Hoi roadside shack with the pig in the toilet but all with concessions to international taste such as forks, hamburgers, sit-down commodes and huge prices. It's like being in the Vietnam Pavilion at Epcot Center. There's even a bar called Apocalypse Now, decorated with war memorabilia. And plenty of American Vietnam vets are back on vacation, reeling around in shock at discovering their girlfriends have turned forty. An international Marathon had just been run in Saigon, although the Vietnamese are inexperienced in these matters and didn't think to block traffic. And the locals were so intrigued by people running without being chased that they swarmed onto the course, asking, 'Where you from!'

The apartment where the narrator in Graham Greene's *The Quiet American* smoked his opium has been torn down to make way for a 600-room hotel financed by Taiwanese. A floating hotel – which had gone into Chapter 11 on the Great Barrier Reef because Aussies prefer a drink in the room to a room in the drink – has been towed up the Saigon River. I was schmoozed by a woman in the bar there. I assumed she was a prostitute. Worse than that, she sold real estate.

'Joint venture!' is, after 'Where you from!', the most heard phrase in Saigon. Government and private citizens alike are trying to get in on them, though the government is doing so with typical communist confusion. I visited the gigantic state textile company, Legamex, which wants to turn itself into a publicly held corporation. 'The problem now,' an executive told me, 'is how to evaluate our fixed assets.' A value of what people would pay apparently not having occurred to him.

The government has also reopened Ehu Tho racetrack. The grandstands haven't been painted, or swept, since Saigon fell, and the groundskeepers seem to belong to some littering advocacy group, but Ehu Tho is filled with punters. God knows what their handicap method is. The horses are ponies, the jockeys are children and neither seem to be trained for anything particular. Just getting the kids mounted is no sure bet. They are supposed to be sixteen years old but I doubt most are twelve and some looked as young as eight. I watched one trainer hold a tyke in racing silks aloft with both hands and chase a rearing horse around the paddock, trying to slam-dunk his jockey into the saddle. In the first race only one kid had his feet placed properly in the stirrups and he ran second to last.

When the starting gate opens the horses run down the track any old way, like mice let out of a paper sack. Jockeys are launched in every direction. A riderless horse is placed third in one race. The moment the jockeys cross the finish line – or come to in the infield – they have to run back to the tack room and strip. Somebody else needs the jersey for the next race.

Di choi, 'go for fun', the atmosphere in Saigon is called. Gianinni and I tried to have some at the Super Star Disco. Unfortunately, Asia is the continent rhythm forgot. At best Asian music is off-brand American pop, like hiring your cousin's band to play the prom. At worst Asian music sounds as if a truck full of wind chimes collided with a stack of empty oil drums during a bird call contest. The locals boogied away regardless, dancing in the style of parents at a Bar Mitzvah.

Out on the streets the whores were cruising, whores on motor scooters who wear tight jeans, a pound of makeup and elbow-length blue gloves; whores being pedaled around in *cyclos* by their combination pimp/rickshaw driver boyfriends, and whores who stand outside hotel lobbies. 'Where you from! Where you from! Where you from!' There are junkies, too. They can't get needles so they slash their legs with razor blades and rub heroin into the wounds. You see them bandaged and hobbling on crutches like victims of pathetic accidents except for the slow and dreamy way they hobble.

'How is this different from Saigon before it fell?' I asked Gianinni.

'It isn't,' he said.

Hard to believe that the thrilling ideal of human liberty always ends up with people acting so . . . human. Like Americans or something. Reading *The Rights of Man*, the *Declaration of Independence*, the preamble to the *Constitution*, it's something of a disappointment to know that the fruit borne by our founding fathers' noble struggles and hard sacrifices is, um, me. Me and the Vietnamese. Ho Chi Minh, after all, called himself 'the George Washington of Vietnam'.

In the Saigon shops there are thousands of Zippo lighters left behind by US soldiers. Each lighter is engraved with a byword or motto, most often:

> OURS IS NOT TO DO OR DIE
> OURS IS TO SMOKE AND STAY HIGH

SECOND
THOUGHTS

A
SERIOUS
PROBLEM

'Is it serious?' we ask the doctor. 'I'm not kidding,' we tell the child. 'What's so funny?' says the voice of authority from classroom to army camp to editorial page of the *New York Times*. The threat of solemnity haunts our lives. Little profit and less pleasure accrue from most somber occasions. The smiles of people emerging from courtrooms, church services and even wedding ceremonies are usually smiles of relief. Life is weighty, important, grave, critical, momentous, etc. Not for nothing does *Roget's Thesaurus* say '*Antonyms* – See DRUNKENNESS, FRIVOLITY, PLAYFULNESS, UNIMPORTANCE.' Yes, indeed, let's see them right away.

But though wise men spend their days trying to stay out of serious trouble, there are other people who frankly wallow in sobriety. They look serious, think about serious things, pick serious topics and speak about them seriously. These are the dinner partners who discuss famine over oysters, the house guests who lecture infirm great-aunts on the importance of aerobic exercise, the journalists who author articles titled 'Whither Gambia' (a kind of writing known in the trade as MEGO: 'My Eyes Glaze Over'). Why do they do it?

My guess is self-loathing. Self-loathing is one of those odd, illogical leaps of human intuition that is almost always correct.

'Serious' people are dense and know it. But, they think, if they can be grave enough about Yugoslavia their gravity will make up for the fact that – like most people – they don't know what's going on there, and – like all people – they don't know what to do about it. Seriousness is stupidity sent to college.

Serious topics also make unimportant people feel as important as what they're discussing. Of course, it's necessary to make sure everyone understands how important the topic is. Hemingway was just a tourist watching Spaniards tease farm animals. But if he could make cattle-pestering a grand and tragic thing in the eyes of the public, he'd become grand and tragic too, because he'd been there while somebody did it.

Truly serious topics give this kind of bore a rare conversational advantage. There isn't any decent way to shut him up. Nobody wants to be caught saying, 'Who cares if seventy thousand people drowned in Bangladesh?'

Seriousness is also the great excuse for sin. These days anything can be forgiven if the person was sincere about his actions. 'I did what I thought was best at the time' is the modern equivalent of a perfect act of contrition. Personally, I'd be more inclined to absolve George Bush if he'd let Saddam Hussein live from pure good nature. But 'I was acting in what I felt to be the best interests of the nation' seems to be more what the public wants to hear.

Seriousness lends force to bad arguments. If a person is earnest enough about what he says, he must have *some* point. There's a movement in some of our school systems to give creationists equal time in science class. Man was plopped down on earth the week before last, is one rib short on the left, and because silly people are serious about this so are we.

Seriousness is also the only practical tone to take when lying. The phrase 'to lie with a straight face' is prolix. All lies are told with a straight face. It's truth that's said with a dismissive giggle.

Real seriousness is involuntary. If you're held at gunpoint or run over by a bus, you'll be serious about it. If you're a decent person, you'll also have some serious feelings when you see someone else threatened or squashed. In fact, if you're a decent person faced with the world's catastrophes, horrors and pleas for help, you'll do the right thing whether you're serious or not.

Sir Thomas More jested with his head on the block. 'My neck is very short,' he warned the executioner. 'Take heed, therefore, thou strike not awry, for saving of thine honesty.' The Persian king Xerxes was astonished when his scouts told him the Spartans holding the pass at Thermopylae were combing their hair and changing into clean clothes for the battle. Gallantry is the proper tone for those who are worth being taken seriously. With one exception – serious looks and serious voice are absolutely necessary when calling the dog.

What I believed in the sixties

Everything. You name it and I believed it. I believed love was all you need. I believed you should be here now. I believed drugs could make everyone a better person. I believed I could hitchhike to California with thirty-five cents and people would be glad to feed me. I believed Mao was cute. I believed private property was wrong. I believed my girlfriend was a witch. I believed my parents were Nazi space monsters. I believed the university was putting saltpeter in the cafeteria food. I believed stones had souls. I believed the NLF were the good guys in Vietnam. I believed Lyndon Johnson was plotting to murder all the Negroes. I believed Yoko Ono was an artist. I believed Bob Dylan was a musician. I believed I would live forever or until twenty-one, whichever came first. I believed the world was about to end. I believed the Age of Aquarius was about to happen. I believed the *I Ching* said to cut classes and take over the dean's office. I believed wearing my hair long would end poverty and injustice. I believed there was a great throbbing web of psychic mucus and we were all part of it somehow. I managed to believe Gandhi and H. Rap Brown at the same time. With the exception of anything my mom and dad said, I believed everything.

What Caused Me to Have Second Thoughts

One distinct incident sent me scuttling back to Brooks Brothers. From 1969 to 1971 I was a member of a 'collective' running an 'underground' newspaper in Baltimore. The newspaper was called, of all things, *Harry*. When *Harry* was founded, nobody could think what to name the thing so some girl's two-year-old son was asked. His grandfather was Harry and he was calling everything Harry just then so he said, 'Harry', and *Harry* was what the paper was called. It was the spirit of the age.

Harry was filled with the usual hippie blather, yea drugs and revolution, boo war and corporate profits. But it was an easy-going publication and not without a sense of humor. The want-ads section was headlined 'Free Harry Classifieds Help Hep Cats and Kittens Fight Dippy Capitalist Exploitation'. And once when the office was raided by the cops (they were looking for marijuana, I might add, not sedition), *Harry* published a page-one photo of the mess left by the police search. The caption read, 'Harry office after bust by pigs.' Next to it was an identical photo captioned, 'Harry office before bust by pigs.'

Our 'collective' was more interested in listening to Captain Beefheart records and testing that new invention, the water bed, than in overthrowing the state. And some of the more radical types in Baltimore regarded us as lightweights or worse. Thus, one night in the summer of 1970, the *Harry* collective was invaded by some twenty-five blithering Maoists armed with large sticks. They called themselves, and I'm not making this up, the 'Balto Cong'. They claimed they were liberating the paper in the name of 'the people'. In vain we tried to tell them that the only thing the people were going to get by liberating *Harry* was ten thousand dollars in debts and a mouse-infested row house with overdue rent.

There were about eight *Harry* staffers in the office that evening. The Balto Cong held us prisoner all night and subjected each of us to individual 'consciousness-raising' sessions. You'd be hauled off to another room where ten or a dozen of these nutcakes would sit in a circle and scream that you were a revisionist running dog imperialist paper tiger watchama-thing. I don't know about the rest of the staff, but I conceded as quick as I could to every word they said.

Finally, about 6:00 a.m., we mollified the Balto Cong by agreeing to set up a 'people's committee' to run the paper. It would be made up of their group and our staff. We would all meet that night on neutral turf at the Free Clinic. The Balto Cong left in triumph. My airhead girlfriend had been converted to Maoism during her consciousness-raising session. And she left with them.

While the Balto Cong went home to take throat pastilles and make new sticks or whatever, we rolled into action. There were, in those days, about a hundred burned-out 'street people' who depended on peddling *Harry* for their livelihood. We rallied all of these, including several members of a friendly motorcycle gang, and explained to them how little sales appeal *Harry* would have if it were filled with quotations from Ho Chi Minh instead of free-love personals. They saw our point. Then we phoned the Balto Cong crash pad and told them we were ready for the meeting. 'But,' we said, 'is the Free Clinic large enough to hold us all?' 'What do you mean?' they said. 'Well,' we said, 'we're bringing about a hundred of our staff members and there's, what, twenty-five of you, so . . . ' They said, um, they'd get back to us.

We were by no means sure the Balto Cong threat had abated. Therefore the staff photographer, whom I'll call Bob, and I were set to guard the *Harry* household. Bob and I were the only two people on the staff who owned guns. Bob was an ex-Marine and something of a flop as a hippie. He could never get the hair and the clothes right and preferred beer to pot. But he was very enthusiastic about hippie girls. Bob still had his service automatic.

I had a little .22-caliber pistol that I'd bought in a fit of wild self-dramatization during the '68 riots. 'You never know when the heavy shit is going to come down,' I had been fond of saying. Although I'd pictured it 'coming down' more from the Richard Nixon than the Balto Cong direction. Anyway, Bob and I stood guard. We stood anxious guard every night for two weeks, which seemed an immense length of time back in 1970. Of course we began to get slack, not to say stoned, and forgot things like locking the front door. And through that front door, at the end of two weeks, came a half dozen hulking Balto Cong. Bob and I were at the back of the first-floor office. Bob had his pistol in the waistband of his ill-fitting bell-bottoms. He went to fast draw and, instead, knocked the thing down the front of his pants. My pistol was in the top drawer of a desk. I reached in and grabbed it, but I was so nervous that I got my thigh in front of the desk drawer and couldn't get my hand with the pistol in it out. I yanked like mad but I was stuck. I was faced with a terrible dilemma. I could either let go of the pistol and pull my hand out of the drawer or I could keep hold of the pistol and leave my hand stuck in there. It never occurred to me to move my leg.

The invading Balto Cong were faced with one man fishing madly in his crotch and another apparently being eaten by a desk. It stopped them cold. As they stood perplexed I was struck by an inspiration. It was a wooden desk. I would simply fire through it. I flipped the safety off the .22, pointed the barrel at the Balto Cong and was just curling my finger around the trigger when the Maoists parted and there, in the line of fire, stood my airhead ex-girlfriend. 'I've come to get my ironing board and my Hermann Hesse novels,' she said, and led her companions upstairs to our former bedroom.

'It's a trap!' said Bob, extracting his gun from the bottom of a pants leg. When the Balto Cong and the ex-girlfriend came back downstairs they faced two exceedingly wide-eyed guys crouching like leopards behind an impromptu barricade of overturned book cases. They sped for the exit.

It turned out later that Bob was an undercover cop. He'd infiltrated the *Harry* collective shortly after the first issue. All his photos had been developed at the police laboratory. We'd wondered why every time we got busted for marijuana the case was dropped. Bob would always go to the District Attorney's office and convince them a trial would 'blow his cover'. It was important for him to remain undetected so he could keep his eye on . . . well, on a lot of hippie girls. Bob was in no rush to get back to the Grand Theft Auto detail. I eventually read some of the reports Bob filed with the police department. They were made up of '— — is involved in the *Harry* "scene" primarily as a means of upsetting his parents who are socially prominent,' and other such. Today, Bob is an insurance investigator in Baltimore. He's still friends with the old *Harry* staff. And, of the whole bunch of us, I believe there's only one who's far enough to the left to even be called a Democrat.

What I Believe Now

Nothing. Well, nothing much. I mean, I believe things that can be proven by reason and by experiment, and, believe you me, I want to see the logic and the lab equipment. I believe that Western civilization, after some disgusting glitches, has become almost civilized. I believe it is our first duty to protect that civilization. I believe it is our second duty to improve it. I believe it is our third duty to extend it if we can. But let's be careful about that last point. Not everybody is ready to be civilized. I wasn't in 1969.

Is There Anything to Be Gained by Re-Examining All This Nonsense?

I like to think of my behavior in the sixties as a 'learning experience'. Then again, I like to think of anything stupid I've done as a 'learning experience'. It makes me feel less stupid. However, I actually did learn one thing in the 1960s (besides how to make a hash pipe out of an empty toilet-paper roll and some aluminum foil). I learned the awful power of make-believe.

There is a deep-seated and frighteningly strong human need to make believe things are different than they are – that salamanders live forever, we all secretly have three legs and there's an enormous conspiracy somewhere which controls our every thought and deed, etc. And it's not just ignorant heathen, trying to brighten their squalid days, who think up such things. Figments of the imagination can be equally persuasive right here in clean, reasonable, education-chocked middle America. People are greedy. Life is never so full it shouldn't be fuller. What more can Shirley MacLaine, for instance, want from existence? She's already been rewarded far beyond her abilities or worth. But nothing will do until she's also been King Tut and Marie of Romania. It was this kind of hoggish appetite for epistemological romance that sent my spoiled and petulant generation on a journey to Oz, a journey from which some of us are only now straggling back, in intellectual tatters.

Many people think fantastical ideas are limited to the likes of harmonic convergences, quartz crystals that ward off cancer or, at worst, harebrained theories about who killed JFK. Unfortunately, this is not the case, especially not in this century. Two of the most fecund areas for cheap fiction are politics and economics. Which brings me to Marxism.

Marxism is a perfect example of the chimeras that fueled the sixties. And it was probably the most potent one. Albeit, much of this Marxism would have been unrecognizable to Marx. It was Marxism watered down, Marxism spiked wth LSD and Marxism adulterated with mystical food coloring. But it was Marxism nonetheless because the wildest hippie and the sternest member of the Politburo shared the same daydream, the daydream that underlies all Marxism: *that a thing might somehow be worth other than what people will give for it.* This just is not true. And any system that bases itself on such a will-o'-the-wisp is bound to fail. Communes don't work. Cuba doesn't either.

Now this might not seem like much to have learned. You may think I could have gleaned more from a half dozen years spent ruining chromosomes, morals and any chance of ever getting elected to political office. After all, the hippies are gone and – if current events are any indication – the Communists are going. But there is a part of the world where politico-economic fish stories are still greeted with gape-jawed credulity. It's a part of the world that pretty much includes everybody except us, the Japanese, some Europeans and a few of the most cynical Russians. You can call it the Third World, the Underdeveloped World or just the Part of the World That's Completely Screwed.

Over the past eight years, working as a foreign correspondent, I've spent a lot of time in the part of the world that's completely screwed. It's always seemed a comfortable and familiar-feeling place to me. The reason is, Third World countries are undergoing national adolescences very similar to the personal adolescence I underwent in the sixties. Woodstock Nation isn't dead; it's just become poor, brown, distant and filled with chaos and starvation.

Marxism has tremendous appeal in the Third World for exactly the same reason it had tremendous appeal to me in college. It gives you something to believe in when what surrounds you seems unbelievable. It gives you someone to blame besides yourself. It's theoretically tidy. And, best of all, it's fully imaginary so it can never be disproved.

The Third World attitude toward the United States is also easy to understand if you think of it in terms of adolescence. The citizens of the Third World are in a teenage muddle about us – full of envy, imitation, anger and blind puppy love. I have been held at gunpoint by a Shi'ite youth in West Beirut who told me in one breath that America was 'pig Satan devil' and that he planned to go to dental school in Dearborn as soon as he got his green card. In Ulundi, in Zululand, I talked to a young man who, as usual, blamed apartheid on the United States. However, he had just visited the US with a church group and also told me, 'Everything is so wonderful there. The race relations are so good.

And everyone is rich.' Just what part of America had he visited, I asked. 'The South Side of Chicago,' he said.

We are a beautiful twenty-year-old woman and they are a wildly infatuated thirteen-year-old boy. They think of us every moment of the day and we take no notice of them whatsoever. If they can't have a chance to love us, a chance to pester us will do – by becoming 'Communists', for example. Anything for attention.

Isn't this very like the relationship we 'dropouts' of the sixties had to the 'straight' society of our parents? Weren't we citizens of our own Underdeveloped World, the world of American teen-age pop culture?

So what are we supposed to do about all this? How do we keep the disaffected youth of the West out of mental Disney World? How do we keep the poor denizens of Africa, Asia and Latin America from embracing a myth that will make their lives even worse than they are already? How do we keep everyone from falling under the spell of some even more vile and barbaric phantom such as religious fundamentalism? We have to offer an alternative to nonsense, an alternative that is just as engaging but actually means something.

Maybe we should start by remembering that we already live in a highly idealistic, totally revolutionary society. And that our revolution is based on reality, not buncombe. Furthermore, it works. Look at America, Western Europe and Japan. It works like all hell. We have to remember it was the American Revolution, not the Bolshevik, that set the world on fire. Maybe we should start acting like we believe in that American Revolution again. This means turning our face against not only the Saddams, Qaddafis, Castros and Dengs of the world, but also against most of the US House of Representatives and half the Senate.

The President and his advisers will not have to sit up late working on a speech to fire the public in this cause. There's a perfectly suitable text already in print:

> We hold these truths to be self-evident; that all men are created equal; that they are endowed by their Creator with

101

certain unalienable Rights; that among these are Life, Liberty and the pursuit of Happiness; that to secure these rights, Governments are instituted among Men, deriving their just powers from the consent of the governed . . .

And that is a much wilder idea than anything which occurred to me during the 1960s.

FIDDLING
WHILE
AFRICA
STARVES

When the 'We Are the World' video first slithered into public view, I was sitting around with a friend who himself happens to be in show business. The thing gave him the willies. Me too. But neither of us could figure exactly why. 'Whenever you see people that pleased with themselves on a stage,' said my friend, 'you know you're in for a bad show.' And the USA for Africa performers did have that self-satisfied look of toddlers on a pot. But in this world of behemoth evils, such a minor lapse of taste shouldn't have upset us. We changed the channel.

Half a year later, in the middle of the Live Aid broadcast, my friend called me. 'Turn on your television,' he said. 'This is horrible. They're in a frenzy.'

'Well,' I said, 'at least it's a frenzy of charity.'

'Oh, no,' he said, 'it could be *anything*. Next time it might be "Kill the Jews."'

A mob, even an eleemosynary mob, is an ugly thing to see. No good ever came of mass emotion. The audience that's easily moved to tears is as easily moved to sadistic dementia. People are not thinking under such circumstances. And poor, dreadful Africa is something which surely needs thought.

The Band Aid, Live Aid, USA for Africa concerts and records

(and videos, posters, T-shirts, lunch buckets, thermos bottles, bath toys, etc.) are supposed to illuminate the plight of the Africans. Note the insights provided by these lyrics:

> *We are the world* [solipsism], *we are the*
>   *children* [average age near forty]
> *We are the ones to make a brighter day* [unproven]
> *So let's start giving* [logical inference
>   supplied without argument]
> *There's a choice we're making* [true as far
>   as it goes]
> *We're saving our own lives* [absurd]
> *It's true we'll make a better day* [see line 2 above]
> *Just you and me* [statistically unlikely]

That's three palpable untruths, two dubious assertions, nine uses of a first-person pronoun, not a single reference to trouble or anybody in it and no facts. The verse contains, literally, neither rhyme nor reason.

And these musical riots of philanthropy address themselves to the wrong problems. There is, of course, a shortage of food among Africans, but that doesn't mean there's a shortage of food *in* Africa. 'A huge backlog of emergency grain has built up at the Red Sea port of Assab,' says the *Christian Science Monitor*. 'Food sits rotting in Ethiopia,' reads a headline in the *St Louis Post-Dispatch*. And according to hunger maven William Shawcross, 200,000 tons of food aid delivered to Ethiopia is being held in storage by the country's government.

There's also, of course, a lack of transport for that food, but that's not the real problem either. The authorities in Addis Ababa have plenty of trucks for their military operations against the Eritrean rebels, and much of the rest of Ethiopia's haulage is being used for forcibly resettling people instead of feeding them. Western governments are reluctant to send more trucks, for fear they'll be used the same way. And similar behavior can be seen in the rest of miserable Africa.

The African relief fad serves to distract attention from the real issues. There is famine in Ethiopia, Chad, Sudan and areas of

Mozambique. All these countries are involved in pointless civil wars. There are pockets of famine in Mauritania, Niger and Mali – the result of desertification caused mostly by idiot agricultural policies. African famine is not a visitation of fate. It is largely man-made, and the men who made it are largely Africans.

Enormous irrigation projects have been put onto lands that cannot support them and into cultures that cannot use them. Feeble-witted nationalism puts borders in the way of nomadic peoples who used to pick up and move when things got dry. Rural poverty drives populations to African cities where governments keep food prices artificially low, thus increasing rural poverty. Bumbling and corrupt central planning stymies farm production. And the hideous regimes use hunger as a weapon to suppress rebellion. People are not just starving. They are *being* starved.

'Socialist' ideals infest Africa like malaria or dengue fever. African leaders, lost in the frippery of centrist thinking, fail to deal with market forces or any other natural phenomena. Leave it to a Marxist to see the world as the world is not. It's not unusual for African intellectuals to receive their education at such august bodies of learning as Patrice Lumumba U. in Moscow. That is, they are trained by a nation which intentionally starved millions of its citizens in order to collectivize farming.

Death is the result of bad politics. And the Aid concerts are examples of the bad logic that leads to bad politics. It's probably not going too far to say that Africa's problems have been produced by the same kind of dim, ignorant thinking found among American pop artists. 'If we take, say, six months and not spend any money on nuclear weapons, and just spend it on food, I think we could make a big dent,' says Waylon Jennings in the USA for Africa publicity packet. In fact, a small nuclear weapon placed directly under Haile Mariam Mengistu and his pals would probably make a more beneficial dent than a whole US defense budget worth of canned goods.

Anyway, money is not going to solve the problem. Yet the concert nonsense is all put strictly in terms of cash. Perhaps it is the only thing the idiot famous understand.

Getting people to give vast amounts of money when there's no firm idea what that money will do is like throwing maidens down a well. It's an appeal to magic. And the results are likely to be as stupid and disappointing as the results of magic usually are.

But, say some, Live Aid sets a good example for today's selfish youth, reminding them to be socially concerned. Nonsense. The circus atmosphere of the Live Aid concerts makes the world's problems seem easy and fun to solve and implies that the solutions are naturally uncontroversial. As an example of charity, Live Aid couldn't be worse. Charity entails sacrifice. Yet the Live Aid performers are sacrificing nothing. Indeed, they're gaining public adulation and a thoroughly unmerited good opinion of themselves. Plus it's free advertising. These LPs, performances and multiform by-products have nothing in common with charity. Instead they levy a sort of regressive alms tax on the befuddled millions. The performers donate their time, which is wholly worthless. Big corporations donate their services, which are worth little enough. Then the poor audience pledges all the contributions and buys all the trash with money it can ill afford. The worst nineteenth-century robber barons wouldn't have had the cheek to put forward such a bunco scheme. They may have given away tainted money, but at least they didn't ask you to give away yours.

One more thing, the music's lousy. If we must save the world with a song, what's the matter with the Metropolitan Opera Company?

Rock and roll's dopey crusade against African hunger has, I posit, added to the stock of human misery. And not just audibly. Any religious person – whether he worships at a pile of gazelle bones or in the Cathedral of St Paul – will tell you egotism is the source of sin. The lust for power that destroys the benighted Ethiope has the same fountainhead as the lust for fame that propels the lousy pop band. 'Not every one that saith unto me, Lord, Lord, shall enter into the kingdom of heaven.' Let alone everyone that saith sha la la la la and doobie doobie do.

THE
TWO-THOUSAND-
YEAR-OLD
US MIDDLE EAST
POLICY EXPERT

Since we as a nation insist on interfering in the Middle East, it behooves us to do some background reading. One all too appropriate book is *The Jewish War*, written nearly two millennia ago by Flavius Josephus.

Josephus gives a contemporary account of the great Jewish rebellion against Rome. The insurrection began in 66 AD and lasted seven years. The Middle East described by Josephus is perfectly familiar – a politically fractionalized land populated with a jumble of ethnic and religious groups. There are Jews, Arabs, Egyptians, Syrians, Greeks, Italians and (presumably) a smattering of Christians. Each detests the others. Extreme political and theological views prevail. Terrorism and assassination are commonplace. Alliances are momentary. Grudges, perennial. And neither colonial subjugation nor local autonomy suffices to keep the peace.

The political events are familiar, too. Rome first intervened in the region as a peace-keeper, brokering a dispute between Seleucid Mesopotamia and Ptolemaic Egypt. Later the Middle East appeared vital to Rome because Roman trade routes passed through the region and because of the Parthian threat to the empire's eastern frontier. The Romans were lured into deeper military and political involvement, and this triggered continual insurrections.

The rebellion of 66 AD, however, did not begin as a war of national liberation. It began as communal rioting in the seaport town of Caesarea – Greeks versus Jews over an empty lot next to a synagogue. This inspired sympathetic rioting in Jerusalem, and a hamfisted Roman attempt to quell the disturbances worsened them instead. The result was one of those great wallows of siege, massacre, treachery, persecution, revenge, plunder and self-destruction to which the Middle East is so often host.

Before the revolt was fairly under way, quarreling had broken out between radical and moderate factions in Jerusalem. Meanwhile, local government troops withdrew from the fray, leaving a greatly outnumbered Roman garrison trapped in the Palace of Herod. The Romans surrendered to the mob on a guarantee of safe conduct – and were murdered as soon as they laid down their weapons.

The rising in Jerusalem set off a reaction among the non-Jewish inhabitants of the region, who indulged themselves in wild pogroms, with killings taking place as far away as Damascus and Alexandria.

Roman military forces were not sufficient to quash the rebellion. Jewish forces were not sufficient to defeat the Romans in open combat. Guerrilla warfare ensued, with predictable consequences to the populace.

The Romans were notable for vigorous foreign-policy responses. The Emperor Nero sent Vespasian and three legions to pacify Judea.

Using a great deal of slaughter and some tactics, Vespasian drove the rebels back to the environs of Jerusalem. He was prevented from ending the war, however, by political confusion at home. Nero was ousted and three worthless and short-lived emperors followed within the year.

The Jews made use of this breathing space by engaging in urban warfare with themselves and by committing all conceivable and some inconceivable atrocities upon their coreligionists.

Vespasian himself was finally proclaimed emperor by the Roman army, and the war was resumed under the direction of his son Titus.

After a prolonged and disgusting siege, Jerusalem was taken. And after another prolonged and even more disgusting siege, Masada, the last rebel stronghold, fell.

The Temple was destroyed, the Jewish upper classes were dispersed, and a Roman army was permanently stationed in Judea. Even then the peace did not hold, and rebellion would break out anew in the reign of Hadrian.

Normally the patterns of history are reassuring. To hear of tsarist Russia pressing for warm-water ports or eighteenth-century England fighting hegemony on the continent or Ming China clashing with Japan over the fate of Korea is to feel a continuity, a comprehensibility, in human affairs. But in *The Jewish War* the shock of recognition is just a shock. Here, sixty generations ago, is nearly the same cast of characters engaged in exactly the same obsessive, vicious and fatal behavior for the same terrifying reasons on the same cursed, reeking, ugly chunk of land.

Who fails to learn history is doomed to repeat it. But we seemed doomed to repeat this history anyway. And what can we possibly learn from hearing that the man who was to become the most temperate and decent of Roman emperors entered the rebellious city of Gabara and 'put to the sword all but small children . . . showing mercy to neither young nor old through hatred of the nation . . . '? What can we learn by reading how the partisans in besieged Jerusalem tortured the plump in order to find hidden stores of food? And what can we learn from the defenders of Masada, who murdered their wives and children and chose suicide over a final battle so the Romans would be 'dumbfounded by our death and awed by our courage'?

Yet *The Jewish War* fascinates. We are spellbound by the ineluctability of events. This is history taking the tragic form exactly as described by Aristotle in *Poetics*: ' . . . with incidents arousing pity and terror, wherewith to accomplish its catharsis of such emotions.' And there is an even more compelling aspect to the book in the narrator himself. Josephus must be the most unabashedly contemptible character ever to have left an accurate self-portrait in print.

Born Joseph ben Matthais, scion of a well-connected Jewish family, he played an important role in the rebellion from its beginning. He was appointed general of the rebel armies in Galilee, making no protest though he claims he 'saw the inevitable end awaiting the Jews, and knew that their one safety lay in a change of heart.' He goes on to say, 'He himself, he felt sure, would be pardoned if he went over to the Romans.'

During the first year of the war Josephus was surrounded by Vespasian's forces in the hill town of Jotapata. Josephus tried to sneak away, but the towns folk prevented him. Jotapata was stormed, and when the defenses collapsed Josephus took a few remaining soldiers and hid in a cave. After a while he suggested that he surrender himself. His men threatened to kill him if he tried. He then suggested suicide with everyone drawing lots and killing each other in turn. Josephus manipulated the lottery, left himself as the last to die, and surrendered anyway.

He gained favor with his captor by making a shrewd and flattering prophecy that Vespasian would be emperor. When this indeed happened, Josephus was freed with honors. He became an active, if timid, member of Titus's staff. (At one point Titus tried to send Josephus to parlay with a group of wavering rebels. 'But Josephus refused to go himself, since the petitioners meant no good. . . . ')

During the siege of Jerusalem, 'Josephus circled the wall, striving to keep out of range but within hearing. . . . ' He yelled Roman propaganda at the battlements that were protecting, among other things, Josephus's wife and mother. '"It might well be reasonable,"' he quotes himself as hollering, '"to disdain meaner masters, but not the lords of the whole world. What corner of earth has escaped the Romans, unless heat or cold made it of no value to them? From every side fortune has passed on to them, and God, who handed domination over from nation to nation around the world, abode now in Italy."' That can hardly have been an effective tack. And the message was, Josephus admits, 'received by the defenders with howls of derision or execration, sometimes with showers of stones.'

These and many other treasons, peculations and self-seekings Josephus recounts with enthusiasm. He is broad-minded in his shamelessness. He lards every description of Rome and Romans with fawning praise. Then he extols the rebels for their courage and claims himself to be a champion of the Jews. It's worth noting that after the war he retired to an apartment in the Imperial Palace and spent the rest of his life writing best-sellers about his experiences.

Reason dictates we should hate this man. But it's hard to get angry at Josephus. What, after all, did he do? A few soldiers were tricked into suicide. Some demoralizing claptrap was shouted at a beleaguered army. A wife was distressed. (She survived, incidently, and Josephus divorced her for a Roman heiress.) And sundry other crimes were committed, all of which pale by comparison to what the good men did. For it was the loyal, the idealistic and the brave who did the real damage. The devout and patriotic leaders of Jerusalem sacrificed tens of thousands of lives to the cause of freedom. Vespasian and Titus sacrificed tens of thousands more to the cause of civil order. Even Agrippa II, the Roman client king of Judea who did all he could to prevent the war, ended by supervising the destruction of half a dozen of his cities and the sale of their inhabitants into slavery. How much better for everyone if all the principal figures of the region had been slithering filth like Josephus.

The Jewish War is a moral oxymoron. It doesn't help us understand the Middle East or know what to do there. But it does lend a fullness and a depth to our incomprehension. And it provides us with a vast crowd of historical company in our impotence and confusion.

STUDYING
FOR OUR
DRUG TEST

Commercial airline pilots smoke marijuana in the cockpit all the time. They giggle and get silly and make PA announcements like, 'If you look out the left side you'll see a big wing.' Then they gobble up the tourist-class desserts and collide with Piper Cubs. All the high school seniors in America are hooked on crack. They run through band practice tearing the uniforms off majorettes with their teeth. After school they mug their moms and drive the nation's violent crime rate through the roof. Many US submarine captains take PCP, which is why they go into murderous frenzies, release Polaris missiles and start accidental atomic wars so often.

This is the impression I get from newspapers, magazines and the network news. President Reagan and his missis must have gotten the same impression. They went on television together in September 1986, looking worried and a bit peeved. 'Drugs are menacing our society,' said the President. 'They're threatening our values and undercutting our institutions. They're killing our children.'

'Drugs take away the dream from every child's heart and replace it with a nightmare,' said the First Lady, and she pointed out that 'drug criminals are ingenious. They work every day at plotting ways to take our children away from us.'

But, said the President, 'people who are terrorizing America will find themselves facing the greatest force for good in the

112

world.' Then he invoked God, country and US war dead and promised us all drug-free schools and workplaces. Because, you see, there is a solution to the American drug catastrophe, and the President announced it the very next day – drug tests.

On Monday, 15 September 1986, President Reagan signed an executive order requiring drug tests for all US government employees in 'sensitive' positions. This includes federal law-enforcement officers, presidential appointees and people who handle classified information. It also includes everyone whose job is related to national security or public health and the safety or protection of life and property plus anyone in a position requiring a 'high degree of trust and confidence'. Broadly speaking, it means the janitor at the Yosemite National Park comfort station and all the rest of the federal government's 2.8 million civilian employees. Many state and municipal workers can expect to be tested, too. And over twenty-five per cent of US corporations already have employee drug-test programs, with more to come. Soon everyone will be tested for drugs except Mother Teresa (and we can catch her at Customs and Immigration).

What a good idea. Poof! The national cancer of drug abuse will disappear faster than the family farm. All we have to do is whizz in a dish, tinkle in a cup, take a leak in a test tube and generally piddle ourselves dry, and we will never have any accidental atomic wars started by narco-crazed sub commanders again.

Of course, we don't have any accidental atomic wars started by narco-crazed sub commanders now. But never mind, lots of other horrible stuff is caused by drugs. Drugs are tearing our society apart and destroying everything we hold dear. Aren't they? If drugs weren't causing monstrous and terrifying calamities there wouldn't be all this prate and gabble in the media. Would there? I called the Federal Aviation Administration's Office of Aviation Safety and put it to them square. 'How many fatal accidents on major airlines have involved drug use by flight crews, air-traffic controllers or other responsible personnel?' I asked FAA spokesman Fred Farrar.

'None.'

113

'That's it,' I said. 'Just "none"?'

'Yes,' said Farrar. 'The answer is none.'

I called the FBI and asked for statistics from their *United States Uniform Crime Reports*. It turns out the nation's violent crime rate is not through the roof. There was a slight rise, 3.1 per cent, from 1984 to 1985. But, overall, violent crime has dropped 6.4 per cent in the past five years, the first sustained decrease since the Second World War.*

Then I called the Public Health Service's Institute on Drug Abuse. They had just completed a major survey on illegal drugs. 'Is drug use up?' I asked.

'It's basically stable,' said Press Officer Lucy Walker with, I think, a hint of regret in her voice. According to the figures Ms Walker gave me, 22 per cent of young people ages eighteen to twenty-five use marijuana, down from 27 per cent in 1982. Cocaine use is up from 7 per cent to 8 per cent in the same period. And hallucinogens are holding steady at 2 per cent. Among the general population, the trends are about the same. If drugs are tearing our society apart and destroying everything we hold dear, they are taking their time about it.

Now, nobody wants to be quoted as saying drugs are cute or a swell thing to give babies. Drugs are bad. Anybody who's watched *1941* on a videocassette knows this. Drugs have caused a lot of people to do a lot of stupid things, such as hock their kid's Apple II, recite Rod McKuen poetry and stab Nancy Spungen. And drugs have given several of my friends one-way backstage passes to the hereafter. But let's get this thing in perspective. In 1986, 563 people died from cocaine overdoses, 3,170 expired from gallstones, and more than 43,000 kicked just tooling around on the highway. Drugs are a problem. We shouldn't stop worrying about the problem. But maybe we should start worrying about the solution.

Drug tests are justifiable in certain circumstances. As part of

---

* Here the author spoke too soon. Violent crime is through the roof after all. But it's hard to see how drug testing would fix that. It's very difficult to get a urine sample from a crack-addled teenager when he's in the middle of shooting a 7-Eleven clerk.

a drug-rehabilitation program, for example, they make very good sense. And DEA agents should take drug tests. People who've been set to guard the henhouse shouldn't develop a taste for chicken. We the general public have a right, as helpless cowards, to ask that drug tests be given to those who hold our lives in their hands. Marine Corps drill instructors, IRS auditors and US Presidents should all be given drug tests if we think they're acting loopy. Most IRS auditors do act loopy, and all recent Presidents have.

But the current fad for wide-scale drug tests doesn't have much to do with justifiable circumstances. Note that the drug test hubbub began with testing professional athletes. We don't depend on these guys for anything except covering the Superbowl point spread, and there's some doubt about whether they do that better with or without drugs. True, children look up to professional athletes. But children are short and look up to everything.

Also note that there's one drug nobody's saying much about. This is the big drug – tonsil polish, idiot oil, vitamin XXX. When it comes to getting sideways we are not a buzzed nation. We are not a zoned nation. We are Drunk Country. An estimated fourteen million Americans are alcoholics or problem drinkers, me for one. Alcoholism costs us around $116 billion a year in lost work, medical expenses, car wrecks and removal of stubborn carpet stains. Booze is responsible for something like 95,000 deaths per annum and who knows how many dumb marriages.

There are simple, cheap and accurate tests for alcohol use. However, nearly half of American adults drink, and that's a lot of voters. So alcohol testing is done sparingly, with probable cause, under highly justifiable circumstances – usually when you're on your way home from a toga party. Nobody is trying to make alcohol tests a regular feature of work or school, let alone government employment. How many congressmen would care to be tested after 6:00 p.m.? A bird can't fly on one wing. A cat can't walk on three legs. Freshen that up for you, Senator?

Anyway, no drug, not even alcohol, causes the fundamental ills of society. If we're looking for the source of our troubles, we shouldn't test people for drugs, we should test them for stupidity, ignorance, greed and love of power. And we have these tests, too. But IQ scores are kept strictly secret. Releasing IQ scores would cause Congress more embarrassment than a boxcar of Breathalysers. And no one is ever sent to Daytop Center because he flunked civics. PE is substituted instead. And, if you get a positive result on life's tests for greed and power lust, you don't lose your job, you get rich and elected.

So it's much better to test for drugs. What the hell, they're illegal, so all we're going to catch is criminals anyway. And drugs make a great patsy. Why blame crime and poverty on something complicated and difficult to fix like the disintegration of family structure or Phil Donahue? Blame them on drugs.

Actually, using drugs as a scapegoat shows we're making social progress. It's a big improvement over 'The Freemasons are poisoning the wells.' But the logic is just as bad. And this bad logic is probably inescapable. Drugs are just too good as a political issue. Drug abuse is one of those home-and-mother oratorical points that let politicians bray without fear of offending any powerful lobbying groups, unless they're running for President of Colombia. Nobody except Timothy Leary and me at about four in the morning is going to say a word in defense of illegal drugs.

And drug tests are an ideal way to use the drug issue. Widespread drug tests make it look like our national leaders are 'doing something about the problem'. To be 'doing something about the problem' is a fundamental American trait and by and large a good one. But, in our love of problem-solving, we sometimes forget to ask what the problem is or even whether it's a problem. And once we start doing something, we often lose sight of whether that something is the thing to do. I give you Vietnam, just for instance.

Drug abuse *is* a problem. But the real solutions – education, rehabilitation and medical research – are difficult, complex and uncertain of success. In other words, the real solutions are like reality itself. And reality has never been anything politicians could stand much of. Besides, some of the solutions to the drug problem are politically suicidal. One of the most terrible proven side effects of illegal drug use is jail. Jail will screw up your life worse than a whole Glad bag full of daffy dust. But with drug hysteria in the air, no politico is going to advocate legalization of even the lamest grade of Oaxacan ditch weed. And drug education, to be effective, would be controversial, too. It would have to speak the truth. We can't tell monsters-under-the-bed stories if we want children to believe us about dope. We can't tell them that they'll turn into hydrocephalic unwed welfare mothers if they get downwind from one whiff of crack. Children are dumb enough to try drugs, but they aren't dumb enough to listen to this.

Drug tests are no solution whatsoever. They're just a method of avoiding the problem, and not a harmless method either. Drug tests are inaccurate. The Federal Centers for Disease Control studied thirteen drug-testing laboratories from 1972 to 1981. They found that only one out of eleven of these laboratories could test accurately for cocaine. And the Centers for Disease Control considered eighty per cent accuracy acceptable. Common urine-analysis tests for marijuana can show false-positive results from painkillers such as Advil and Nuprin. Contac will trigger false positives for amphetamines. And tonic water can make it look like you're shooting smack. Even the most sophisticated gas-chromatography and mass-spectrometry tests are only accurate in the ninety-five per cent range. This means one out of twenty people tested could end up driving a school bus on LSD or going to jail because he sipped a G&T last week.

A person who got a false-positive result on a drug test and held one of those ill-defined 'sensitive' jobs would face . . . I hardly have the stomach to write about it. At best he would, like Hamilton Jordan in the Carter administration, emerge from a bureaucratic tag-team match and ugly court fight with his reputation indelibly smeared. No doubt some government agency will be established to prevent such miscarriages of justice. Government agencies being what they are, this should make things much worse.

And drug tests are expensive. The most accurate kind cost $100 each, which gives new meaning to the words 'piddling sum'. Between $200 and $300 million a year is already being spent on drug testing. The military alone spent $47.6 million last year. And the *New York Times* estimates that if annual drug tests were to be given to the whole work force, the cost would be several billion dollars. Surely there is something that we need several billion dollars worth of more than we need several billion dollars worth of falsely accused citizens and scot-free hopheads.

But even if drug tests were free and one hundred per cent accurate they would still be unconstitutional. There is going to be a lot of legal rhubarb over this. And I don't know what the Supreme Court is finally going to decide. But I take the same attitude toward the Constitution that Reformation Protestants took toward the Bible: anyone can read it and witness the truth thereof. Amendment 4 is perfectly straightforward:

> The right of the people to be secure in their persons, houses, papers, and effects, against unreasonable searches and seizures, shall not be violated, and no warrants shall issue, but upon probable cause, supported by an oath or affirmation, and particularly describing the place to be searched, and the persons or things to be seized.

It's hard to see how scattershot drug testing could be legal under the Fourth Amendment, no matter how particularly the government describes the way you take a leak.

And the Fifth Amendment is also clear: 'No person . . . shall be compelled in any criminal case to be a witness against himself.' If using the contents of your bladder isn't making you a witness against yourself, then I suggest that crapping on a Supreme Court justice isn't assault and battery.

Furthermore, the president of Beth Israel hospital in New York has been quoted as saying that during drug tests, someone 'must watch each person urinate into a bottle. If that is not done, it's a sham.' I haven't gone through the Constitution with a fine comb, but I'm sure our Founding Fathers wouldn't have let this nation get off the ground without putting something in there about the natural rights of man to go to the bathroom alone.

Drug tests are illegal, expensive, inaccurate and stupid, and those are their comforting aspects. More frightening is what widespread drug tests would do to our country. They would create a national atmosphere of distrust, resentment and demoralization. We all remember how we felt when dad sniffed our breath for beer after we came home on Saturday night. We all remember how we acted when mom went through our dresser drawers looking for cigarettes. And we remember what we wanted to do when our parents peeked through the rec-room door to see if we'd arrived at second base with our dates. Does any country in its right mind want an entire population feeling this way about its government? We will have a nationwide outbreak of adolescent tantrums, sulks and screaming matches, but it will be the Mom-and-Pop elected officials who may find themselves grounded without TV forever.

And it will be worse if the nation doesn't blow up. We will have allowed the government to make an unprecedented and probably irreversible intrusion into our private lives. This is the first step toward totalitarianism. Of course it won't be the breadline and barbed-wire totalitarianism the North Koreans have. It will be an all-American, clean-cut, safety-first, goody-two-shoes totalitarianism where everybody takes care of his health, keeps his lawn nice and never ever does anything naughty or dirty or fun. And there won't be any troublesome, offbeat creative people left to screw it up either. Try giving drug tests to the great men of arts and letters. There goes Coleridge, Poe, Freud, William James, Rimbaud, Aldous Huxley, and the whole cast of *National Lampoon's Animal House*.

I can think of only one good thing about drug tests. All important government officials will have to take them, and we get to watch. We get to stand and stare while the powers that be go potty. This is a democracy and we're all equal before the law. If they don't trust us, why should we trust them? I think this will be a salutary experience. The high and the mighty will be humbled in the public eye, always a good thing. And – when it comes to certain members of Congress and the administration – we the people will have it confirmed once and for all that they are lacking two specific bits of anatomy.

AN ARGUMENT IN FAVOR OF AUTOMOBILES VS PEDESTRIANS

We often hear automobiles criticized. Safety experts say they are dangerous. Ecologists tell us they pollute the air. Economists claim cars are responsible for US trade deficits and high energy costs. Social scientists blame them for the deterioration of our inner cities. And aesthetes damn them for roadside blight. But even if all these accusations are true, the automobile is still an improvement on its principal alternative, the pedestrian.

Pedestrians are easily damaged. Try this test: Hit a pedestrian with a car. Now have the pedestrian hit the car back. Then roll a pedestrian and a car through four inches of slush and road salt at sixty miles an hour. Take a coin-operated spray gun and hose off their undersides. Which is in better shape? Also, most automobiles have 5 m.p.h. bumpers. But a pedestrian cannot be run into a wall at even 3 m.p.h. (approximate walking speed) without getting a bloody nose. And pedestrians are notoriously expensive to repair.

Automobiles are cleaner than pedestrians. Even diesel exhaust smells better than a dirty human. Pedestrians wiggle and squeal when you try to scrub them, and they are hard to wax. A dented and rusty automobile is still more attractive than the average pedestrian. Strip a car of its paint. Strip a person of his clothes. Which looks worse in broad daylight?

Cars last a hundred thousand miles or so. Just try to take anybody that far on foot.

Pedestrians are slow, require complex maintenance procedures and have bewildering fuel requirements.

There are no quality-control or safety standards for pedestrians. And if the anti-abortion lobby gets its way, we won't even be able to recall them.

Most of the time you can predict what an automobile will do. And if you lose control of an automobile you can jump out of it. But pedestrians are completely unpredictable. And when you're a pedestrian it's difficult to jump out of yourself.

Not only are automobiles better than people in most respects but people behave better when they are in automobiles than they do when they are on foot. A great big crowd of people in automobiles is a traffic jam. It's unpleasant, yes – horns honk, tempers flare, etc. But a great big crowd of people *out* of automobiles is a mob. And that's worse. No traffic jam ever stormed the Winter Palace, cheered a lynching or voted Adolf Hitler into power.

Most good things can be experienced in a car – eating, sleeping, sex, listening to Handel's *Water Music*. But the experience of evil is severely limited. Think how much less evil Central America would have experienced if, for example, all the Sandinistas had been in cars. They would have been stuck in the jungle, axle-deep in mud, and would never have been able to enslave peasants, kill Contras or get any Russian weapons into El Salvador.

It's hard for people to mug you from inside an automobile, and virtually impossible for them to rob your apartment without getting out of the car.

People on foot are more likely not only to steal, but to litter. The normal business suit has no convenient place, such as the backseat floor, to toss candy wrappers, old newspapers and empty beer cans.

When people are in a car driving down the road it's hard to hear them lie, complain, argue and spread malicious gossip – especially if you're in your own car headed the other way.

Consider how much better the United Nations Assembly

would be if all the delegates were speeding around the Assembly floor in old junkers having a figure-eight race and smashing into each other. It would be more interesting for everybody, and the intellectual quality of debate would be greatly improved. The same goes double for Congress.

True, some trouble, such as drive-by shootings and fatal crashes, can be caused in an automobile. But often it's just a pedestrian who gets killed. And though drunk drivers are a menace, drunk parents are a worse one. They do more damage to society stumbling around the house than anybody ever did in a head-on collision.

All children should be given a car as soon as they are old enough to wash it and vacuum the seats. Owning and caring for an automobile builds good citizenship. Children can learn a great deal by watching their automobile and following its example. Automobiles are democratic. A Plymouth Belvedere is more than a match for a Lamborghini in a six-car pile-up. Automobiles are egalitarian, as anybody who's ever drag raced a Bentley in an old Mustang knows.

Automobiles are strangers to sexism. You can't possibly say that a car's place is in the kitchen. And there's never been any such thing as distaff automobiles that couldn't vote or Chinese wire-wheel binding.

Automobiles have no unfortunate allegorical connotations. A man on horseback is a symbol of authoritarianism. But a man on a car roof is just silly.

There are no religious controversies among automobiles. Automobiles belong to no race and have no political opinions (though a Trabant, if it could, would probably wish it had been designed by somebody other than a drunk Communist).

Automobiles are free of egotism, passion, prejudice and stupid ideas about where to have dinner. They are, literally, selfless. A world designed for automobiles instead of people would have wider streets, larger dining rooms, fewer stairs to climb and no smelly, dangerous subway stations.

Indeed, we would lead better lives and be a wiser nation if we placed the automobile, instead of our own ambition and greed, at the center of our society. This should be taken into consideration the next time we amend our Constitution:

Article I

Congress shall make no law respecting the establishment of a boring old 55 m.p.h. speed limit; or prohibiting the free exercise of performance cars on empty winding roads; or abridging the freedom to cruise around aimlessly; or the right of the people to remove those annoying voice boxes that tell you to buckle your seat belt.

Article II

Contented Yahoos being necessary for the amusement of a free state, the right of Texans (and people who act like Texans) to drive around with guns in the gunracks of their pick-up trucks and shoot varmints and critters out the window shall not be infringed.

Article III

No driver's education student or School Safety Patrol member shall, in time of peace, be quartered in any house if he won't shovel the driveway.

Article IV

The right of the people to be secure in their cars, trucks, vans and RVs against unreasonable nosiness shall not be violated, and no policemen with flashlights or irate parents shall come poking around country lanes or scenic overlooks while couples are parked and necking.

Article V

Excessive bail shall not be required, nor excessive fines imposed, nor cruel and unusual wisecracks by local traffic cops made just because somebody forgot to get their car inspected or was going 38 in a 35 m.p.h. zone.

And so on. It would give us a federal charter that really has something to do with our day-to-day lives. And it would keep our legislators and Supreme Court busy with important things instead of school prayer and covert CIA antics. Plus – and this is very important – parking would be an unalienable right.

A CALL FOR
A
NEW
McCARTHYISM

NOTES TOWARD A BLACKLIST FOR THE 1990s

Our era is supposed to be the 1950s all over again. Indeed, we are experiencing anew many of the pleasures and benefits of that excellent decade: a salubrious prudery, a sensible avariciousness, a healthy dose of social conformity, a much-needed narrowing of minds and a return to commonsense American political troglodytism. But there's one delightful and entertaining feature of the Eisenhower years which is wholly absent from the contemporary scene – old-fashioned red-baiting. Where's our McCarthyism? Who's our Tailgunner Joe? Why don't we get to look for Communists under our beds or – considering the social changes of the past thirty-five years – *in* them? ('Good night, honey, and are you now or have you ever been a member of the Committee in Solidarity with the People of El Salvador?')

God knows the problem is not a lack of Commies. There are more fuzzy-minded one-worlders, pasty-faced peace creeps and bleeding-heart bedwetters in America now than there ever were in 1954. The redskis have infiltrated the all-important exercise-video industry, not to mention movies and TV. Academia, too, is a veritable compost heap of Bolshie brain mulch. Beardo the Weirdo may have been laughed out of real life during the 1970s, but he found a home in our nation's colleges, where he whiles away the wait for Woodstock Nation II by pestering undergraduates with cultural diversity and collectivist twaddle when they should be thinking about better car stereos. And fellow travelers in the State Department? Jeeze, the situation is so bad at Foggy Bottom that we'd better *hope* it's caused by spies. If it's stupidity, we're really in trouble.

So how come the HUAC staff isn't returning my phone calls? Who's keeping *I Led Three Lives* from being remade starring Tom Selleck and Arnold Schwarzenegger? And why aren't we making sure that that Fidel-snuggler Ron Dellums never works again? Whoops, we already did that. We elected him to Congress. And, come to think of it, there are other problems with an up-to-date nineties-style witch hunt. For one thing, it's no use going after real, card-carrying Communists any more. Hard-core Party apparatchiks are already being persecuted by organizations more brutally efficient than anything we've got in the US, organizations such as the Union of Soviet Socialist Republics. Plus accusing somebody of being a 'comsymp' just isn't the same since Gorbachev began his three-hankie *perestroika* performance. Even Margaret Thatcher said she sympathized with Ole Splotch-Top. And when it comes to the International Communist Conspiracy to Enslave Europe, Asia and the Third World – well, somebody's got to do *something* with those people. Good luck to the Patrice Lumumba University Class of '89.

No, a modern McCarthyism is going to have to concentrate on other things besides the Big Lie and the Red Menace. In fact, if we examine even a brief selection of people who should be tarred and feathered and run out of town on a rail (or, to be more contemporary, oat-branned and goose-downed and jogged out of the condominium complex on an exercise track), we see that they are not necessarily Marxist or even socialist in their thinking because that would presuppose thinking in the first place. Nobody is ever going to accuse us of being *thought* police for going after the like of Kris Kristofferson, Phil Donahue, Marlo Thomas, Dr Benjamin Spock, Yoko Ono, Dave Dellinger, Ben & Jerry's ice-cream, the World Council of Churches, Ed Asner, Michelle Shocked, Lenora Fulani, Robert Redford and people who think quartz crystals cure herpes.

The distinguishing feature of this cluster of dunces is not subversion but silliness. If we hope to wreck careers, destroy reputations and drive holistic Ortega fans into exile in Sausalito and Amherst, Massachusetts, we're going to need tactics very different from those used by Roy Cohn, Bobby Kennedy and the distinguished senator from the great state famous for its La Follette and cheese. A traditional 'black list' will never work. Put some *sandalista* on your black list and you probably guarantee him a MacArthur genius grant and a seat on the ACLU national board of directors. But maybe we can tear a page from the *Très Riches Heures* of Tipper Gore and insist upon a rating system for music, film, television and the *Boston Globe* editorial page. A warning would have to be prominently displayed: 'OH-OH, A PERSON INVOLVED WITH THIS UNAPPEALING ITEM OF MASS COMMUNICATION HOLDS SILLY OPINIONS ON MATTERS ABOUT WHICH HE OR SHE IS LARGELY OR ABYSMALLY UNINFORMED.' There'd be three ratings:

S = Silly
VS = Very Silly
SML = Shirley MacLaine

Thus a return of *M*A*S*H* featuring Alan Alda would get an 'S' rating. Any public pronouncement by a member of the innumerable Phoenix family, such as River, Leaf, Summer, Stump, Ditch or Pond Scum Phoenix, would get a 'VS' rating. And the next Tracy Chapman album will get an 'SML' with oak-leaf cluster.

No, this isn't going to work either. You can't shame or humiliate modern celebrities. What used to be called shame and humiliation is now called publicity. And forget traditional character assassination. If you say a modern celebrity is an adulterer, a pervert and a drug addict, all it means is that you've read his autobiography.

We have to come up with more clever ways to ruin these people. Perhaps we can spread rumors that they performed in South Africa before Nelson Mandela was released. I was in South Africa myself a few years ago, and I'm almost certain that was Sinéad O'Connor singing back-up for Frank Sinatra at Sun City. Or perhaps we can direct the wrath of the remarkably terrifying animal-rights activists against them. I'm going to write a letter to People for the Ethical Treatment of Animals about how Susan Sontag allows her intellectual ideas to be tried on innocent laboratory rabbits before humans are exposed to them. (As for the animal-rights activists, we can turn the animals loose on them later.)

But the worst punishment for dupes, pink-wieners and dialectical immaterialists might be a kind of reverse black list. We don't prevent them from writing, speaking, performing and otherwise being their usual nuisance selves. Instead, we hang on their every word, beg them to work, drag them onto all available TV and radio chat shows and write hundreds of fawning newspaper and magazine articles about their wonderful swellness. In other words, we subject them to the monstrous, gross and irreversible late-twentieth-century phenomenon of Media Overexposure so that a surfeited public rebels in disgust. This is the Burt Reynolds/Loni Anderson treatment, and for condemning people to obscurity, it beats the Smith Act hollow.

Anyway, I'm sure we'll find some way to chastise these buggers of sense, to bully, torment, harry them and generally make a workers' paradise of their lives. In the meantime, the fun part of McCarthyism is, as it always was, *writing out the enemies list** Heh-heh:

Sting

Gore Vidal

The Institute for Policy Studies

Tom Hayden (Hope you didn't give Jane your ideals in the divorce settlement, Tom.)

Victor Navasky

Angela Davis

William Sloane Coffin

Noam Chomsky

Abbie Hoffman (I guess we can cross him off; he was on God's list.)

* What follows was compiled in 1989 and is thus in dire need of amendment. Readers may use the endpapers and the inside of the dust cover.

Ralph Nader

Anthony Lewis

William 'The Client Is Obviously Guilty' Kunstler

Jackson Browne

Allen Ginsberg

Norman Lear

Meryl Streep

Peter, Paul and Mary (Yes, they're still alive.)

The Christic Institute

Common Cause

Center for Constitutional Rights

Anybody whose last name is Cockburn

Anybody who inherited so much money and so little sense that
  her last name might become Cockburn

Cockburn wannabe Christopher Hitchens (Christ, who's checking the green cards around here?)

The Order of Maryknoll Nuns

Amy Carter

Susan Sarandon

The Redgrave family

Patty Duke

Casey Kasem

Daniel and Philip Berrigan (Yes, *they're* still alive.)

Jesse Jackson

The New York Review of Books

The New York Times Book Review

That poor man's Walt Kelly, Garry Trudeau

That poor man's Garry Trudeau, Berke Breathed

The Sandinista's Oliphant, Paul Conrad

The National Resources Defense Council

Lawyers Guild

The DC Statehood Party

Mayor of Burlington, Vermont, Peter Clavelle

The Berkeley City Council

Berkeley

Mother Jones

The Nation

The Village Voice

Any organization with 'Peace' in its name

The English Department at Duke

The Law School at Harvard

The Liberal Arts faculty at Stanford

Any educator using the term 'Eurocentric' (While we're at it, let's reintroduce corporal punishment in the schools – and apply it to the teachers.)

Salman Rushdie (Kick 'em when they're down is what I say.)

Martin Sheen

Charlie Sheen

The rest of the Sheen family plus Rob Lowe, Judd Nelson, Demi Moore, Molly Ringwald and all the other Brat Pack members (Which brings to mind another idea for a modified black list – this list would *require* left-wingers to write movie scripts, but only for Brat Pack movies.)

And let's not forget that most subversive of all organizations in America, the American government:

Senator Tom Harkin, D., IA

Senator Ted Kennedy, D., MA

Senator John Kerry, D., MA

Senator Chris Dodd, D., CT

Representative Pete Stark, D., CA

Representative Barbara Boxer, D., CA

Representative Ed Markey, D., MA

Representative Gerry Studds, D., MA

Representative Gus Savage, D., IL

Representative Barbara Mikulski, D., MD

And from Michigan – an improbable place to find a nest of Jacobin nogoodniks – these Not-the-Reagan-Democrats:

Representative George Crockett

Representative David Bonior

Representative John Conyers

And that's just a beginning. Let's make this a blood bath – well, a phlegm-and-bile bath anyway. Maybe we can reconquer our body politic. Maybe we can sweep the ideologically homeless from the streets of our Shining City on a Hill. Or maybe we can't. It might all backfire the way the splendid fifties backfired and led to the wretched and unspeakable sixties. Still, it's worth a try. At the very least 'Red Scare – The Sequel' will rile the lefties and get them out demonstrating again so policemen can hit them on the head. The police have been having a rough time in recent years, what with crack and Miranda rights. They need some fun. And one other great good will have been accomplished. We will have found a job for J. Danforth Quayle. He's the perfect point man for Nouvelle McCarthyism, a Senator Joe Lite if ever there was one. Besides, I'm sure he'd much rather have a reputation for evil than the reputation he's got now.

SEX
WITH
DR RUTH

I t's question-and-answer period at Central Connecticut State University, where Dr Ruth Westheimer is giving a lecture to eighteen hundred students in a packed auditorium and I am dying of boredom in the audience.

A boy in the front row stands up. He's blushing hideously and surrounded by a half dozen seated, snickering pals. Maybe he's a fraternity pledge, or maybe he's just one of those kids who can be talked into anything. His friends have gotten him to ask a question about the most embarrassing sex act they can think of. A serious question, mind you, but embarrassing. He asks it.

' . . . and, anyway,' finishes the stammering youth, 'why do some girls like that and some girls *hate* it?'

Dr Westheimer is whatever the complete opposite of embarrassed is called, 'antichagrined', perhaps, or 'hyperconcerted'. She doesn't, however, answer his question. She deflects it into one of her miniature homilies. Maybe it's 'Most People Want to Have One Significant Other' or 'The Need for a Sexually Literate Society' or 'Don't Stint on Foreplay, Be Inventive!' There are dozens of these – obvious, pat and nearly irrefutable. And they are repeated endlessly, apropos anything.

More questions follow.

Student: 'What about bondage?'

Dr Westheimer: 'Anything that pleases two consenting adults and doesn't hurt anybody is fine.'

Student: 'What's the most sexually stimulating thing you can do to a woman?'

Dr Westheimer: 'Love her.'

Student: 'Is the sponge a good method of birth control?'

I ask a question of my own. I tap the kid in front of me and ask, 'Why are all these people here?' He says, 'Everybody has boyfriend or girlfriend problems, or thinks they do.' Or thinks they do?

Student: 'What exercises can I do to improve my sex life?'

Dr Westheimer: 'The only exercises you can do are in your brain.'

The questions continue. They are almost innocent enough to be exciting, but not quite. There are no questions about AIDS, not even any about herpes. None of the questions is antagonistic Only a few are intended as jokes.

And Dr Westheimer continues. She informs. She educates. She charms. She giggles. Dr Westheimer is effervescently sincere. Her singsong voice burbles on, sensible, understanding, wise and just about impossible to shut up.

Weeks later I'm at the typewriter, circled by background material and notes, and I am plagued. Dr Westheimer reminds me of something, something half-glimpsed, something partly remembered. I know it's significant. I go through her book and her bio sheet, through the articles about her in *Newsweek*, *Playboy*, *People*, *T.V. Guide*, the *New York Times Magazine* and, it seems, every newspaper feature section in the country. Then, while I'm watching *Terrific Sex*, her new how-to videotape, I see it:

Dr Westheimer is standing in a mock living-room set, her clothing casual and homey. She is looking directly into the camera, speaking slowly. Her voice is soothing, perky and earnest all at once. She is saying, 'How open can *you* be? Can *you* say to your partner, "Look at my penis. Do you like it?"'

Yow! I jump away from the VHS. It's Mister Rogers run amuck!

And back there in the drab confines of Central Connecticut

State University, that's the Mister Rogers generation, isn't it? They want security even when they have their pants around their ankles.

I try to imagine my own generation putting up with anything like this. True, we did crowd the lectures of another Ph.D, one Dr Leary. And, yes, he too said it was all right for us to take our clothes off and cohabitate. But he also said it was all right for us to paint our behinds Day-Glo orange and burn down our parents' summer homes. And he never said anything about 'most people want to have one significant other'. We would have hooted him out of the geodesic dome.

Anyway, what year is this? Aren't we too hip for 'don't stint on foreplay, be inventive'? The sexual revolution is over and the microbes won.

But of all the sexual contagions rampant in our society, Dr Westheimer seems to be the one most difficult to avoid.

This is a list of what Dr Westheimer is doing or selling, though I'm a couple of hours out of date, and a line of perfume and a signature-model first-baseman's mitt may have been added by now:

- Private sex therapy practice at Bellevue Hospital and Kingsbrook Jewish Medical Center
- Teaching at Cornell University
- A weekly radio talk show, *Sexually Speaking*
- A cable television program, *The Dr Ruth Show*, nightly Monday through Friday
- Three books: *Dr Ruth's Guide to Good Sex; First Love: A Young People's Guide to Sexual Information* and *Dr Ruth's Guide for Married Lovers*
- The college lecture circuit
- The aforementioned *Terrific Sex* videotape
- A semiweekly syndicated newspaper column
- A monthly column for *Playgirl* magazine
- A board game called 'Dr Ruth's Game of Good Sex'
- Television commercials for Dr Pepper, Smith-Corona and Lifestyles condoms

- A principal role in the Sigourney Weaver, Gerard Depardieu movie, *A Woman or Two*
- Frequent guest appearances on the *Tonight* show and *Late Night with David Letterman*

Maybe Dr Westheimer is another spasm of celebrity, one more in the ten thousand such seizures which have wracked our nation. Maybe in six months she'll be as dimly remembered as the Bay City Rollers. But, temporary or not, the public appetite for her chitchat must say something about the public. Backstage at Central Connecticut State a dozen mature, adult newspaper reporters were asking for her autograph.

Neither WYNY-FM, originator of the *Sexually Speaking* radio program, now heard in forty-eight markets, nor Lifetime cable network, syndicator of *The Dr Ruth Show* to twenty-four million homes, had any idea what popular enormities they were about to commit. There is a vacuum in the lives of the great unwashed (but pretty well-deodorized). And Dr Westheimer fills it. Says Michael Capes, Lifetime's Manager of Public Affairs, 'There was such a void that no one knew it existed.'

I go to see Dr Westheimer do her cable television show. Two programs each week are live, three are taped. The viewer phone-ins are done by appointment. While *The Dr Ruth Show* is being broadcast, an assistant takes the callers' numbers. Those with the most promising difficulties are phoned during future shows and asked if they still have problems and is there anyone home they shouldn't talk in front of.

There are also famous people who appear on the show. 'These are pure entertainment, an audience builder,' says Executive Producer Robert McBride. Tonight one famous person is David Huddleston, who plays Santa Claus in the movie of the same name. Another is jazz drummer Buddy Rich. As to what they're doing on the program, Huddleston looks slightly confused, Rich looks very. Dr Westheimer does her best to tie it all in with sex somehow. 'Drumming has a rhythm,' she ventures. 'Drums in primitive societies are often involved with sex.'

'Yes,' says Buddy Rich, 'I've had some discussions about that and it's been very enlightening but we'll be off the air if I repeat them.'

And he's right. After all, Dr Westheimer's much-mentioned frankness is nothing but using the dictionary to call things what they're called. Neither the form nor the content of her language is anything compared to the dialogue in a typical one-act play.

Tonight, the first call-in is from a woman whose child has died. Now her husband is impotent and she's not interested in making love. The next caller's romance has disappeared with age and child-bearing. The next is worried her husband is homosexual. Their children's friends all call him 'faggot'. Only journalistic professionalism and thoughts of the mortgage payment keep me from running out the studio door. Is life so empty of solace and aid that these poor folk must call up a shrimpy TV personality and wail lamentations via satellite link?

There's nothing wrong with what Dr Westheimer tells them, nothing that looks cheap or facile in the sympathy she shows, but it's like fighting evil with room freshener.

When she's on the telephone, Dr Westheimer is frank, even adamant, that she's not a therapist. 'Go to a professional,' she says. She says, 'I'm not a physician.' 'I'm not a psychiatrist.' 'I'm not a research scientist'. 'I'm not a rabbi.' Until you wonder what it is she *is*.

Well, she is a conservative libertine:

> Human sexuality is best kept within the protection of a relationship.
>
> *Dr Ruth's Guide to Good Sex*, p.242

She is an absolutist of moral relativism. It's all right to try unusual things, she avers, even really unusual things like being a devout Catholic or an Orthodox Jew:

> I tell people . . . not to offend your family or religion if you can reasonably avoid it – and often you can.
>
> Ibid., p. 13

Her philosophy is what you'd get if Norman Vincent Peale and Hugh Hefner had a raging (but monogamous) affair:

> You should like yourself, the special way you are and God made you – and remember that while you are alive you are a sexual being with sexual thoughts and feelings.
>
> Ibid., p. 12

She's giving us permission to do anything we want, now that we don't want to do anything much:

> . . . being sure to have contraception and knowing the lady well enough, so you're almost sure she doesn't have herpes . . .
>
> Ibid., p. 309

But the annoying truth is, when you listen to Dr Westheimer, you *do* learn something. For instance, I learned that women have a pubococcygeus muscle. Rest assured I won't describe the item. But it is a fascinating piece of biology. And Dr Westheimer has nonfamous guests on her show, such as Dr Mary Ellen Brademas, director of the Sexually Transmitted Disease Clinic at Bellevue Hospital, who discusses chlamydia. It's a malady I've never heard of that's not only double-horrible but also completely asymptomatic. I gather it infects all cute girls I'd like to fool around with.

Also, let's face it, listening to Dr Westheimer's call-ins is awful but as compelling as eating Cheez Doodles – people with children who touch themselves, people who've never touched anything, wives who won't do something or won't stop, husbands who snooze *in flagrante delicto*, and teenagers thinking they can't get pregnant doing the only thing that can make them that way.

It can be hard for those of us with SAT scores exceeding our golf handicaps to remember that ignorance is a renewable resource. Dr Westheimer has tapped into vast proven reserves of it. *Whatever* she tells these people is bound to be an improvement on what they think now.

Another call comes in on the studio phone. A thirty-two-year-old woman says she cannot have an orgasm without lesbian fantasies. She has never made love to a woman. She enjoys being with men. But she can't have an orgasm without her fantasies.

Dr Westheimer says nothing but, 'Fantasies are only fantasies. Don't worry about it.'

'*Really?*' says the woman. There's a buoyant pause. 'Okay!' she chirps.

Yet another call: A middle-aged woman has caught her husband masturbating in front of the television.

Dr Westheimer: 'What was he watching?'

Caller: '*Wild Kingdom*, it was about rhinos.'

Dr Westheimer: 'Did he know you saw him?'

Caller: 'No.'

Dr Westheimer: 'Don't tell him. For all you know, he was thinking of you.'

(Actually, I don't believe Dr Westheimer heard the part about the rhinos. She's usually not this funny on purpose.)

I try to get her to sit still for an interview. She is as overactive as her curriculum vitae would imply. But once you have her attention, you have a very great deal of attention indeed. The husband of one Lifetime Television executive has coined a word for her: 'endearritating'.

In person, Dr Westheimer is not so easy to make fun of. Beneath an unflattering hairstyle and too much New York matron makeup, Dr Westheimer is an attractive woman, a zaftig gamin. Not commonly pretty, perhaps, but she has perfect eyes, cute lips and a hint of the Tigris and Euphrates in the bones of her face. Thirty years ago she was a sniper in the Haganah underground during the Israeli rebellion in Palestine. I commend to your imagination her elfin figure on the rooftops, in khakis as adorably oversized as anything from Kenzo.

I ask her, 'Is there any danger in treating humans as if they were rational?'

'I believe in that. I believe people basically know what's needed and what's good for them,' she says. She will not tell me if she's found any good excuse for social reticence about sex. 'It's only in the late stages of civilization that all this prudishness comes about.' (So the clock is running backward for the Western democracies, I guess.)

'Isn't this subject intellectually limiting?'

'Yes. If the questions were only on sex, I'd be bored. But the questions are about relationships. The nice thing for me is this is all coming together with my doctorate, which is Interdisciplinary Study of the Family.'

'What purpose does human sexuality serve?'

'Bonding,' says Dr Westheimer. 'It needs two people to raise that gene. Monogamy is inherent in humans.'

That's a truth this particular human has been known to fumble with. I blurt out, 'Is it possible to be satisfied with just one partner?' (After all, the woman knows a lot and there's some information I'd like, just for personal reference.)

'We don't have another form,' she says. And she's emphatic.

Dr Westheimer interrupts the interview. A group of disabled teenagers have come to see the taping. Most of them are suffering from a genetic disease that has twisted their bodies. It's hard not to stare at them, also hard to really look. Dr Westheimer talks merrily, patting shoulders and signing autographs, pleased with them as if they were Junior Olympians training for the synchronized swim or high hurdles. The kids beam.

When she gets back I ask her if she's familiar with Nathanael West's novel *Miss Lonelyhearts*. 'No thank you,' she says. 'It won't happen to me.' I tell her I detect a sense of mission. She backtracks to say sometimes she gets very sad. Then, 'Mission?' she says. 'I'm not sure about the sense of mission. Ten years ago I would have said yes.'

For a quarter of a minute I feel I've escaped Dr Westheimer's mental desktop filled with answer stamp pads. Then I ask for her utopia.

'People would have good communication with each other. Not *one* unwanted pregnancy. Abortion must remain legal.' Her staccato becomes staccato now, 'Prostitution should be legal. No person would ever be violent or rape another one. Homosexuals who do not want to be homosexuals, there would be a way we could help them. Peace, of course. No hunger. My program on a regular network,' she giggles. 'Sex education would be a combination of the efforts of parents, churches, community centers, schools and anybody who is interested in the next generation. The disabled would have satisfaction.'

Reasonable enough, now try getting it through Congress.

I ask her, 'How do you reconcile reason with the bigotries of deeply held faith?'

'To give successful advice I have to connect, give information within the realm of your values, hopefully with a grain of joie de vivre.'

'But what about a clear-cut conflict between values and sense?'

'That's not my role. I have to know my limitations.' She sighs, but not unhappily. 'It's a cop-out but a cop-out I have to use or I'd be ineffectual.'

Perhaps Dr Westheimer has earned some intellectual half measures. She's been through the horrors of ideological extremes. She was slipped out of Germany and put in a Swiss orphanage when World War II started. Her parents disappeared in concentration camps. She was nearly crippled by an artillery shell in Palestine, lived the life of an impoverished student in Paris, then worked as a housemaid in Manhattan to put herself through graduate school. Now she has two grown children, a third husband, a BA in Psychology from the Sorbonne, an MA in Sociology from the New School for Social Research and her Ph.D from Columbia University. She says she doesn't expect this limelight to last. She says she'll enjoy it while it does.

Her live broadcast begins. I page through my notebook. 'Common sense,' I've jotted. 'Common-sensical attitude.' 'Philosophy is common sense.' 'Sensible.' 'Just applies good sense to things.' 'Sensible answers to questions.'

I begin to feel myself mired in clearheadedness. There's a frightening rush of unbiased practicality. I am being overwhelmed by a great, gooey wave of prudent liberalism.

I go home and say to my own Significant Other, 'No, really, dear, Dr Westheimer is great. You'd love her. Do you know about the pubococcygeus muscle? It's right down . . .'

142

'Oh, wince,' she says.

'And there are all sorts of really basic and straightforward things,' I say, 'that can be done for people if they're educated about it, for instance, if a man has a problem with premature ejaculation he can take his erect penis . . . '

'And get out of town.'

The fog of common sense clears. I'm suddenly myself again. I put my pajamas on and fix a sandwich.

No, everything will not be all right if we just talk it over, face facts, use our noodles.

And you can't tell the truth and remain morally neutral. Religions have actual laws against doing the right and the reasonable thing. Clitorectomies are sacred in some parts of Africa, and contraception is a sin in a Catholic country, no matter if the children are stacked three deep. Stay within our own religious guidelines, says Dr Westheimer. And get advice about Shi'ite suicide sex?

And maybe our inhibitions are not as otiose as they seem. Dr Westheimer cites 1.5 million unwanted children a year as evidence of a need for education. But forty years ago young women were less educated in you-know-what, and there weren't 1.5 million unwanted children. It's not sexual ignorance making all those babies, it's sex.

Taboos have something to do with keeping human behavior in line. Given the record of human behavior lately, should we be throwing ancient restraints away? Is sexual modesty just a vermiform appendix of the conscience?

Life is not simple, let alone love. Maybe guilt and fear actually increase sexual desire. They did in the backseats of cars when I was younger. Or maybe the very obscurity of sex solders the bond between lovers. Maybe there's even something to that sublimation business. Errol Flynn slept around a lot and I notice he didn't come up with the Special Theory of Relativity.

Anyway, new inhibitions arise as quickly as the old ones wilt. I could never have brought myself to ask Dr Westheimer how much she's making from this.

The physician Galen, in the second century AD, said that man

143

and nearly all other creatures feel shame and fatigue after coitus. Or maybe after talking about it for hours.

Please, Dr Westheimer, go home and go to bed – on the couch.

THE
DEEP
THOUGHTS
OF
LEE IACOCCA

Y ou see the poor bastards at every airport in the country and all the Ramada Inns, Avis counters and Beef-and-Blank restaurants. They have shoes with metal dingles, vinyl briefcases, Seiko watches. They're dressed in poly-blend vested suits and don't know not to wear a belt with the vest. Horrible Yves Saint Laurent buckles peek out the bottoms of their waistcoats. They are America's young management meatballs. And every man jack of them has a copy of *Iacocca: An Autobiography* under his arm. It is the *New York Times* number-one nonfiction best-seller. It has overtaken *In Search of Excellence* as the nation's most popular business book. So far, 1.4 million copies have been printed, and each is being read by someone who moves his lips.

The secret is in there. The meatball knows it. If he can just read carefully enough he'll crack the code: 'How I turned personal failure, corporate debt, the two-bit K-car and a goofy last name into glory, fame and worldwide respect.'

Lee Iacocca is a hero for our time – a conceited big-mouth glad-handing huckster who talked the government into loaning his company piles of money. And *Iacocca: An Autobiography* is literature for our time. That is, it stinks. My copy looks like some origami-instruction manual, it is so dog-eared from marking idiocies.

First there is the beastly style – coarse, disorganized, repetitious and bulked with oatmeal filler:

> During that time the factories were simply not operating, which meant that both the machinery and the workers were idle.

> John Riccardo and his wife, Thelma, were two of the finest people I've ever met. Unfortunately, the crisis at Chrysler was so severe that I never really got to know them.

> To say the least, testifying before Congressional and Senate committees has never been my idea of fun and games.

> But then came the Depression. No one who's lived through it can ever forget.

Also, there's the earthy wit:

> This was probably the greatest jolt I've ever had in my business career. When I thought about it, I was bereft. (That's a euphemism for feeling lower than whale shit!)

This much can be blamed on the amanuensis, William Novak, who knows better and ought to be held by his heels and shaken until his brains run out his ears and some more useful innard slides down and fills his skull.

The rest of the problems are Iacocca's own. He is a paranoid and an egomaniac. But those are not the terms. They are too clinical and blame-evading. We need older, stricter words. The man is consumed by pride and besotted with vanity. Every nit-pick in his life must be of compelling interest to us, his co-adulators:

> When I was in sixth grade there was an election for captain of the student patrol. The patrolmen all wore white belts with a silver badge, but the lieutenant and the captain got to wear special uniforms with special badges . . . I loved the idea of wearing that uniform, and I was determined to be the captain.

146

A number of journalists have reported (or repeated) that my parents went to Lido Beach in Venice for their honeymoon and that I was named Lido to commemorate that Happy week. It's a wonderful story, except for one problem: it's not true.

There is persistent name-dropping done mostly with a degree of deftness thus:

Once, at a private dinner with Vince Lombardi, the legendary football coach and friend of mine . . .

And every now and then we are treated to a passage of the following kind:

Once [Henry Ford] and his wife, Christina, came to our house for dinner. My parents were there, too, and Henry spent half the night telling them how great I was and that without me there wouldn't be a Ford Motor Company. On another occasion, he took me to meet his good friend L.B.J.

Of course self-love cannot be displayed in full bloom without a leafy green background of hatred for others. Chapter 10 begins with the sentence, 'In 1975, Henry Ford started his month-by-month premeditated plan to destroy me.'

Darn that old Henry Ford, anyhow. And he's just got done telling Lee's mom and dad what a swell kid they'd raised, too. Well, Lee is not going to take this lying down, not when he's got a whole book of his own to say things in. Iacocca launches a rhetorical assault the likes of which has not been heard since Cicero indicted Marc Antony. Rapier thrust follows rapier thrust: Lee wanted a signed photograph of Henry Ford, but Henry never got around to signing it. Henry sold the company plane to the Shah of Iran for five million dollars and 'The company lost a bundle on the deal.' Henry used tax shelters. Henry told his executives to 'get off your asses and do what needs to be done for the black community,' then later that day used the word 'coon'. And Henry Ford and women?

Actually I always thought he hated women – except for his
mother. When Henry's father died, Eleanor Clay Ford had taken
over the family and put her son Henry in charge. She also kept
him somewhat in line.

But when she died in 1976, his whole world came tumbling
down.

One sick puppy, that Henry Ford. What's more he likes to have
a few shooters and get wide:

Henry tried to be sophisticated and European ... . But it was
all a façade. After the third bottle of wine, all bets were off.

(With Iacocca in the next office, his head as large as a haystack
and barbering from nine to five about what a big lasagna he is,
who wouldn't need a drink?)

Anything can be excused by genius, and Iacocca has been
called one. But where's this genius parked?

Iacocca's book is filled with managerial balloon juice. 'The
only way you can motivate people is to communicate with them.'
'The speed of the boss is the speed of the team.' 'In addition to
being decision makers, managers also have to be motivators.' 'To
sum up: nothing stands still in this world.'

He exhibits general ignorance of business fundamentals. 'A
couple of months after I arrived [at Chrysler], something hit me
like a ton of bricks. We were running out of cash!' He berates
the Federal Reserve Board for being primarily concerned with
banking. He blasts America as 'a nation enamored with investing
in paper,' as though the cash represented by stocks, bonds and
certificates of deposit were all jammed in a sock under Carl
Icahn's mattress. He discusses the overseas retail prices of
Japanese cars without reference to value added tax, accuses the
Japanese of exporting unemployment to the United States (How
do they pack it? Does it spoil?), and he claims this for the United
Auto Workers' reaction to his ballyhooed 1980 salary of one dollar
a year:

From that day on I was their pal. The union loved me. They said: 'This guy is going to lead us to the promised land.'

Moreover, Iacocca exhibits *specific* ignorance of the automobile business. He says, 'Now, it's true that you can't make money on small cars – at least not in this country.' But Honda does at its Marysville, Ohio, plant. And General Motors is investing 1.5 billion dollars in a new domestic small-car division, presumably not for kicks. Iacocca calls the Mustang II 'a terrific design'. It sucked. He says, 'The K-car is a sensational product.' It is adequate. He claims the Chevrolet Vega had a 'pancake aluminum engine'. It had nothing of the kind. And he proudly takes credit for the stupid seat-belt interlock ignition system that appeared on 1973 cars and disappeared as quickly as owners could unhook it.

Iacocca's idea of engineering:

The [Mercury] Marquis had achieved . . . the softest, plushest ride in the world.

His idea of design:

My plan was to create a new car using the same platform, engine, and even the roof, but to make enough changes so that the car really *looked* new and not like a spinoff of the T-Bird.

And the following explains better than John Stuart Mill himself could what it is Lee Iacocca does for a living:

. . . on the island of St Thomas, we unveiled the new Cougar. At a beach lit by clusters of brilliant torches, a World War II landing craft pulled up to the shore and lowered its ramp. The audience was breathless as a shining white Cougar drove onto the sand. The door opened, and out stepped singer Vic Damone, who began to entertain.

But let's be fair. The man works hard. He took a risky job at a

troubled company and managed to put it in the black. He . . .
Oh, let's *not* be fair. This book is rubbish. The meatballs in the
airports would be better off reading the phone book. Check under
Brooks Brothers. A banker-gray two-piece chalk-stripe with a
buttondown shirt and a pin-dot tie and at least you'll 'really *look*'
like you've got some sense.

As for Lee Iacocca, he's being bruited about as a Democratic
presidential candidate. The man deserves no better.

Review of *Everything to Gain:*

Making the Most of the Rest of

Your Life by Jimmy and Rosalynn

Carter, Random House, 1987

THE VERY DEEP THOUGHTS OF JIMMY AND ROSALYNN CARTER

Jimmy and Rosalynn Carter, who used to be employed as a live-in couple in Washington, have written a book. Actually, it's more than a book. Around my house *Everything to Gain* has become a complete home-entertainment center. Using the Carter opus, I've developed no fewer than five swell new parlor games. They are better than Trivial Pursuit, charades and nude Scruples combined. The rules are printed below. Try them yourself.

D-U-M Dumb

The object of D-U-M Dumb is to find the dumbest sentence in *Everything to Gain*. And, let me tell you, it's a toughie. The book is passed around and each player notes a passage. The winner is determined by the amount of laughter in the room when the quotation is read.

In the case of a tie, handicap points are subtracted according to the 'dumbness potential' of the section of the book from which the quote was drawn. *E to G* is divided into little bits and pieces, some written by Jimmy and Rosalynn together, some by Jimmy

151

alone and some by Rosalynn all by herself. Of course, the dumber the section, the easier it is to find a dumb quote in it. Professional help seems to have been applied to the parts written in duet. These get a handicap of −1. Dim Jimmy gets a handicap of −2. Learning-impaired Rosalynn gets −4. Cover blurbs and dust-jacket copy, written by actual literate humans, get no handicap.

There are two game categories, 'Form' and 'Content'.

Overall winner of the first D-U-M Dumb tournament and undefeated champion to date in the 'Content' category is Ms D.B., a New York TV executive. Even though D.B. was working with a Rosalynn quotation and, hence, a −4 handicap, no one has yet been able to top the gem she found on page 59:

> I have worked with the problems of the mentally afflicted for years, ever since I first became aware of the needs while campaigning for Jimmy for Governor.

D.B.'s victory was, however, marred by rules protest. A fellow contestant held that this sentence properly belonged in a third, 'Honest Confessions', category. D.B. replied to the challenge by offering an alternative Rosalynn quote, 'We need people for shelving [which I learned was putting books back on the shelves] . . . '

I myself am a top competitor in the 'Form' category. I won my last match with this topic sentence:

> Their search for a new life over the next few years led them eventually to Koinonia Farms, a nonprofit farm that uses its income to help the needy, not far from Plains.

That nosed out another −1 handicap entry backed by my lawyer:

> And having our mothers close by to call or visit every day was a particular joy.

D-U-M can be played with children, even preschoolers, since the Carter prose style makes advanced reading skills unnecessary.

Finish That Thought

The object of this game is to find a Carter thought (be sure to allow adequate time!) and take it to its logical conclusion. Examples are given below with the contestants' additional material marked in italics:

It was good therapy . . . to be able to go to my shop and design, cut, fit and finish a piece that was useful, permanent and sometimes beautiful – or just to bang on something *the way I used to bang on the economy.*

We savored the different seasons of nature and gathered wild fruits, such as plums, blackberries, mayhaws, grapes, blueberries and persimmons that grow along or near the rural trails, *paths, pathways, tracks, walks, passages, bypaths, lanes, roads and routes.*

I even surprised myself with some of the things I could write. *Words, for instance. All spelled out and everything.*

When together for meals . . . our family almost invariably had freewheeling political discussions or arguments on controversial issues of the day. Quite early Amy learned to join in and *that's how we figured out what to do about the Iran hostages.*

Sometimes an unpleasant or even catastrophic event can transform one's life and reveal opportunities that could never have been envisioned. *Take Hiroshima . . .*

That night when we called [Amy] to dinner and she didn't come, we found her outside in a tree *eating bananas with Abbie Hoffman.*

So often, the best therapy for a mentally ill person is just knowing that someone cares. *So Jimmy and I gave John Hinckley a call.*

Riposte

This is similar to Finish That Thought, but instead of adding material to different passages, a single passage is read and players compete to see who can come up with the most appropriate response. Examples:

I had so much information written down about the earlier period of my life that I didn't have room to include much of it in my book. For instance, I learned that my daddy's mother climbed out the window at age sixteen and eloped with a traveling salesman named Mr Smith, who was crippled and twenty-five years older than she was. I'm saving these anecdotes for our grandchildren.

Thank you.

Marriage was not seriously considered with girls known to 'go all the way'.

Which must have made for great honeymoons.

I've already mentioned that Jimmy also has an amazing capacity to sleep all night, even in times of incredible pressure.

Pressure on what, Rosalynn?
(or)
And the nation rested easier, too, knowing the son of a bitch was off duty for at least eight hours every day.

My wife has never been more beautiful than when her face was covered with black smut from scraping burned ceiling joists, and streaked with sweat from carrying sheets of plywood . . .

Okay, okay, we believe you.

We needed a lot more volunteers in 1980!

Pal, what you needed was votes.

154

You Don't Say

In this game selections of incredibly looney, puerile and ignorant prose are written on a piece of paper. Players then try to guess whether the selections come from *Everything to Gain* or from something else, such as an Andrea Dworkin tract or the *Washington Post* editorial page. Here's a sample game card:

On Japanese War Guilt

When I was young and in high school, during World War II, I thought Hirohito was the cruelest man in the world next to Hitler. I blamed the whole Pacific conflict on him. Years later . . . we went to Tokyo and called on a sweet little elderly man, who raised flowers in his hothouse at the palace . . . This was Emperor Hirohito – as far removed from my conception of him as he possibly could be.

☐ The Carters
☐ Barbara Walters

On the Sandinistas and US Central American Foreign Policy

A Habitat project was started in northwest Nicaragua in 1985. . . . Habitat volunteers are teaching the local people how to build good homes – without interference.

☐ The Carters
☐ *The Village Voice*

On Watergate and Its Aftermath

. . . we were joined by Chuck Colson, whom we had personally never met before, but for whom we had little respect because of his statements and actions during the Watergate years . . . We were also somewhat cynical about his supposed religious 'conversion'. . . . We quickly saw that he was at ease about his past. . . . In just a short time our remaining doubts were removed by his enthusiasm and persistence.

☐ The Carters
☐ Tammy Faye Bakker

On the Need For an Expanded Federal Health-Care Program
By strict disciplinary measures, possible only in a totalitarian society, and using intensive educational programs and trained paramedics who work closely with village leaders, the Chinese have reduced their infant mortality rate, carried out a broad immunization program, practically eradicated venereal disease, and lowered the annual population growth rate.
☐ The Carters
☐ Mao Tse-tung

On Tibetan Buddhism, Not Heretofore Known to Be Polytheistic
I have memories of prayer wheels, large and small, which spin prayers up to heaven, and of prayer flags that flap their messages to the gods . . .
☐ The Carters
☐ Shirley MacLaine

On Soviet–American Relations
During the service different members of the Soviet delegation were called on to speak, and each said that though we have different languages, there is room for friendship and peaceful coexistence. The very conservative residents of this north Georgia community listened intently to the interpreter, and, when the speeches were over, spontaneously rose to their feet in a standing ovation.
☐ The Carters
☐ Tass

If you guessed 'The Carters' on all six selections, you win.

I've also invented a great Carter Book Drinking Game. You just open the book at random and, boy, do you need a drink.

So that's *Everything to Gain* – a perfect icebreaker for any party and enjoyed by family members of all ages. But what – you may be asking – is the book *about*? It's about 193 pages. Ha. Ha. Ha. Excuse me. Spend a couple of hours with Jimmy and Roz and you get silly. I don't know what the hell the book's about. I mean, I read it and everything, but I haven't got the faintest idea. It just sounded to me like a couple of prissy old ratchet-jaw hicks yammering away about nothing until you wanted to stuff them headfirst through the outhouse seat.

Maybe we'd better ask the *New York Times*. After all, the *New York Times* is so much smarter than the rest of us. Let's see . . . here we go, the 31 May, 1987, issue of the *NYT Book Review*. Therein a certain Letty Cottin Pogrebin casts an overeducated eye made wide by thought provocation upon the Carter tome and concludes it's 'autobiography that is part confession, part pep talk and part hand-book for activism . . . an inspiring account of the creation of a meaningful life.' I don't know if we should listen to a woman from a family so obviously bad at spelling, but, what the heck, let's take Letty Cottin Pogrebin's word for it. Any questions? I don't want to keep seeing the same hands.

You know, the Carters may be onto something here – autobiography/confession/pep talk/handbook for activism *and* blueprint for meaningful life. I'd like to try one of those myself and give Jimmy a little of his own back. Let's see if I can do it in twenty-five words or less:

> I was born in Ohio. I drink. Hooray for the Red Cross. Send contributions to 17th and D NW, Wash., 20006. Get a job, Goofy-tooth.

We didn't really elect this hamster President of the United States, did we? Naw, get outta here. It was *Gerry*, Gerry Ford. That was the one we elected. Jimmy, Gerry – easy to get the two mixed up. And you know how vague we Americans are about history. We've just plumb forgot which fellow we voted in.

Whoops. I looked it up. We *did* elect Jimmy Carter President. Although, I notice, we unelected him as soon as we possibly could.

So now what are we going to do with him, him and his nitwit wife? We can't go on letting them write books. It's too embarrassing. This is an industrialized, Western nation. We can't have things like this in our bookstores. We'll get drummed out of the English-Speaking League. We've got to find some other line of work for these two before they, oh God, write again.

Television evangelists
Permanent guest hosts on *Hee Haw*
Carnival sideshow attractions
Goodwill ambassadors to Sri Lanka

Those possibilities leap to mind. But I have a better suggestion. Let's put them back in the White House.

All right, it sounds insane. But think about it for a minute. We've got all our seventies' debts paid off with cheap eighties' dollars. We've got low mortgage rates locked in on our houses. Now, if we could just get T-bills to yield twenty per cent again, we'd be fixed. We're *ready* for double-digit inflation.

Then there're the Russians. Carter would keep them worried and off balance. When you've got a guy as dumb as this in the White House, hell, he might *sit* on the button. The Soviets would be shaking.

And Carter has this remarkable peace-making ability. Reading *E to G* makes it suddenly clear how he managed the Camp David Accord. Begin and Sadat were so bored by the blubber-skulled Carter family that they were willing to do *anything* to get out of Camp David. It might just work again with Syria or Jordan.

Plus there's the matter of kick-ass patriotism, which has been slipping in the aftermath of the Iran-Contra hearings. With J.C. at the helm, there'd be another disaster such as the hostage crisis. That might be what we need to put some lead back in the national pencil and get us started whooping on creepy foreigners again.

Furthermore there'd be no obnoxious big-government activism in a new Carter administration. This is because of the people Carter would appoint. As soon as they were in office they'd run down to the South African embassy to protest apartheid. And they'd get thrown into jail and wouldn't be able to cause trouble.

The country's editorial cartoons would become hilarious again because Carter is funnier looking than Reagan. Indeed, as Jimmy gets older, he's funnier looking than *anyone* – a sort of Don Knotts of the undead.

And here, *here*, is the kicker. If Jimmy comes back, Billy comes back. Damn it, don't we all miss Billy Carter!*

So run right out and buy a copy of *Everything to Gain*, and write and tell Jimmy and Rosalynn just how much fun you had with it. (I've found my copy is also great for playing fetch with the dog.) Do everything to encourage the fellow. Maybe he'll make a comeback.

It's increasingly clear that nobody in his right mind wants to be President of the United States. Therefore let's, as Rosalynn doubtless says, 'go with the flow' and put somebody in the White House with no mind at all.

---

*Almost all the predicted benefits of a Carter presidency have been, amazingly enough, provided by the Bush administration. The exceptions being twenty per cent T-bill yields and, of course, a return of Billy Carter to the public eye. (Also, Bush's political associates tend to run afoul of the law for reasons other than protesting apartheid.)

Review of *The Kennedys:*

An American Drama by Peter

Collier and David Horowitz,

Summit Books, 1984

MORDRED HAD A POINT — CAMELOT REVISITED

This is a wonderful hater-of-Kennedys guide, an assemblage of ugly facts and rude anecdotes about this large and dirty family. It is not, of course, a complete collection. Deforestation of North America would be needed to print a book that size. But it will suffice.

Here, for those who have forgotten or just love to hear it all again, is the fulsome scurvy truth: Old Joseph P. Kennedy was a liar and a greedy thief, an ignoramus, adulterer, vile anti-Semite, coward and pompous ass. His wife, Rose, was a frigid martinet, unashamed to suckle at the teat of shabby lucre, awash in pietism and Tartuffery, filled with the letter of Catholicism and empty of its spirit. They raised their nine whelps in an atmosphere of brutal pride and stupid competition. When the hapless Rosemary turned out to be retarded, they had her lobotomized and parked her with the nuns. The remaining eight turned out foolhardy, arrogant, unprincipled, and wholly lacking in sense of consequences. This last trait caused Joe Jr and Kathleen to die in airplane crashes and allowed Jack to get his PT boat T-boned by a Japanese destroyer. (A tale of heroism was manufactured from that incident. The family wasn't so lucky with Teddy's Chappaquiddick skin-diving efforts three decades later.)

The Kennedys, however, continued to wax. Elections, intellectuals and press adulation were purchased. One family member rose, briefly, to great political power and almost unlimited sexual excess. Some others nearly achieved the same results. Two were shot, but under the most romantic circumstances and not, as might have been hoped, after due process of law. A third remains a fat dog in a Senate manger that's overdue for mucking out. Thus the Kennedys excelled in every Irish vice and learned others strange to the sons of Erin, such as simony and lust.

Then comes the morally satisfying third act, when the last generation of Kennedys reap the trust-fund dividends of sin. They wallow in drugs and indolence, perform wild acts of self-destruction and roll in social manure. At Studio 54, Xenon and Danceteria, they fritter away the advantage and wealth gained by their loathsome ancestors. They overdose and get arrested and, best of all, disappear from the public eye. Just desserts! Just hors d'oeuvres! A just main course of crow!

What fun this book is, what a storehouse of chortles and gloatings. It satisfies the streak of mean self-righteousness in us all. But that is just the problem. After reading *The Kennedys* one feels a little guilty for wasting the time and even a bit embarrassed at watching such manful thwacks being given to this dead equine. Why bother? The Kennedy pitchmen have folded their tents. The bogtrotters' circus has left town. Everywhere, except perhaps in benighted Massachusetts, the Kennedys are defeated and gone. What's the point of hating them anymore? Well, there are several points.

The Kennedys were more than a rich, bad family who gained temporary political power. They were demagogues of oligarchy. Disguised as populists, they championed the definitely privileged and supposedly enlightened few. These few, when ensconced in the offices of government, would decide what was best for the many. The Kennedys saw political office as the source, rather than the result, of social order. They held government to be the fountainhead of all privilege, responsibility, benefit and constraint. They did not know and probably couldn't understand the idea of a free people chartering a government for the sake of convenience and paved roads. It never occurred to a Kennedy that the proper role of federal administration might be to guard the coasts and let UPS deliver the mail. And only in the vaguest, election-fixing way did any Kennedy realize that public officials serve at the people's sufferance.

What's worse, the Kennedys not only believed in the primacy of government but believed it to be good. With the exception of the disgusting Joe Sr, there was genuine idealism in the tribe. The rotting leftovers can still be whiffed in Teddy Kennedy's speeches. There is something more horrible than hoodlums, churls and vipers, and this is knaves with moral justification for their cause. The Kennedys thought the world would be a better place for having them run it. And thus their every excess and corruption could be excused as contributing to a larger good.

Peter Collier and David Horowitz are not as alert as they might be to this idealistic evil. Collier and Horowitz have abandoned the leftism of their youth, but they retain something of a social-activist point of view. They see the Kennedys as doomed figures who failed to accomplish noble objectives because of moral shortcomings. But the Kennedys didn't have a tragic flaw. The Kennedys were themselves a tragic flaw of ours. And, in fact, they accomplished lots. They changed the nature of election-eering forever with thespian talents and piles of cash. They expanded executive power to do things like make war without Congressional permission or even public knowledge. They helped bring on the age of truly elephantine government programs. And they nearly established America's first hereditary political dynasty. To the extent the Kennedys succeeded, they did so precisely because of their unscrupulousness, never in spite of it. By having us hate the sinners rather than the sins, Collier and Horowitz distract us from the proper vein of bile.

Collier and Horowitz also fail to explain how these sewer trout managed to swim upstream into our body politic. The authors attribute the Kennedy rise to the family's pet intellectuals. This is giving the American public too little credit. We may be dumb, but we're not so dumb that we ever spent a minute listening to Theodore Sorensen. Neither were lick-spittle journalists at fault (though not through lack of trying by the likes of Joe

Alsop and Philip Graham). We have no one to blame for the Kennedys but ourselves. We took the Kennedys to heart of our own accord. And it is my opinion that we did it not because we respected them or thought what they proposed was good, but because they were pretty. We, the electorate, were smitten with this handsome, vivacious family.

> It's always tempting to impute
> Unlikely virtues to the cute.

We got a mad crush on the lot of them. They were so stylish, so charming, and – at least in their public moments – so gracefully behaved. We wanted to hug their golden tousled heads to our dumpy breasts.

This may be the stupidest thing that has ever happened in a democracy. And certainly it shows an emptiness at the center of our idea of government, if not at the center of our lives. A desire to adore a head of state is a grim transgression against republicanism. It is worse than having a head of state who demands to be adored. It is worse even than the forced adoration of the state itself. And this puts the Collier-Horowitz book in another light. It's ourselves we should be flailing. Trust hubris to bring such trash as the Kennedys to their knees. They are but few and a passing evil. We are another matter. There are 230 some million of us, and we'd better start talking sense to ourselves soon. The President of the United States is our employee. The services he and his legislative cohorts contract for us are not gifts or benefices. We have to pay for every one of them, sometimes with our money, sometimes with our skins.

If we can remember this we'll get a good, dull Cincinnatus like Eisenhower or Coolidge. Our governance will be managed with quiet and economy. We'll have no need to go looking for Kennedys to love. And no need to boil over with hatred for them later.

GIVE
WAR
A
CHANCE

DISPATCHES

FROM

THE

GULF WAR

ar! War! Blood-red savage war! Cry havoc and loose the dogs of ditto. Saddam Hussein – he's worse than Hitler, worse than Stalin, worse than waking up wearing a wedding ring next to Roseanne Barr. He invaded Iran. He invaded Kuwait. He even invaded some parts of the country he already lives in, that's how crazy Saddam Hussein is. He's got chemical weapons filled with . . . with . . . *chemicals*. Maybe he's got The Bomb. And missiles that can reach Riyadh, Tel Aviv, Spokane. Stock up on nonperishable foodstuffs. Grab those Diet Coke cans you were supposed to take to the recycling center and fill them with home heating oil. Bury the Hummel figurines in the yard. We're all going to die. Details at eleven.

It's lots of fun being in the panic industry. If you can't convince the world to love you, then scaring everyone out of their Bart Simpson Underachiever-and-Proud-of-It T-shirts is the next best way to get attention and feel needed. My fellow members of the news media and I have been pursuing this strategy with zest since 2 August. 'Horror Show', 'Talk of War', 'Must This Mean War?', 'Should War Come: A Scenario', read the headlines. *Time* ran a cover bannered 'Is the World Ready for This?', showing a photo of what looks like a cellular phone wrapped in a table napkin wearing Ray-Bans and a shower cap but which was

167

labeled 'US soldier testing chemical warfare gear in Saudi Arabia'. The daily papers and the nightly news are festooned with maps – arrows going every which way, little silhouettes of tanks and planes and proposed casualty figures that look like long-distance phone numbers.

The US government has also been pretty good at spreading alarm – not to mention money and guns – all over the place. We are sending 250,000 troops, six hundred fighter planes, three naval carrier groups and twenty-six B-52 bombers to the Persian Gulf, a little late to save Kuwait, maybe, but just in time to rescue the US defense budget. One well-placed ICBM and Saddam Hussein would get the message, but that wouldn't prevent Congress from taking all our Stealth Bomber money and giving it to naked NEA performance artists to rub on their bodies while denouncing male taxpayers.

Everybody's been cashing in on Hussein Hysteria. The Soviet Union is accumulating points in the civilized-nation lookalike contest. The UN thinks it might finally have found something to do for a living. My own fiancée plans to make a fortune selling 'FUQ IRAQ' bumper stickers. Literary agents are lining up hostage tell-alls and sending faxes to Baghdad instructing trapped Americans to have poignant thoughts and spiritual insights and to get tortured a little, if possible. So many TV camera crews have descended on the Middle East that Arab authorities are rushing to tourist hotels to check the Gideon Bibles – Exodus, chapters 7 through 12 – on the subject of plagues: blood, frogs, lice, flies, dead cattle, boils, hail, locusts, darkness, firstborn sons and, yep, network anchormen. Of course, Jesse Jackson is on hand, warning the world in *vers de société* couplets about a situation 'Where the price of oil would go up / And the price of blood would go down.' The occasion being too solemn for rhyme.

So I figured I'd better get over there. I've been to the Middle East three whole times before and know several words in Arabic, including *la* ('no') and *Ayna akrab mal'ab golf?* ('Where's the nearest golf course?'), therefore I'm an expert, too, and can put things into perspective, give you a clearer picture of unfolding events and maybe relieve some of the unnecessary fears and needless

JORDAN

anxieties stirred up by cynical, sensationalistic journalists like me.

I know what you readers are saying to yourselves. You're saying, 'P.J., P.J., how can you possibly tell us what these people are going to do? Here they are gadding about in their mothers' nightgowns, playing with pop beads and going, "Muhammad this" and "Muhammad that", when they've got to know Ali is pushing fifty and has Parkinson's disease and couldn't go half a round with Razor Ruddock.'

Well, that just shows how ignorant of Arabic culture you readers are. Ali could go the distance with Ruddock any day of the week standing on one foot, I don't care whose disease he's got. Besides, the Arab peoples possess an ancient and highly developed civilization that is in many ways more sophisticated than our own. For instance, they invented algebra. And this is why we have to go to war with Saddam Hussein this minute and bomb the shish kebab out of him before he invents trig and chemistry and the whole of America flunks high school.

Sending everything we've got short of Dan Quayle in a National Guard uniform to the Middle East to keep Saddam Hussein from doing whatever it is that he hasn't managed to do already is called 'being the world's policeman'. There's a lot of argument about this, mostly from American newspaper editorial writers who like to begin paragraphs with, 'America isn't the world's policeman'. But you'll notice that when Kuwait got invaded, nobody called Sweden.

So here we are, running around armed to the eyeballs in the same kind of weather you can get at the laundromat by putting two quarters in the dryer, while our domestic economy deflates like a cheap beach toy. And do we hear any thank yous?

I hadn't even gotten out of the Kennedy Airport Royal Jordanian Airline first-class lounge (a windowless room with two bottles of Johnnie Walker, no ice, a bowl of pistachios and a television permanently tuned to *Wheel of Fortune*) before a Jordanian started in on me: 'When Israel invades Sinai, did America send troops? When Israel invades the West Bank, did America send troops? When Israel invades Lebanon, did America send troops?' Of course he was being very unfair. We didn't send troops but we *did* send arms, material and a great deal of financial assistance. Albeit we sent them to Israel.

At the baggage carrousel in Amman, a Jordanian-American businessman, when asked where the *bureau de change* was answered with an impassioned defense of Saddam Hussein. 'Again and again and again Iraq asked Kuwait to quit violating OPEC guidelines. Again and again and . . . '

I bought a copy of the *Jordan Times*. They wanted the Cold War restarted:

> . . . it is most unfortunate that the Soviet glasnost and peres-
> troika policy has meant giving the Americans more leeway to
> do what they want with the smaller countries in the world . . .

Like, you know, save their butts.

At my hotel an organization called the Child Welfare Committee of the General Union of Voluntary Services was handing out press releases about a 'Women's and Children's March' to protest the trade embargo on Iraq:

> Such a blockade constitutes no less than an act of savagery,
> unprecedented in recent history . . .

The march was organized by the same kind of earnest wholegrain busybodies we have in the States, wearing Birkenstock sandals and primitive jewelry and arriving at the demo in their husbands' Volvos. They were trying to get seven or eight hundred kids under twelve to quit dropping, losing and smacking each other over the head with printed signs reading, 'ARAB WORLD IS MY WORLD', 'IRAQI CHILDREN = ARAB CHILDREN', 'HOW MANY KIDS' LIVES FOR A BARREL OF OIL?' and 'DO NOT KILL MOM'.

Do-gooders are always hard to figure, but watching the

Women's and Children's March was – considering the porky guy with the poison gas who stands to benefit – like being a spectator at an Earth First! spotted-owl shoot.

And one more thing I discovered on my first day in Jordan: The Jordanian American Friendship Society had been dissolved. (Though its president, Muhammad Kamal, admitted, 'The organization . . . has really been dormant since its establishment.')

America is the world's policeman, all right – a big, dumb mick flatfoot in the middle of the one thing cops dread most, a 'domestic disturbance'.

To the uninitiated, what Iraq did to Kuwait seems like regular war: Country A whacks Country B, which screams bloody murder, dragging Countries C, D and E into the fray. But within the large, noisy and exceedingly fractious family of Arabs, it's not that simple. Iraq, Kuwait, Jordan, Syria, Saudi Arabia and so forth are hardly nations as we understand the term. They are quarrels with borders.

Until 1918 the Arabian peninsula was ruled by the Ottoman Empire, so called because it had the same amount of intelligence and energy as a footstool. When the Turks backed the wrong horse in World War I, the French and English divvied up the region in a manner both completely self-serving and unbelievably haphazard, like monkeys at a salad bar. The huge, senseless notch in Jordan's border with Saudi Arabia, for instance, is known as 'Winston's Hiccup' because the then head of the British Colonial Office, Winston Churchill, is supposed to have drawn this line on a map after a very long lunch.

The British were fans of one Hussein ibn Ali, the Grand Sherif of Mecca, who led the Arab revolt against the Turks that Lawrence of Arabia claimed to be such an important part of. The British wanted to make members of Hussein's Hashemite family kings of what-all and which-ever. They crowned Hussein himself King of the Hejaz, the Red Sea coast of the Arabian peninsula. They put his son Faisal on the throne of Syria. But the French threw a fit, so the Brits moved Faisal to Iraq. And Faisal's brother Abudullah – grandfather of the King Hussein we've got these days – was given the booby prize of Transjordan, an area previously known as 'to-hell-and-gone-out-in-the-desert' when it was called anything at all.

In the 1920s, Ibn Saud – the man who put the 'Saudi' in Saudi Arabia – chased Hussein ibn Ali out of the Hejaz. This is why the Jordanians hate the Saudis.

The Jordanians should hate the Iraqis, too, because the military government that Saddam Hussein now runs killed every available member of the Iraqi branch of the Hashemite family in 1958. But Jordan and Iraq are both too busy hating Syria for Syria's attempt to achieve Arab hegemony by allying with Iran, invading Lebanon and trying to gain control of the Palestine Liberation Organization.

The PLO, meanwhile, nearly toppled King Hussein in 1970, whereupon the king, with Iraqi support, exterminated thousands of Palestians. Thus the Palestinians should hate the Jordanians and vice versa, but since sixty-five per cent of Jordanians *are* Palestinians, it's easier for everybody to hate Israel.

Which still doesn't explain why the people in Jordan are furious at the United States for coming to the aid of Kuwait. Unless it does.

Amman is a pretty dangerous place for an American to go – you wouldn't believe the traffic. Everybody in Jordan drives everywhere at top speed. They parallel park at sixty miles an hour. And Jordanians never touch the brakes, turn signals, dimmer switch or even the steering wheel. All driving is done by horn.

Amman's street layout was designed using the splatter technique popular with action painters of the post-abstract expressionist school. The idea of numbering buildings and naming streets has been taken up, but in a grudging, desultory manner, the way baby boomers practice dental flossing.

There are no major intersections in Amman. Instead there are roundabouts, from which radiate four, six, eight, twelve or thirty

avenues. There's really no telling because, although it's possible
to enter a roundabout from virtually any street in the city, it's
not possible ever to exit again.

This is why I missed a special Rotary Club of Jordan meeting
called to protest America's unfairness to Iraq. I had been eager
to see the results of backslapping Rotarian boosterism applied to
Islamic *jihad*: 'Okay, fellows, any member who hasn't drunk the
blood of an infidel dog since the last meeting has to stand on his
chair and sing "I'm a Little Teapot."'

Rotary International is just the thing for Amman, a bland,
clean, busy, humdrum, commercial city, a kind of Arab Brussels,
although perched on spectacular hills.

The buildings are all cement block made to look like limestone, except for some made of the limestone the cement's supposed to look like. By day the whole town is the color of those
afternoons at the beach when you can't tell where the sea ends
and the sky begins, and by night it's alive with the headlights of
drivers lost in roundabouts. All the modest one- and two-floor
cement homes have metal rebars left sticking up from their roofs
like whiskers – a Third World symbol of hope, meaning the
residents are planning to make enough money to add another
story to the house. Even the poorest parts of the city are tidy
and unodoriferous, thanks, in part, to huge subsidies Jordan
receives from the oil-rich Gulf states such as Kuwait.

But subsidies or no, pictures of Saddam Hussein were beginning to appear on the smaller and shabbier storefronts and in
the rear windows of taxicabs. Copies of that old anti-Semitic
forgery *The Protocols of the Elders of Zion* were stacked next to the
cash register in an expensive bookstore. And, according to the
Amman Star, University of Jordan students 'from all political
trends' were condemning 'Arab traitors, Saudi Arabia and
Kuwait, for inviting foreign troops into Arab and Islamic lands',
and calling for 'a battle of honor against the United States, the
Zionists and all other treacherous forces'.

The students had formed something called the Preparatory
Committee for the General Union of Jordanian Students. One
of their spokesmen said the Gulf crisis 'pushed us to political

extremism that hopes for an Arab-American confrontation that will lead to re-drawing the map of the Arab world.' In which case I hope they get New Jersey.

I did manage to find – by just leaving my car in a roundabout and walking – the University of Jordan, a handsome, shady campus filled with polite kids. The members of the infelicitously acronymed PCGUJS said, however, that only the head of their Information Sub-Committee was authorized to make statements to the international press. To my relief, they couldn't find him.

Most of the students at UJ were dressed like students anywhere, or better than that, Jordan being more or less a Mediterranean country and quite stylish. But about a third of the women students were wearing no makeup, scarves covering all their hair and drab ankle-length dresses. This in adherence to fundamentalist Muslim rules of decorum which mean, basically, dressing the way middle-aged dads with teenage daughters think girls should. To judge by the amount of fiddling, tugging and adjusting of the scarves, it was a fashion that had just come in. It's been a long time since I was in college, so maybe I've forgotten how these things work, but a campus fad for looking like a Russian cleaning lady and acting like a nun seems odd.

When I got back to my hotel Saddam Hussein was on the English-language TV news, pestering a group of British expats he had stuck somewhere in Baghdad.

'Your presence here and in other places is best to avoid the scourge of war,' said Saddam through a not very competent translator. 'Are you having recreational facilities?' Not waiting for an answer, he suggested they take a group photograph 'about preserving the memory of this time', then said, 'Let's put this on TV!' as though struck with a remarkable inspiration having nothing to do with the video cameras, soundmen and lighting crews in the room. Saddam reached out with a beefy mitt and petted the head of a freckled little English kid later identified as Stewart Lockwood. 'Are you playing volleyball with Iraqis?' asked Saddam, pawing the youngster's face, kneading his cheeks and playing with his nose. Young Stewart – sturdy chap – bore it all with more disgust than fear. A week later I was in Abu

Dhabi, watching English-language news again, this time about Jesse Jackson's return from putzing around in Iraq. And there was poor Stewart, now gripped by Jesse like a pet being taken to the veterinarian and giving Jackson exactly the same look he'd given Saddam. If we're serious about achieving world peace, we could start by getting international political leaders to leave Stewart Lockwood alone.

I drove out to Ruwayshid, the Jordanian checkpoint where the refugees from Iraq and Kuwait were beginning to arrive in large numbers. It's 250 kilometers through desert waste. Those of us brought up on Disney 'The Living Desert' films expect time-lapse blooming century plants and lizards with funny tongues pursuing bugs all over the place. But in fact this desert looks like house plants do after six months in a bachelor's apartment. It's flat and featureless with nothing sentient visible. At noon the temperature is in the hundreds. Dust devils slop back and forth in dirty spirals across the plain. And the whole is bathed in a nasty shimmy of mirage. Mirage being not an optical illusion of a palm-fringed oasis, but the constant glare of hot sunlight reflected by an even hotter layer of air along ground that's too hot to talk about.

There is one real oasis 100 kilometers from Amman, Al Azraq, a nasty littered collection of concrete-block buildings with a salt marsh and about fifteen half-dead date palms. This was Lawrence of Arabia's headquarters and, for five dinars, an ancient worthy will tell you, 'This was Lawrence of Arabia's headquarters.'

Beyond Al Azraq the desert gets worse, all covered with small chunks of basalt that absorb and compound the nauseating heat. This is the Black Desert, where even Bedouin caravans wouldn't go, because the sharp, heated stones destroyed the feet of their camels. After another seventy-five kilometers the desert gets worse yet. Solid lava flows with the texture of piles of razor blades are interspersed with lumps of basalt now big as chairs and sofas. And if you roll down your car window swarms of tiny flies cover every part of your exposed flesh.

Lawrence called Al Azraq a 'luminous silky Eden', and by

the time you get back from Ruwayshid it actually looks that way.

This two-lane asphalt highway across the desert is the only ground link to Iraq, and there was plenty of blockade-violating traffic on it. The Iraqis seemed to be running every old tanker truck they could get started, trying to get cash for their oil in Jordan. But the return traffic was not exactly a good-buddy, that's-a-big-10-4 version of the Berlin airlift. Many of the trucks headed toward Baghdad were empty, very few seemed to be carrying food and a number of them were loaded with two-by-fours or immense rolls of pulp paper, playing what part in the war effort I'm not sure.

The road is straight and paved in a sort of folk-craft blacktop. The truck drivers go right down the center crown to avoid as many potholes as they can, and nobody dawdles out here. It is a memorable experience to roll head-on with a closing speed of 240 kilometers per hour at a fully loaded eighteen-wheel gasoline truck being driven by somebody dressed like Yasir Arafat.

The rest of the traffic coming toward me was made up of refugees. I guess I'd expected them to be pushing all their belongings in baby carriages or something, the way movie newsreel refugees always were when I was a kid. That type of refugee would sizzle and pop open like a weenie on a grill in this climate. Besides, these were affluent refugees – at least they had been until recently – in Chevrolet Caprice Classics, 200-series Mercedes, Peugeots and BMWs. And they were very modern refugees, people making a run for it not because Stukas were strafing their villages but because their bank cards wouldn't work in Kuwaiti cash machines anymore.

Every refugee car carried suitcases tied on the roof, the immense vinyl suitcases of the underdeveloped world, big as folded-up rollaway beds. Each car was more splendidly loaded than the last, bearing huge swollen stacks of luggage, and every moment that these stacks stayed in place was a tribute to Middle Eastern knotwork. But now and then some vast baby-blue portmanteau would pitch loose and go vaulting down the highway berm like a rectangular Olympic gymnast, until it exploded – an underwear bomb.

Less affluent refugees were packed into buses. And refugees less affluent than that were standing in the back of open trucks. You'd see one of these trucks pulled to the side of the road for a piss break, its occupants scattered across acres of featureless landscape, squatting in their *disdasha* robes to preserve some modesty during the call of nature.

At the Ruwayshid checkpoint thousands more refugees were arguing with officials and one another, standing in petrified lines, wandering around bedraggled or patiently hunkering in whatever shade they could find. They were contained in a five-acre barbed-wire space with a dozen smelly cement buildings between two border-guard posts that looked like turnpike tollbooths. The compound was covered with shit and litter and aflutter with the Oriental mania for making copies of documents in triplicate and stamping everything with rubber stamps six or seven times. There seemed to be some food and water available, and a mosque where, when the *muezzin* made the midday call to prayer, nobody went.

These were the lucky refugees. Out in the desert toward Iraq, beyond the Jordanian border guards who refused to let me pass, were thousands and thousands more people with no shelter at all – thirsty, hungry and desperate to get into Ruwayshid, the first-class section of hell.

I talked to a Jordanian named Abnan abu Sherke who'd waited two and a half days out there. He owned a store in Kuwait that he had abandoned and had five thousand dinars in a Kuwaiti bank which were gone forever, and he'd driven 1,750 kilometers so far trying to get back to his family in Jordan.

'We are Arabs,' said Mr Sherke in a pleasant and conversational tone of voice. 'We are very happy because Iraq is face-to-face with the US. I have the admiration for Saddam Hussein. I lose everything but I am happy.'

The next day I drove the new four-lane desert highway out to Aqaba, Jordan's only port and a would-be Red Sea tourist resort that looks like a Bulgarian's idea of Ford Lauderdale.

This is another crucial chink in the international cordon that's supposed to convince Saddam Hussein to act like Dag Hammarskjöld. At the quays I counted two ships loading Jordanian phosphate, one rusty tramp steamer from Bombay and a grossly overloaded car ferry full of Egyptian refugees headed for Suez. If Saddam is going to feed a nation of eighteen million people by way of Aqaba, they'd better start eating Egyptians and their automobiles.

In an absolutely empty souvenir shop downtown the doddering owner told me, 'Jordan is a friend to all nations.' His thirty-year-old son said, 'You know almost all the taxes you pay in America go to Israel, eighty per cent.' He said he wasn't anti-Semitic, either, because he'd gone to college in Romania and had a Jewish girlfriend there for six months.

I drove back to Amman by the old mountain route, 360 kilometers of goats in the right of way and spectacular cliff-top views of the Dead Sea that will kill you in a second if you take your eyes off the road. I passed through Wadi Musa, the Springs of Moses, where he struck the rock with his staff and brought forth water; and past the picturesque Bedouins with their flocks and tents and dreams of running a grocery store in Detroit.

I traversed the ancient lands of Ammon and Moab and Edom and viewed the sites of King Solomon's Mines and the Palace of Herod where Salome danced for the head of John the Baptist. The mountain highway follows the same path that the Roman road took two thousand years ago, beside the ruined line of Crusader castles with remains of Byzantine, Ottoman and British forts in between. It's a kind of Grayline Tour of failed foreign policy initiatives.

These heights above the Jordan valley, along the great rift that runs from Africa almost to Europe, are the home and hearth of the entire world's culture. The oldest remains of fixed human habitations – houses from eleven thousand years ago – have been found here in Beida and Jericho. These people buried dead children in jars under their living-room floors. No kidding. I checked up on it at the Archeological Museum in Amman – evidence that not only the Arab world but our entire civilization was founded by crazy people.

Near Wadi Musa, about ninety-five kilometers north of Aqaba, I stopped for a few hours to look at the ruins of Petra. This was the great stronghold of the Nabataean Arabs who flourished from the fourth century BC until the first century of the Christian era by straddling the caravan route from Arabia Felix to the Tigris-Euphrates valley. They made their money by helping themselves to some of everything that went by – a previous example of vast, unearned wealth in the Middle East.

The Nabataeans used their swag to build Petra, which can be reached only by traveling down the floor of an unnerving canyon called the *Siq* – three hundred feet deep and barely wide enough for three people to walk abreast. At the end of this passage is a two-square-mile city of tombs, temples, houses and public buildings all carved into the face of living rock in the most elaborate Greek and Roman styles. It is a monumental hidey-hole, a thing done by mad children with unlimited resources.

Trade routes shifted. Petra lost its livelihood. The very location of the place was forgotten, and it wasn't rediscovered until the early nineteenth century. Bedouins were still building their cooking fires in the palaces of Petra until a few years ago, when the Jordanian government's Department of Antiquities shooed them out. They come back to water their flocks and lead tourists around. A kid of about fourteen was showing me a spectacular Doric cavern with a strong smell inside. 'Is here was the great temple,' I said in profound and solemn pigdin, 'and now is used to pen goats.' The Bedouin kid looked at me like I was a big dope. I had some better idea what to use it for?

UNITED
ARAB
EMIRATES

September 1990

The situation down in the Gulf States is, of course, very different from that in Jordan. For one thing, the guy who stamped my passport at the Abu Dhabi airport was wearing a wristwatch worth more than my car. Also, we've got a quarter of a million troops around here keeping the locals from being pounded like cheap veal, so they're very pro-American. Well, sort of pro-American. 'The foreign forces will leave the area as soon as the reasons for which they came are ended,' said United Arab Emirates Defense Minister Shaikh Mohammed bin Tashid in an interview with the UAE *Khaleej Times*, which also ran an editorial blaming the whole Gulf crisis on 'big powers':

> The big powers have only themselves to blame for what is happening now. Greedy for money they and unscrupulous arms dealers in Western countries have supplied Iraq with all the weapons now being pointed at themselves.

So maybe they're not very pro-American, but they're very pro-not getting pounded like cheap veal. The exiled Defense Minister of Kuwait told the *Gulf Times* that he'd order an immediate attack on Iraq if he were commanding the US troops in Saudi Arabia, and as I got into the elevator to go to my room at the Abu Dhabi Sheraton, a Kuwaiti in a perfectly pressed *disdasha* and carefully draped *ghutra* headdress began to speak to me in high-speed Arabic, 'America something-something-something-something.' I shrugged and he held up an admonishing index finger. 'Quickly! Quickly!' he said.

The Gulf is a place that does not surrender itself easily to mere description. The weather, to begin with, is so bad in September that people *long* for the interior of Saudi Arabia. When I was there the temperature was over 110 degrees every day, but with a dampness that can't be possible under skies as blue as a vinyl swimming-pool liner. The windows of my hotel room were frosted like an iced-tea pitcher. One afternoon the humidity was actually 100 per cent, at which point air isn't even vapor. I was breathing soup. A poison gas attack would be wholly redundant here.

Everything is air-conditioned, but not for comfort. An air-conditioned car is like a space suit. Step outside it for more than a few seconds at midday and you get dizzy, sick and as wet as if you'd been flushed down a toilet.

And there's the architecture. Abu Dhabi is new, really new, with a half million people packed into an unrelenting pre-post-modernism worse than Epcot Center. I've seen a photograph of old Abu Dhabi. There was a mud fort, of exactly the kind used as the set of *Beau Geste*. There was a mud mosque. There was the home of the British Colonial Officer and a few Bedouin tents. That was it. That was the whole town. The picture was taken in 1966.

Now buildings tower, ooze and mushroom in every shape that concrete can be poured. Some are trimmed in chrome and smoked glass like the coffee tables in time-share condos, and others make a daffy nod to Islamic tradition with pointless pointed arches opening to nowhere or senseless spreads of mosaics on ceilings instead of floors. My hotel was supposed to evoke, with rounded crenelations and brown tints, the mud fort in the center of town. But it only succeeded in looking like a grain elevator.

The city is laid out in an uncompromised grid which should make it easy to get around in even during the twilight 500SEL Benz-lock. But, instead of a few numbered addresses like Amman, there are none, and no concept that a street, once named, should keep that name for any length of its existence. Thus in a downtown as simple as a tic-tac-toe board, I lost the whole Saudi embassy, and two street maps, the concierges at three hotels, the Avis rent-a-car girl, the Marines on duty at the US embassy, several shopkeepers, an Iman at a mosque and the guards at the ambassador of Saudi Arabia's own residence were unable to direct me there.

When I did find the Saudi embassy, two days later, it was a big and obviously expensive building with not only no style but no discernible front. The reception room was bare except for chrome and Naugahyde conference-room chairs, one dusty formica-topped table and a standing ashtray. The floor was cheap terrazzo, the walls shabby stucco, but the ceiling was covered with rococo plaster work painted in pink and aqua and highlighted with gold leaf. On the wall was an official Saudi government map of the Arabian peninsula, which – in case you think the Kuwait fracas is the last we're going to hear from this neck of the woods – indicated disputed borders with the UAE, Oman, Qatar and Yemen.

There is no charm in Abu Dhabi. As the *Economist Business Traveler's Guide to the Arabian Peninsula* puts it, 'There are virtually no "sights" as such.' And the only place I've ever seen with worse aesthetics or a greater taste for flash and fake was Jim and Tammy Bakker's Heritage Village USA. To which place the UAE bears other similarities as well. 'Oil wealth has also reinforced the religious basis of society in the Emirates,' says a locally printed tourist booklet. 'Today, in the cities, no one need walk further than half a kilometer to the mosque.'

There are beautiful gardens, however, along all the streets and in every open space, all brought to blooming, verdant life by that thing which, in the desert, is more precious than gold –

money. Even the superhighways have gardens. The road that runs 130 kilometers to the oasis of Al Ain in the mountains on the Oman border is irrigated and landscaped the entire way, sleeved in date palms and tamarisk trees and flowering shrubs, the plants tended by brown, sweating people from Pakistan, Bangladesh, India and Egypt. Only here and there can you see what's behind the mask of greenery, which is nothing, the true, complete nothing of the sand desert. There are not only no plants or animals but not even any objects, just creeping, blowing, red-blond sand in dunes that rise as high as three hundred feet.

I went, in the early mornings when I could almost stand the heat, to the *suqs*, the open-air markets in Abu Dhabi and Dubai. Though almost nothing is manufactured in the Emirates, or, really, anywhere in the Arabian peninsula, shops were stuffed with goods, a barbaric splendor of merchandise – truly barbaric. That is, synthetic fabrics of astonishing ugliness, shoddy housewares, bad appliances, every kind of electronic gimcrack known to East Asia, a million overpriced Rolexes, garish nylon carpets in lampoons of Persian designs, gold necklaces with medallions bigger than salad plates, gems cut and set like carnival prizes, furniture to make a Mafia wife wince and table lamps Liberace wouldn't have owned.

We think of a barbarian as somebody with a bone in his nose. But, in fact, a barbarian is more likely to have his nose full of a Hong Kong Shalimar knock-off. I wonder if all the polyester and highway beautification will weather as well as the ruins of Petra.

But, never mind. World peace and international order must prevail, so we're going to sacrifice ourselves and our treasure . . . Well, not actually our own personal selves. More like eighteen-to twenty-year-old selves who couldn't find worthwhile civilian jobs. And the treasure is borrowed, like the rest of the national debt. But you know what we mean. We're going to make the same brave, selfless sacrifices to save the Arabs from Saddam Hussein's crazed aggression that we made to save the Jews from Hitler's death camps, the Cambodians from Pol Pot's massacres and the Poles, Hungarians and Czechoslovaks from Stalin's terror . . . That is, the same brave, selfless sacrifice that we were going to make as soon as the Jews, Cambodians, Poles, Hungarians and Czechoslovaks struck oil.

'SOMEWHERE IN EASTERN SAUDI ARABIA'

This is the first globally broadcast, real-time, live, on-camera, televised war. It's so televised, in fact, that increasing CNN's Nielsen share seems to be an allied war aim only slightly less important than degrading Saddam Hussein's command-and-control capability. However, what you're reading at the moment is, as you may have noticed, print. This report is not electronic, maybe not even electric (to judge by the sound of this rented typewriter, I've got one of the early IBM diesel models). These words are thus as out-of-date as the US State Department's tilt toward Iraq in the last Gulf war. By the time you read this we may be up to our Kevlar underpants in the kind of bloody trench warfare not seen since the French got their crêpes folded at the Somme. Or we may be drinking Saudi near-beer out of the open-toed slippers of Saddam Hussein's harem concubines in liberated Baghdad. Who knows? Truth is the first casualty of war, but, in this particular conflict, print journalism took the second hit.

What you're reading is not only out-of-date, it's hastily written and disorganized, too. This is war, for chrissake. At least that's my excuse. Actually, the best thing about this war has been all the new excuses generated by the Pentagon briefing officers. These will doubtless prove handy to Americans in all walks of life, especially school kids who haven't done their homework:

> My book report impacted harmlessly in an unpopulated area.
>
> I can't tell you what happened in 1066, we're waiting on the bomb-damage-assessment reports.
>
> I'm sorry but units of elite Republican Guards were dispersed and dug in around my algebra problem.

I arrived in Saudi Arabia thirty-two hours after the war began having taken a sixteen-hour flight in the cargo hold of an Air Force C-141 Starlifter. There were 126 other journalists on the trip. Now that 2 Live Crew has been arrested, the C-141 Starlifter is the single noisiest thing on earth. The journalists couldn't hear themselves think. Of course there's nothing unusual about 127 journalists not thinking, but the Starlifter was so loud that the journalists couldn't even talk. And 127 journalists silent for sixteen hours is another first for this war.

We had a brief stop in Frankfurt, where we received what the Air Force called 'a hot Italian food meal' followed by everybody's last Scotch until the war is over. We landed 'somewhere in eastern Saudi Arabia', which means the port area of Dhahran on the Persian Gulf about 180 miles south of the Kuwaiti border – as Saddam Hussein has surely figured out by now. Then we were herded into a US military briefing where it was explained to us that we could do absolutely nothing as journalists without US military permission to do it, and whatever it was that we got permission to do, we might not be able to do that either.

In fact – as of this writing – the military has been reasonably helpful in dragging journalists out to places of moderate discomfort and/or mild danger and letting those journalists ask Oprah Winfrey-quality interview questions. But the military press office – the Joint Information Bureau, or JIB – has a strictly grade-school field-trip mentality with much posting of rules, schedules and little lists of things reporters are expected to bring along. The JIB will be requiring notes from our parents next.

Reporters used to covering 'low-intensity conflicts' – where we took taxis to the fighting and it was the US military advisers who weren't supposed to be there – are, in a word, bored. But, in an *un*-low-intensity conflict, bored is the way to be. It means you're still alive. Besides, what's really hurting journalism around here isn't military censorship, it's military jargon. Spend more than an hour at the JIB and you begin calling the staircase 'a foot-impelled bi-directional vertical transport asset'.

I haven't been to the front yet. There are more than seven hundred journalists here – far more newsmen than there is news – and there's only room for about one hundred of them on the military 'pools' covering the troops. Also, I'm here as a radio journalist but am not even sure which part of a tape recorder takes the pictures.

I'd been trying to get a Saudi Arabian visa since Iraq invaded Kuwait last August, but when the name of your magazine means 'a large rock that moves around' and its pages are filled with pictures of Madonna wearing cookie tins on her chest, you don't get taken as seriously as the guys from *Time*. John Lyons, an old friend of mine at ABC Radio, got me a slot as an emergency incompetent broadcast correspondent, and I'm left in the rear manning the phones and explaining the Gulf Crisis to Blitzo Bob and Rocket Jaw Jim on the WONK morning drive-time zoo.

That's all right. The rear is where the action's been. We call it 'Club Scud'. We've had missile attacks almost every night. When the first attack came, ABC-TV producer Derwin Johnson and I got in a car and began driving around Dhahran looking for missile damage. We heard sirens and saw flashing lights on one of the main roads. We rushed to the scene and discovered a car wreck. Then we heard more sirens and saw other flashing lights. We rushed to that scene and discovered another car wreck. We saw four or five smash-ups that night, including one involving a police car. When the air-raid sirens go off everybody starts looking at the sky instead of the road, and Saddam Hussein's most fearsome weapon of the war's first week was the unguided Chevrolet Caprice Classic sedan.

The first sign of a Scud attack is a deep, vibrant *whoosh* from the Patriot anti-missile missile being fired. Then there's a *crack* when the Patriot breaks the sound barrier, followed by a light in the sky and a huge *boom* from the Scud being destroyed. After that there's a brief pause followed by an incredibly loud air-raid siren which our hotel sets off to let us know that the Scud attack that has just happened is expected soon. This sends the Filipino waiters and Indian busboys into a panic. They go running down the stairs to the air-raid shelter, colliding, on the way, with journalists running up the stairs to see the Scud fireworks from the hotel roof. Getting out on the roof is the third most dangerous thing about the Scuds – after car wrecks and falls on the staircase. You have to go through the blacked-out kitchen of the Chinese restaurant on the top floor, and there's considerable danger of falling into a big pot of stewed cat.

A Scud only carries about 250 pounds of explosives which – assuming the Patriots don't get it first – would create a blast a hundred yards wide at the most. These missiles are being lobbed into an area of eastern Saudi Arabia that's roughly fifty miles long and thirty miles wide. That's 4,626,400,000 square yards. The actual chance of this taking a direct Scud hit is two in a million. Don't tell CNN this, however. Their nightly Scud watch – called the 'Range-Finder Show' for its comments on where the missiles seem to be headed – is about all we have in the way of entertainment here.

Not only is this the first live televised war, it's also the first war ever covered by sober journalists. There is nothing available in Saudi Arabia with more 'command-and-control capability' than Moussy. Which explains why a lot of the coverage from here seems a bit, well, sober. (Some of us journalists have discovered, by the way, that what we'd thought for years was the pain of genius was, in fact, a hangover.)

Coverage from here has been sober and – as sobriety often is – uninformative. After five months of the United States being about as involved with another country as it's possible to get, most folks back home still don't know what Saudi Arabia looks like. Sand and camels, they think. Sand and Marlboros and Pepsi would be more like it. Eastern Saudi Arabia looks like Arizona would if Arizona had beautiful beaches. There's the same big sky, the same sparse vegetation and the same modern architecture – most of it ugly, just like in Phoenix.

Local mores do not, however, allow for much in the way of beach-blanket bingo or *Sports Illustrated* swimsuit-edition photo ops. And there are no movie theaters, night clubs, discos or rock concerts either. And no Victoria's Secret catalogues or even lingerie ads from the *New York Times Magazine*. But there are superhighways, supermarkets and malls. Most of the power shoppers are men. What few women you see are all in black, veiled up past the forehead and draped down to the ground. When the women want a better look at things in the market, they pull the hems of their veils out and over the merchandise like nineteenth-century photographers taking tintypes.

Saudi Arabia is perhaps the richest country on earth, and there are some big houses here and some Mercedes-Benzes that aren't much smaller. But it's not an ostentatious nation. Saudi men all dress the same no matter their wealth or importance. They wear sandals and a long nightshirt of a *disdasha* or *thobe*, in white cotton or brown wool according to the season. They wear white or red-checked *ghutra* headdresses held in place by the *igal* headband, a cord that was once used by Bedouins to hobble their camels. Status is told by the details – a Rolex watch, a Mont Blanc pen, a gold Dunhill lighter.

Saudi mansions are built close to each other. The two- or three-storey houses are always plastered white and usually roofed in red tile. The architecture is grand in scale but austere in form – a sort of cousin-on-steroids of the Spanish colonial style. Each home is enclosed in a small garden. You don't see that slew of leisure toys with which rich Americans clutter their yards. There are no ski boats, ATVs, dirt bikes, camper vehicles, ultralight airplanes, hang gliders or whatnot. The desert comes right up to the garden walls.

Not that Saudi Arabia is all desert. There are large oases along the Persian Gulf coast. These contain thousands of date palms in a landscape so ripe, wet and buggy that it could come out of central Florida. Except that these groves of palm trees have been occupied by the same clans of strict and pious Arabs for fourteen centuries. Imagine Disney World without the Disney and without the world.

Most native Saudi Arabians adhere to the orthodox Sunni Muslim Wahabi sect. Wahabis are strict like old-fashioned American Baptists are – no drinking, dating, mixed dancing or movie going. But the Wahabis are not looney televangelist-with-a-gun fanatics of the Ayatollah Khomeini stripe. The religious practices and attitudes of Saudi Arabia are no more peculiar than those of Billy Graham. A church-going, small-town American from forty years ago would be perfectly familiar with the public morality here. Only the absolute segregation of the sexes would seem strange. And I'm not so sure about that. At O'Rourke family Thanksgiving dinners in the fifties all the men were in the living room watching bowl games and the women were in the kitchen washing dishes.

During the nine days that I've been here I have, of course, spent most of my time watching CNN to see what's happening to me. But I've also managed to visit the markets, or *suqs*, in the various towns along the Gulf coast – Dammam, Al Khubar, Qatif, Tarout. It's nice for an American to be someplace where people love the country he comes from – a big change from being in America.

I've tried to get some 'man in the *suq*' radio interviews but without much success. People are shy of the tape-recorder microphone. But they're eager to shake hands, say *'Marhaba'* ('Hello'), buy me a cup of coffee and ask about the war. 'You are the journalist but now we will interview *you*,' said a wholesaler in the Dammam fruit and vegetable market. I asked why he wanted to do that. 'Because you have talked to too many people' – an accurate solecism if ever I've heard one. The people in the market wanted to know how dangerous the Scuds were, how the air war was going, when the ground war would start. They said they didn't trust the information they were getting. They wanted to talk to a newsman and hear the real story. I asked where they were getting this information that they didn't trust. 'From the news,' they said.

People in eastern Saudi Arabia are still worried about poison-gas attacks. Nobody here goes anyplace without a gas mask. The masks come in imitation leather shoulder bags. Every man on the street has one. Dhahran looks like it's hosting an international convention of purse-snatchers. Nothing could be further from the truth. There is virtually no crime in Saudi Arabia. You can leave the key in your car ignition here and leave your wallet and watch on the car roof, for that matter. This is one of the most honest places on earth and for good reason. Under Shari'ah religious law murder is considered a mere civil matter, involving monetary compensation of some kind, but theft can be punished by amputation of a hand. There's also no begging or importuning or wheedling of any kind. I don't know what they amputate for this offense, but whatever it is, I suggest we start cutting it off in New York City.

The Dhahran area seems a bit empty and, at the same time, overpopulated with foreigners – sort of like Paris in August. Many local residents have decided that Scud month is a good time to visit relatives down around Yemen somewhere. But other than light traffic and everpresent gas masks, life is normal. Food prices have actually gone down and the only notable shortage is of AA batteries. This tells us that the US troops are moving up to the front. As the troops leave, they empty the battery racks, stocking up to keep their Walkmans running. This is – one more first – the first war where everybody gets to pick his or her own theme music.

In case you're wondering, a gallon of premium gasoline costs 58¢, and, no, you don't get your windshield washed. The gas stations are just like ours, including the bathrooms. Most bathrooms in this part of the world are Turkish style – you put a foot on either side of a hole in the floor and hunker down. But Saudi Arabian gas stations are equipped with American facilities. Some of the local people are unaccustomed to using these, however, which leads to one little problem – footprints on the toilet seats.

US troop morale seems to be ridiculously good. I ran into some members of the 101st Airborne Division buying art supplies in downtown Al Khubar. I'd say that indicates confidence (not to mention a previously little-suspected creative bent among our nation's paratroopers). The soldiers, sailors, marines, airmen, coast guarders and whatever in Dhahran are cheerful. Maybe they're cheerful because they're not off in hell's outhouse somewhere sleeping in sand holes and eating MREs ('Meals Ready to Eat' or, as they're called, 'Meals Refused by Ethiopians'). But from what we've been seeing in the 'pool' reports and hearing from the reporters who've been to forward positions, the troops up there are in a pretty good mood, too.

It's important to remember that the 1991 US military is not made up of Oliver Stone and his hootch-torching platoon of hopheads. These young men and women were barely born then. They're the Reagan Kids. They took one look at the sixties leftovers which littered their childhoods and said, 'Give me a haircut and a job.' They've got skills, training, education, and if they'd just quit calling me 'sir' and telling me, 'You're the same age as my mom,' they'd be the salt of the earth.

*

One more thing about this generation of soldiers – they grew up in video arcades. It's no coincidence that watching the Gulf War's high-tech weapons on our TV screens is so much like watching computer games. The war is the daddy of all Mario Brothers, the Gog and Magog of hacker networks, the devil's own personal core dump. And our soldiers have an absolutely intuitive, Donkey Kong-honed, gut-level understanding of the technology behind it. Thank God they do. It's why we're winning. So here's what you folks back home can do to help with the war effort. If you happen to have any kids and they're outdoors exercising in the healthy fresh air and sunshine, give them hell: 'YOU GET IN HERE RIGHT NOW AND PLAY NINTENDO!' The future of our nation may depend on it.

MONDAY, 28 JANUARY,
DAMMAM SUQ   It's supposed to be a male-dominated society in
Saudi Arabia, but I'm not so sure. There are amazing dresses for
sale in the stores here – loud-colored silks and violently patterned
satins with gold embroidery and gem-stone trimmings. Under
those black *abayas* Saudi women are wearing some important
fashion statements. There are also a lot of jewelry stores with big
gold necklaces and big ruby bracelets and diamond rings so large
that you'd practically have to wear them on both hands at once
just to lift the things. I'm a married man. You can't fool me. If this
were *really* a male-dominated society, the jewelry stores would be
stocked with plastic pop beads and the only thing the dress shops
would be selling is aprons.

Since the time of the Crusades we in the West have been using
so-called 'Arabic numerals'. But the numerals actually used in
Arabia are different from ours. The 1s are the same, but an Arabic
2 looks like a backward 7. An Arabic 4 is a backward 3. A 7 is
a 6. A 0 is a 5. And a little dot is a 0. I don't know why the
two systems of numbers are different, but I can guess. I'll
bet if we went back and examined the Crusaders' expense-

account receipts, we'd find out that Richard the Lion-Heart got skinned.

TUESDAY, 29 JANUARY, HALF MOON BAY Oil is so important in Saudi Arabia that thoughts of 'Liquid MasterCard' seem to pervade everything. The US Consulate in Dhahran hands out a pamphlet to visiting Americans. The pamphlet gives tips on tourism and recreational activities. But a suggested picnic outing is described by the US Consulate in these terms: 'The beaches nearby are open to the general public and afford a good view of the oil terminal.'

WEDNESDAY, 30 JANUARY, AL KHUBAR One of the pleasures of going someplace where people don't speak English is making fun of the English the people don't speak there. Many of the commercial signs in Saudi Arabia are printed in English – more or less. I've seen the 'Decent Barber Shop' and the 'Meat Cow Fresh Butcher Shop', also 'Wow' brand toilet paper, a fast-food restaurant advertising 'humburgers' (ham being illegal) and a fancy model of running shoe called, in all innocence, the 'Crack'.

Of course, when it comes to truly not speaking English, it's impossible to top the US Department of Defense. The DOD calls a metal nut – the metal nut that goes on a bolt – I'm not kidding about this – a 'hexaform rotatable surface compression unit'.

One peculiar feature of Saudi Arabia is intersection art. There are lots of traffic circles, and in the middle of each traffic circle is . . . something. Devout Muslims don't approve of statues of people, so there aren't any of those. But, just in the Al Khubar area alone, there is a giant cement Arab coffeepot (a symbol of hospitality), a scale model of the Space Shuttle (because a Saudi Prince was a crew member on one mission), a real, twenty-foot-long fishing boat mounted on a concrete plinth, a large jet airplane engine in a glass case and an entire mosque, utterly isolated and unreachable on its island in the highway. There's also a lot of abstract stuff, such as a huge metal spiral (representing oil prices?) and two immense stucco triangles flanking what appears to be the robot vacuum cleaner from 'The Jetsons'. What I have not seen in a traffic circle – and don't think I will see – is a monument to the first Saudi Arabian who learns how to signal a turn or a lane change.

THURSDAY, 31 JANUARY, INTERNATIONAL PRESS HEAD-QUARTERS, DHAHRAN   There don't seem to be a lot of celebrities protesting against this war. New Kid on the Block Donnie Wahlberg did wear a 'War Sucks' T-shirt at the Grammy awards, but that's about it. In fact, I've heard that Jane Fonda has decided to maintain public silence on the subject of Desert Storm. Getting Jane Fonda to be quiet – this alone makes fighting Iraq worthwhile.

The Saudi Arabian beach resort of Khafji has been retaken. Which leaves us with the question: what do Saudi Arabians do at a beach resort? The women are dressed in tents, you can't get a beer to save your life and it's hard to play beach volleyball in robes that drag on the ground. As much as I can figure, the only amusement that's ever been available in Khafji is the one we've just witnessed – shooting Iraqis.

You may wonder what the job of being a Gulf War journalist is like. Well, we spend all day broadcasting on the radio and TV telling people back home what's happening over here. And we learn what's happening over here by spending all day monitoring the radio and TV broadcasts from back home. You may also wonder how any actual information ever gets into this loop. If you find out, please call.

FRIDAY, 1 FEBRUARY, INTERNATIONAL PRESS HEADQUARTERS, DHAHRAN   Dogs are considered 'unclean' in Saudi Arabia. Which, if you think about it, is true so far as it goes. Sport does like to get mud on the bedspread and roll in stuff on the lawn. But camels are *not* considered unclean in Saudi Arabia. This leads

196

me to believe that the Saudi Arabians know something about house-training animals that we do not.

Members of the press corps have been trying to figure out what the US military means when it talks about 'air supremacy'. We think it means that American Air Force pilots bombing Iraq are the only people in the world who can take a long trip by air and not have to change planes in Atlanta.

The so-called 'pool' system of reporting the war is causing a lot of frustration. The US military puts together groups, or pools, of reporters – one reporter from each kind of media. Then the military takes these pools on little trips to see things. This is like not being able to go to a football game unless Joe Montana invites you personally. If the pool system were used in dating, two hundred people would all . . . well, it would be the 1960s all over again. If we got our news at home the way we're getting it here, the only time you'd know about a fire would be when kids playing with matches phoned the local newspaper before they lit the living-room drapes.

SUNDAY, 3 FEBRUARY, DHAHRAN AIR BASE I was interviewing some British Tornado pilots who've been flying missions deep into Iraq – missions that sometimes take four or five hours. And I asked them the question that was foremost in *my* mind: 'Isn't that a long time to go without taking a leak?'

It turns out the pilots do have 'relief sacs'. But they're wearing so much clothing – flight suits, G-suits, chemical-weapon-protection suits – that it takes them ten minutes just to get ready to use these aerial bedpans. So they avoid liquids for a couple of hours before they fly and, so far, only one Tornado pilot has actually relieved himself over Iraq. And, no, he did not target civilian areas.

MONDAY, 4 FEBRUARY, THE ROAD TO ABQAIQ   Out in the Saudi desert I came across one of the strangest road-hazard signs I've ever seen. I was driving through a region of huge sand dunes, and every mile or so there would be a triangular sign – the kind that says 'SLOW, CHILDREN' or 'DEER CROSSING' in the States. But these signs said 'SAND DUNES!' Sand dunes drift at a rate of about thirty feet a year. Saudi Arabians are fabulously bad drivers, but even they should be able to avoid something that's moving at less than one millionth of a mile per hour.

WEDNESDAY, 6 FEBRUARY, KING FAHD AIR BASE   I was with a couple of US Air Force officers, and they were complaining how everything has to be shipped in here – food, water, even the most primitive construction materials. While they were grousing I was looking around at all the bunkers, gun emplacements and air-raid shelters built out of sand bags – thousands and thousands of sand bags. 'Well,' I said, 'I bet there's one thing you guys can get locally . . . '

'You're *wrong*,' said the Air Force officers. 'We know what you're going to say, but the sand here isn't the right kind of sand to make sand bags – too powdery.' So the US military is buying sand in Saudi Arabia.

Because of the time difference, we get the late-night TV talk shows here early in the morning. Arsenio Hall by himself is plenty alarming enough at 8:00 a.m. but this morning he had Sandra Bernhard on and, whoa, talk about something that doesn't go with breakfast. At least she makes the troops feel a little better about there being no USO shows here.

We've been having an informal competition to come up with the worst movie idea based on this war. Here's a strong contender:

A group of American war correspondents somehow gets trapped behind enemy lines, and they have to complain and exaggerate their way out of Iraq.

THURSDAY, 7 FEBRUARY, HOFUF This is an ancient oasis town a hundred miles off into the Saudi desert, and it's one of the few places in this country which retains any character or visual charm. It has narrow-roofed streets in the *suq*. There's a bit of Ottoman Empire architecture left mid the concrete-block modernism. And Hofuf has one of the world's largest mud forts, a place that looks like . . . one of the world's largest mud forts.

It must have been interesting to live here. I guess when you grow up in a mud fort, Mom yells, 'You kids take your shoes off before you leave – I don't want you tracking our house all over the outdoors.'

FRIDAY, 8 FEBRUARY, INTERNATIONAL PRESS HEADQUARTERS, DHAHRAN I watched Secretary of State Baker's speech to the House Foreign Relations Subcommittee the night before last, and I actually heard the secretary say that America will help rebuild the economy of Iraq after this war. Mr Secretary, I just can't tell you what enthusiasm your plan has inspired here in Saudi Arabia. First, let's donate the American savings-and-loan industry to the Iraqis. Then we'll give them Michael Milken so he can set up a Baghdad junk-bond market. And, when we're done with that, we'll send in Michael Dukakis for a repeat performance of his Massachusetts Miracle.

As everyone knows, the US military censors our news 'pool reports'. We're not supposed to tell specific locations – cities, military bases, etc. We're only allowed to name the country or, at most, the general region of that country. Hence, 'somewhere in eastern Saudi Arabia'.

One of my radio pool-report tapes came back from the censors with a so-called red flag and a note saying, 'You cannot mention "Thumerate" in Oman.' I'd never heard of Thumerate. In vain I searched the map of Oman for Thumerate. Finally I played the tape back. What the military censors were sure was a city or vital base – Thumerate – was an Air Force Colonel from North Carolina saying, *'The Emirate* of Oman'.

GIVE WAR A CHANCE

We keep hearing about Iraq's 'elite Republican Guard'. Well, if they're so elite why don't they have better jobs than sitting around getting the stuffing bombed out of them in Kuwait? And what are they guarding anyway – big charred wrecks of buildings and blown-up bridges? And one more thing – how many of these elite Republican guards are really still Republicans?

Early February 1991

Halfway through a ninety-minute flight to the front lines aboard a C-130 Hercules cargo plane, Colonel Clay Bailey, Commander of the US Air Force's 317th Tactical Airlift Wing, began explaining that this particular Hercules was patched together from two other C-130s which had crashed. 'The crew calls it "Franken-Herc",' said the Colonel with the large smile that military men get when they're scaring civilians.

The inside of a Hercules is like an airborne basement, with wires, pipes and ductwork covering whatever you call an airplane's walls and ceiling. There's room for 42,000 pounds of cargo. Colonel Bailey wouldn't tell me what this cargo was, a secret which made me sincerely hope his crew would avoid air turbulence, let alone enemy anti-aircraft fire.

The cargo was in wooden boxes held in place by what looked like women's hairnets. That is, if a woman had big wooden boxes for a head and was wearing a hairnet, she'd look like this. Each netful rested on a metal plate as wide as the plane, and the plates sat on a wheel-covered deck – a kind of reverse skateboard or roller-floor which allows the cargo to be rapidly shoved out the back when the plane lands or even when it doesn't land, if parachutes are used.

We were flying at 6,000 feet with fighter planes somewhere above and below us so that we were the tuna fish in a giant airlift sandwich. There was nothing to see from the cockpit except winter desert haze – endless murky gray-brown ground and murky gray-blue sky with a smudge of horizon in between. We seemed to be inside a bad Mark Rothko painting. But if I looked straight below us and concentrated, I could pick things out, things that looked like random scatterings of runes or Arabic letters – wiggles and dots in the sand. The wiggles were berms – bull-dozed ridges of sand pushed up around the tents, tanks, guns and trucks, which were the dots. Berms are this war's trenches. You get dug in, but first you get bermed up. There was nothing actually random about the wiggles. This was a modern front with soldiers and weapons carefully spread around thousands of square miles. It is to the front lines of past wars as today's pro football defense is to the way football was played in the 1950s. The troops don't just line up and crouch anymore.

At first a modern front didn't seem impressive, and then I realized how long I'd been looking at wiggles and dots while flying by at 300 miles an hour. This is a big, but uncrowded, war. The sky isn't black with airplanes. The ground isn't honeycombed with bunkers. Everything in this war is so powerful, so fast and has so much range and reach that a roomy bloodbath is required.

The C-130 landed on a mile-long blocked-off section of two-lane highway about fifteen miles from the Iraqi border. The plane came in at the same angle that's used for bobsled runs. The pavement was only twenty feet wider than the landing-gear track. This is not a large margin of error when crosswinds are blowing, and they always are. Outside the scenery was similar to that photographed on Mars by the *Viking* spacecraft – so similar as to be identical and I think a NASA audit is called for.

The land was hard-packed grit the color of blood and diarrhea. It was strewn with mud-pie-looking rocks and was so awful in its perfect flatness that I thought I could see the curvature of the earth. Anywhere I stood I seemed to be standing on high ground. The horizon fell away in every direction. I got dizzy when I stared into the distance.

A cold and arid wind seemed to come from every direction at once. A few tents had been pitched. They had grit all over them and drifts of grit coming in under the tent flaps. A few soldiers were there, grit all over them, too. One of the Air Force officers had just come back from a year-long tour of duty in Greenland. 'When I got off the airplane in Greenland,' he said, 'I thought, "I've found the end of the earth."' I asked him what he thought now. 'I've found the other end.'

Army Specialists Forest Chester of Aberdeen, Washington, Michael Lindstrom of Reno, Nevada, and Sherrie Murry of Lyons, Georgia, were using a tent pole to scratch a map of the United States into the dirt, making the outline as nearly life-size as they could. They'd been five months in Saudi Arabia without leave, and they'd been a month in this particular Satan's parking lot. The fact that I was from *Rolling Stone* magazine was the most interesting thing they'd heard in days, although that wasn't saying much. They wanted me to please tell John Prine to do another album, quick.

Listening to Walkmans is about the only fun American troops are having in a place where there's no booze and most of the women either are covered with the front-hall rug or they outrank you. By now every American soldier has listened to every cassette and CD in Saudi Arabia at least twice. I was talking to a sergeant in a Dhahran record store, a black woman from Chicago. She said, 'Who's that girl who's got the song that goes "da-da-da-da-da" forever?'

I said, 'Suzanne Vega?'

'Yeah,' she said, 'I'm even going to listen to her.'

Peacenik types say there would be no war if people truly understood how horrible war is. They're wrong. People don't mind a little horror. They can even be enthusiastic about it if the horror is happening to somebody else. But everybody hates to be bored and uncomfortable. If people truly understood how much sleeping on rocks, how much eating things rejected by high school cafeterias, how much washing small parts of the body in cold water and how much sheer sitting around in the dirt war entails, we might have world peace after all.

The dirty little secret of this war is that we all privately hoped the Israelis would get fed up with being Scud-whipped and break down, drop the big one and fuse the sands of Iraq into one vast sheet of glass so we could go in there and finish this thing with Windex. That isn't going to happen. And so the war drags on – a whole three weeks now. Jeeze, this thing is turning out to be longer than the Civil War miniseries on PBS.

Boredom aside, US troop morale seems to be fine, whatever that means. You'll notice that the term 'morale' is never used except in reference to soldiers or people in analogous positions, such as employees of large corporations or prison inmates. Even educational institutions have 'school spirit' or 'the mood on campus' rather than 'morale'. Nobody ever talks about the morale of participants in a passionate love affair, nor does the word come up in discussions of wild drinking sprees, marathon poker games or visits to whorehouses in Bangkok.

'Morale' apparently means 'how well people are doing when they're not doing well at all'. In that sense, US troop morale is, as I said, fine. Nobody has painted a peace symbol on his helmet. And nobody – except journalists dealing with the military's Joint Information Bureau – has threatened to frag an officer. Everybody has a pretty good idea why he's here. And just about any Pfc can articulate it better than President Bush: A whole bunch of US citizens are facing a tin-pot dictator with the fourth-largest army in the world so that the tin-pot dictators with the fifth-, sixth-, seventh- and eighth-largest armies in the world won't dis Uncle. Or anybody else. One of the war's favorite T-shirts bears a takeoff of the *Ghostbusters* logo with Saddam Hussein in place of the ghost. 'Who Ya Gonna Call?' it says, and below that are the numbers 001, the international telephone-access code for the United States.

Morale is particularly fine in the air. Air forces own the franchise for this war so far. Even the crews from the British Tornado fighter-bomber wing which has had four of its planes shot down were full of smiles and sang-froid. A half dozen Tornado fliers were trotted out to endure the press. When asked the inevitable age-of-sensitivity 'How does it feel?' question, the crew members gave answers better suited to a gardening column than the Phil Donahue show.

'One of the things that obviously you can't train for and get used to is the amount of flak and missiles coming up,' said pilot Richard Goodwin. 'It does look very, very spectacular.'

'I'm still amazed at the sort of sparkling lights of the anti-aircraft fire and the missiles and so forth,' said Goodwin's navigator Dave Chatterson, 'and I stupidly enough still find them quite pretty.'

A lieutenant colonel in the Kuwaiti Air Force – who'd managed to escape to Saudi Arabia in his A-4 jet last August – was even more cheerful. 'It's, kind of, happy feelings to get into Kuwait,' he said. 'After six months we didn't see Kuwait. And then we fly inside Kuwait. You see the country. At the same time, you know, we bomb our country.' Though this didn't seem to upset him. After all, anybody who's been a bored schoolboy has fantasized about doing that. 'But we try to avoid to bomb which is populated areas,' he added.

Morale is fine and boredom is preferable to getting shot, but Saudi Arabia is off the hit parade. Very few people who came here for Desert Storm will be coming back on vacation. It's not that the Saudis aren't fighting. Saudi troops – uncouth-looking fellows who seem to be from the boonies of Asir and the Yemen border – fought well if not wisely at the battle of Khafji. (The Saudi brass have explained to everyone who will listen that they didn't allow the Iraqis to slip into Khafji and they won't do it again, also it wasn't their fault and furthermore it was part of a plan.) But the drab sanctimoniousness of Saudi Arabia is getting on everybody's nerves. There's no noise, no fun, no movies, no Christmas and our military chaplains have to be called – that word again – 'morale officers'.

Our Father, who art in . . . um . . . the gym at the Y . . . Give
us this day our daily hobby- and leisure-time activities . . . And
forgive us if we get in a bad mood.

And civilian Saudis themselves aren't acting much like American
civilians would if the fourth-largest army in the world were
massed on the Canadian border. Nobody is up in the master-
bedroom window with his duck-hunting shotgun or out fixing
punji sticks in the herbaceous borders. The Saudis aren't doing
much of anything, which is par. They pray five times a day and
everything shuts down for about five hours at every prayer time
– you figure it out. All real work in Saudi Arabia is done by
dark-skinned poor people – from India, Egypt, Thailand and the
Philippines. (Of course, you could make a somewhat similar
argument about the US military, but don't make it in front of
General Powell.) There's a standing wager in the press corps, a
free bottle of postwar champagne to the first person who sees a
Saudi lift anything heavier than money.

The entire Saudi civilian war effort in Dhahran has consisted
of half the Saudis leaving town, even though Dhahran is separated from the front by 180 miles of desert and all the US Army,
Air Force and Marines in the world. I talked to an Indian who
was managing a Dhahran sportswear store. About two-thirds of
the shops on the block were closed. I asked when they'd shut.
'From the beginning of the war,' he said.

'Was it the Scud missiles that scared the shopkeepers away?'

'Oh, no,' said the Indian. 'Just the war. They never know
what is going to happen.'

'Where'd they go?' I said.

'Maybe some went to Jiddah. Maybe some are sleeping at
home. All the stores open here, they are open by Indians and
Filipinos.'

I said, 'I guess it's too far for you to go back home?'

He frowned and shook his head and said it wasn't too far at
all. 'My sponsor has my passport.' He couldn't leave.

So far no pejorative term has been coined for Iraqis. There's
no 'Gook' or 'Kraut' or 'Nip' for this war. And the only Iraqi

jokes I've heard, I've heard on the telephone from back home. As a matter of fact there's only one war joke going around in Saudi Arabia:

What's the name of the Saudi national anthem?
   'Onward, Christian Soldiers.'

GULF

DIARY

Monday, 11 February,

DHARAN   One thing all of us here sincerely regret is that John Tower was not confirmed by the Senate as US Secretary of Defense. You can bet we'd be able to get a drink in Saudi if Good-Time Johnny Tower were in charge of Desert Storm. Either that or we'd be fighting this war someplace where we could – New Orleans during Mardi Gras, for instance.

TUESDAY, 12 FEBRUARY, DHAHRAN AIR BASE   Ever since bombs were invented it's been customary to personalize them with messages written on the shells: 'Stick this in your mustache, Saddam,' that sort of thing. We've been trying, however, to improve the quality of bomb graffiti, make it a little more clever. Not that we've had much success so far:

STEALTH PILOTS DO IT IN THE PLACE WHERE YOU LEAST EXPECT THEM TO DO IT

IF YOU CAN READ THIS YOU'RE DEAD

MY OTHER BOMB IS ATOMIC

Anyway, we're open to suggestions.

WEDNESDAY, 13 FEBRUARY, DHAHRAN An Iraqi air-raid shelter was hit by American bombers. Initial estimates from Baghdad of the casualty figures ranged from 40 to 1,500. This illustrates a persistent problem in the Middle East. The zero was invented by the Arabs, but so were the next six or eight zeros after that. Americans should be warned that you will hear a lot of numbers coming out of this part of the world, but don't count on them.

THURSDAY, 14 FEBRUARY, DHAHRAN It's Valentine's Day, time for romance. And what could be more romantic than sex toys? We've been trying to figure out what Saudi Arabian sex toys would be . . . edible veils? Inflatable plastic airline tickets to Europe? But in a country where a man may have as many as four wives, the most popular marital aid is probably ear plugs.

Have you noticed Saddam Hussein's furniture? You can see it in the background in his CNN interview or when he's having a photo opportunity with international peace-pest diplomats. Is this stuff Cosa Nostra Rococo, or what? Now we know why the Iraqi Air Force disappeared – they didn't want to get the white velvet upholstery in their MIG cockpits messed up flying combat missions.

If we want to demoralize the population of Iraq and sap their will to fight, we ought to show them videotapes of the South Bronx, Detroit City and the West Side of Chicago. Take a look, you Iraqis – this is what we do to our own cities in peacetime. Just think what we're going to do to yours in a war.

FRIDAY, 15 FEBRUARY, DHAHRAN Maybe Kuwait really *was* a threat to Iraq. I talked to a Kuwaiti Air Force colonel who thought it had been. He explained that Kuwait was using all its oil money to buy things for its citizens while Iraq was using all its oil money for military hardware. 'Iraq,' the colonel said, 'either had to bring its citizens up to the Kuwaiti level or bring Kuwaiti citizens down to the Iraqi level.' In other words, Kuwait caused the war by shopping too much. This leaves us with little hope of overall world peace as long as wives are allowed to hold credit cards in their own names.

I passed a Saudi bus on the highway last night. US soldiers had written in the dust on the back and sides. 'Iraq sucks', said one message, but most of the graffiti was home towns – Mobile, El Paso, Detroit, Des Moines. And way up in the corner of the bus's back window one soldier had written the name of that quintessential home town of almost all us Americans – 'Suburbia'.

SUNDAY, 17 FEBRUARY, RIYADH   I came to the Saudi capital to attend a couple of the military briefings in person.

The journalists in Riyadh are even more earnest, whiney and weenie-like than the journalists with the troops in Dhahran. One long-haired worrywart who was with either the *Village Voice* or National Public Radio was concerned that we were bombing every one of the government buildings in Baghdad. 'Are we going to leave Iraq without *any* government departments?' he asked the briefing officer indignantly. Not all the reporters in Riyadh are like that, of course; the British newspaperman sitting next to me said, 'We'll leave them the Department of Tourism – "See the Ruins".'

We're used to not getting much information during the question-and-answer periods at the military briefings. But the Saudi briefing today won the prize. A reporter asked the Saudi general in charge, 'What's the weather like in Saudi Arabia in March?' Said the Saudi general, 'I will try to find this out for you.'

MONDAY, 18 FEBRUARY, WADI AS SAHBA   I got stuck out in the desert. I pulled off the road to take a leak and my car went down in the sand like the *Andrea Doria*. I didn't have a shovel. I tried to dig the car out with a hubcap – the car went in deeper. I tried

210

to put brush and rocks under the wheels – the car went in deeper. I had the car in sand up past the doorsills by the time the Saudi police happened by. They almost got their car stuck in the sand, too. They didn't have any rope so they flagged down a trucker. He didn't have any rope either so we used one of the canvas straps from his freight load. We got my car out, but the canvas strap became completely snarled in my front bumper and tangled in the police car's back axle and none of us had a knife. We spent the next half hour sawing at the cargo strap with the edge of a flattened soft-drink can.

America has all the guns and Saudi Arabia has all the money, but it's no wonder the Japanese are ruling the world.

WEDNESDAY, 20 FEBRUARY, DHAHRAN I read today on the AP wire that our loyal NATO ally Turkey is sending two generals and three colonels to Saudi Arabia. No soldiers or anything, just generals and colonels. 'Forward, me!' 'About my face!' 'Self, I am hereby recommending that a medal for heroism be awarded to me for saving the life of everyone under my command – which action was accomplished by my sitting myself down right here in a Riyadh hotel room.'

Between 350 and 400 Iraqi soldiers just surrendered to US helicopters flying hundreds of feet in the air. Not long before, another group of Iraqi soldiers had surrendered to three *Life* photographers. The Iraqis seem willing to surrender to anything. The Saudis have promised that all prisoners of war will be given adequate food and shelter, kept away from the fighting and released when the war is over. Adequate food and shelter? Kept away from the fighting? Released when the war is over? The press corps must have surrendered months ago.

THURSDAY, 21 FEBRUARY, DHAHRAN Personally, I'm coming back to the United States as a big supporter of atomic power. It's worth the risk just to make sure that this part of the world *never* has any political, strategic or economic significance again. That done, we can use the Middle East for the purpose to which it is so ideally suited – dumping nuclear waste. Watch out for the nine-legged camels.

Every time I look at American TV I see these 'defense experts' – former generals now being paid large fees to go on *Nightline* and talk about the Gulf War. Well, I'm a former hippie. Maybe I can get a job as a 'protest expert'.

Ted Koppel will say: 'P.J., does your expertise as a retired long-haired butt-head lead you to think that the protesters will continue to beat drums outside the White House or will they begin chanting "No Blood for Oil?"

And I'll say, 'Well, Ted, I believe that we will see continuation of a primarily drum-focused activity here although we cannot rule out the possibility that the protesters may eventually utilize "Draft Neil Bush" signs. We know they have the capability.'

FRIDAY, 22 FEBRUARY, DAMMAM I've mentioned before that Saudi Arabia is an incredibly honest country – as well it might be, since they cut your hand off if you're caught stealing. But although there seems to be no theft here, there are enormous padlocks on all the shops and offices – sometimes four or five of them on a single door. Maybe there's a side to Saudi Arabia I don't know about. Whatever, I've decided to stay out of neighborhoods full of one-handed men.

MONDAY, 25 FEBRUARY, DHAHRAN One terrible problem confronting Iraqi troops is finding something white to wave when surrendering. They've run out of pocket hankies. The Iraqi army doesn't issue bedsheets. And, since the Iraqi soldiers have been at the front lines for a long time without adequate supplies, their underwear is, frankly, gray and dingy. So, if anti-war organizations back home want to stop the fighting in the Gulf, they should send some Clorox to Iraq, quick.

We hear the Iraqi army is systematically blowing up buildings in downtown Kuwait City. If the architecture in Kuwait resembles the architecture in Saudi Arabia, the Iraqi army will have done one good deed, anyway. As soon as the Iraqis have all surrendered, let's send them to New York and let them take a whack at Trump Tower.

RIYADH
AND
THE
DESERT

Late February 1991

Certain of the ancient moral philosophers – Norman Mailer comes to mind – hold that every man should experience war because war, like love, is one of the central mysteries of life.

Central? Let's hope not. Mysterious? And how. Even the most modern and baffling romances, with their diseases, divorces, custody battles over the dog and years spent afterward in therapy and Woody Allen movies are not more mysterious than combat. For example, during the past week and a half we've been facing the worst threat of this war so far – peace. Giving the Iraqi armed forces a chance to go home, simonize their tanks and think up new ways to amaze the world is the most terrifying imaginable outcome to the Gulf conflict.

But we were reasonably confident that bloody, murderous peace wouldn't break out. We'd managed to survive Saddam Hussein's first call for a cease-fire, 'The Dog Ate Kuwait' peace initiative, which he presented last week. Then there was the Soviet-brokered 'I'll Pull Out in Time, Honey, Honest I Will' peace plan. We endured that. So we figured we could get through George Bush's noon on 23 February deadline.

214

And, indeed, as I write this, on Sunday, the 24th, word comes that the ground war has started. Word also comes that we're going to learn nothing about that ground war. The secretary of defense tells us we are entering a period of 'media blackout'. Thus war grows more mysterious still. And so does war reporting. Here I sit scribbling trivia while the most serious events of a generation take place so close that I can see the haze from the oil-well fires in Kuwait.

War is mysterious but never more so than when it involves two of life's other big mysteries, Saudi Arabia and the US military mind.

Nothing about the US military – except killing bad guys – makes sense. The military mind is unfathomable even in the most minute and specific details of its operation. Inside each MRE field-ration kit there's a pouch containing salt and pepper, gum, napkins, other odds and ends and a pack of matches. The matchbook cover is plain olive drab and bears the message:

> These matches are designed especially for damp climates but they will not light when wet.

As for Saudi Arabia, the English-language newspaper here, *Arab News*, has an Islamic agony column where readers can write in with the kind of questions Ann Landers would get if she were a Muslim scholar:

> Q. What lesson do we draw from knowing that a certain person died in the toilet?

The answer being no particular lesson to speak of. But some of the replies in the *Arab News* leave a westerner feeling that he has encountered a mentality almost as foreign as the one which produced the MRE matchbook:

> A. The rule is that when you put your socks on in the morning

215

> you should have a full ablution, washing your feet. Then before
> that ablution is invalidated, you put on your socks . . . If you
> need to do ablution again that day, you need not take off your
> socks. You simply wet your hand and, using your fingers, you
> pass them over the top of your feet.

Simply as a physical locale Saudi Arabia is incomprehensible. It's not a matter of, 'What are we doing in this place?' It's a matter of, 'What is this place doing in existence?' The two-hundred-mile stretch of desert between the Persian Gulf and the Saudi capital of Riyadh is so scruffy, flattened-looking and devoid of physical features that it hardly seems to be part of nature. The land appears to have been cleared by a bulldozer the size of the Hoover Dam. It's God's Vacant Lot. There's a whole section of Saudi Arabia called the Rub al Khali, the 'Empty Quarter', and the frightening thing is, this isn't it. The Rub al Khali is somehow emptier yet.

An ugly four-lane highway runs through the ugly desert from Dhahran to Riyadh. Junk is strewn all along it – rusted mufflers, empty water bottles, waste paper, lengths of cable, old truck tires, construction detritus and a thousand bright pink and yellow plastic shopping bags floating like jelly fish on the breeze.

We Americans are long trained in highway citizenship. It's been thirty-five years since I threw something out a car window without guilt. I'd forgotten the pure exhilaration of littering and found myself heaving Coke cans and half-eaten sandwiches into the ether at every opportunity.

The other signs of human life along the Riyadh road are oil wells and oil storage tanks, a few plumber's nightmare petrochemical factories and an occasional gas station.

The Saudi landscape, when there's a landscape at all, is utilitarian, industrial and dumpy – grimly practical stuff. But what is the practical result of all this practicality? There's no clue in Riyadh. It is a city with two million people and uncountable wealth, and there is no reason on earth to go there. A large, glossy picture book, *The Kingdom of Saudi Arabia*, commissioned by the Saudi government itself, says of Riyadh:

> With its flyovers and tree-lined boulevards, its first-class hotels and . . .

Here is a glowing official description of a nation's capital, and the first thing that the first sentence mentions is highway overpasses.

Rightly so. Riyadh is almost all new, with the worst kind of urban newness – a grid of lifeless streets in a cage of freeways, and every little rectangle is filled with modern architecture. There are miles of the usual high-rise concrete and steel self-storage-in-the-sky buildings. But the Saudis can afford the creative kind of modern architecture, too. You can always tell when modern architecture is being creative – the rest of the thing looks like the same old curtain-wall rabbit hutch but the roof is nutty. Lumpy roofs, wavy roofs, roofs in curlicues and roofs puckered in the middle like assholes – Riyadh has them. Also, like Abu Dhabi and Dubai, it has modernism that gives a nudge and a wink to Arab traditions – giant cement Bedouin tent shapes serving no purpose and enormous onion-shaped arches in the middle of nowhere. And there are all the other varieties of contemporary design: Havatrail Modern, Brobdingnagian Lego Block, Behemoth Tinker Toy, Cheese Grater of the Titans, plus some of those buildings that are wider at the top than they are at the bottom, who knows why?

The Saudis are guaranteeing the safety of all surrendering Iraqi troops, and they're also providing asylum to everybody who ever got kicked out of architecture school.

Only a few of the traditional mud houses of the Nadj, or central Arabian highlands, are left in Riyadh, and the Saudis are tearing these down as fast as they can. The flat-roofed buildings are reddish-beige, the color of a frostbitten nose. More vertical and austere than American adobe homes, each is a sort of private tower keep with only a few small, deep-set and shuttered windows. The floors are made of palm-trunk beams covered in layers of thatch. Simple pie-crust and pinking-shear patterns are traced around the edges of the roofs. By watching the demolition work I acquired a sort of X-ray vision. Where walls were toppled, I could look inside the houses and see the steep switchback staircases with their rounded mud steps leading to snug rooms all white-washed, with borders around the windows and doors painted in brilliant blues and greens.

Around the corner from the demolition site I found several dozen Filipino construction workers shoveling wet dirt and straw into a cement mixer. They were building a brand-new mud structure. This, I was given to understand, would be ready for tours in a month – the traditional architecture of Old Riyadh painstakingly reconstructed within two hundred yards of Old Riyadh being torn down.

I drove southeast out of the capital, following a line of oasis towns in the riverless riverbed of the Wadi as Sahba. Each town was a miniature of Riyadh in its up-to-date ugliness and sat in a nasty little tangle of date palms that looked like the cat had gotten into the potted plants.

The road was two-laned here and the driving was, as it is everywhere in Saudi Arabia, horrific – conducted at absolute top speed with no thought for consequences. Though there were plenty of consequences to be seen. Amazing car wrecks lay beside the road, sometimes a dozen of them in a mile, things you would never know had been cars if a couple of car wheels weren't sticking up out of them. Whole Chevrolets were crumpled like gum wrappers. And these wrecks had taken place without collision on a perfectly straight and level road that is absolutely free of obstructions. Cars just somehow go blooey and wind up in a wad beside the highway.

Running parallel to the road was a railroad track that was also perfectly straight and level and absolutely free of obstructions. And – sure enough – amazing train wrecks lay beside the rails, things that you would never know had been trains if a couple of train wheels weren't sticking up out of them.

I stopped in one of the oasis towns to get gas and some more Coke cans to throw out the window. There was a Bedouin kid about fourteen years old at the little store there. Most Saudis are – whether they take their socks off during ablution or not – fastidiously clean, and they are polite to the point of cold formality. But this kid was pesky and dirty and determined to practice his nonexistent English. 'Riyadh? Riyadh? Riyadh?' he said. Yes, I'd come from Riyadh. 'Is seeing George Bush?! George Bush?! George Bush?!' George Bush is a president. Riyadh is a capital. Naturally I'd seen him there. Then the kid tried to sell me something. It was a photograph of a girl – with her veil off. I've been here so long I blushed.

Turning back toward the Persian Gulf, I drove northwest through the 150-mile-long Ghawar oil field. The whole way I could see an immense natural gas burn-off flaring on the horizon like the pillar of fire that guided the Hebrew tribes by night when they were fleeing from Egypt. Above the flame was a huge vertical cloud like the pillar of smoke that guided the Hebrew tribes by day. But the Hebrew tribes wound up in Israel and the oil wound up here. Those Hebrews took a serious wrong turn.

Is this empty, dusty, cheerless, oily, fun-free place making the American military crazy? Here's another mystery of war – no. Even being in the American military isn't making the American military crazy. I visited an Army motor pool where the soldiers had – with the exceptions of a few forays into the shockingly dull local town – been confined for five months to one vast expanse of asphalt surrounded by razor wire. Specialist Hefner of St Mary's County, Maryland, and Specialist Jonas of Bay City, Texas, both streaked with grease like zebras, were happily wrenching on a large truck. 'She's our best mechanic,' said Specialist Hefner of Specialist Jonas, who had left a baby behind in the States to come do this. Specialist Jonas gave a shy smile of nondenial. 'We don't like it here too much – nothing to do,' said Specialist Hefner. But that was all I could get out of them in the way of complaints, although Specialist Hefner did allow that the Saudis 'drive like fools'.

At Saudi Arabia's main Persian Gulf port facilities in Dammam, I talked to Captain Johnny L. Sawyer from Detroit, Michigan, Commander of the 551st Transportation Company. His job is to unload boats. Captain Sawyer said, 'When we initially arrived here, we worked the soldiers eighteen hours a day, gave them four to six hours rest, at most, and put them back to work. There weren't any complaints whatsoever. That's seven days a week, and we've been doing that for the past six months. They're down to a twelve-hour schedule now but we still have soldiers that are willing to work extra hours without being told. They stay behind just to finish a job.' Captain Sawyer had been in the Army for thirteen years and had come up through the ranks. 'The quality of the soldiers, from then to now,' he said, 'has improved drastically. I don't think that a soldier that we would have called standard then would be allowed to join the Army today.'

I talked to a medical officer at one of the British field hospitals. He'd been in Vietnam and this was his first contact with the American military since. 'I was astonished when I got here,' he said. 'Every American soldier I met was tidy, cheerful, eager to help, glad to be here – well, not precisely *glad*, but you know what I mean. This had not been my experience in Vietnam. It is as if the American soldiers here come from a different nation.'

And that is one last mystery of war – where did the addled, sniveling, pointless America of the past quarter century go? There's no trace of it in these parts. The catch phrases of this war are 'I'll make it happen', 'not a problem', 'good to go' and 'hoo-ah!', a sort of all-purpose noise of enthusiasm. When the chairman of the Joint Chiefs of Staff visited here, the soldiers asked him for his autograph. A sense of doing something worthwhile and important has even infected a few members of the press corps. Some reporters were ready to check into the local clinic after experiencing a strange and frightening choked-up feeling when looking at the American flag.

At the King Fahd Air Base, west of Dhahran, there's a small sign posted in one of the buildings taken over by the US Air Force:

GIVE WAR A CHANCE

W e couldn't go to war, but war
came to us. Two days into the ground assault on Iraq the majority
of the press corps was stuck, as usual, in the press headquarters
at the Dhahran International Hotel. There was a Scud missile
attack on Monday night, one of dozens since the war began. We
didn't think much about it. Some of the technicians on the out-
door TV platforms – where you see correspondents stand with
the foolish blue-domed roof of the hotel's pool cabana in the
background – watched the Scud go down. They thought it hit
near the local shopping center and we joked that Saddam Hussein was targeting Dhahran's only decent record store. Then we
went back to the work of pretending we knew more about this
war than people watching television in Cleveland.

The missile had, indeed, struck right behind the record store,
going through the roof of a warehouse that had been converted
to a billet for US troops. We heard nothing about this at the press
headquarters. Almost two hours later I was driving to Dammam
and I saw hundreds of blue police lights blinking in clusters
around the shopping center. A half dozen helicopters hung in the
sky with their searchlights moving back and forth like blackboard

222

pointers. And ambulances were rolling away in long and frighteningly silent convoys.

Saudi police blocked the road. I parked and followed a crowd of robed Saudi onlookers, some of them holding hands, most of them speaking in whispers. They moved across a half mile of open fields toward the shopping center. It didn't seem like a disaster scene. What had been the warehouse with more than one hundred Americans inside didn't look like a building that had been blown up. I thought I was staring at a construction site. The framework of steel girders was mostly still standing. Some of the I-beams were twisted or collapsed, but the ventilation ducts and the electrical conduits remained in place. What I didn't understand was that there had been a roof and walls. And these were utterly blown away.

There was really nothing else to see except slightly panicky Saudi police and very serious American troops. Twenty-seven soldiers were killed and ninety-eight were wounded – more American casualties caused by one unlucky Scud strike two hundred miles behind the lines than had been suffered in the whole rest of the war so far.

As befits a short war, it didn't take me long to readjust to peace – three minutes and forty seconds to be exact, the length of one Billy Idol music video. I was drunk and lying on a hotel bed in Rome. In the previous forty-eight hours I had managed to get myself out of the reeking, scrambled mess of Kuwait, back to the ugly, sterile, unwelcoming Saudi capital of Riyadh. From there I'd driven across hundreds of miles of stupid desert in a disposable diaper of a Korean rental car and finagled a ride out of Dhahran on an airliner chartered by an English TV company to take its people and gear to the next place foreigners decide to get killed.

It didn't seem like it had been a short war at that particular moment, not after two months with the arrogant, lazy Saudi Arabians and nothing to drink. We charter passengers were into the Johnnie Walker miniatures before the plane cleared the runway, and grown men, adult broadcasting executives with serious jobs in a large corporation were kneeling in their seats, trying to swill from three or four little Scotch bottles at once and screaming out the windows at the diminishing landscape, 'FUCK YOU, YOU MOVING TEA TOWELS.'

Anyway, as I was saying, I was lying on a hotel bed in Rome, and I flicked on the television, and there was MTV showing a Billy Idol video. Billy was really going at it, running around the stage in a most histrionic way, thrusting his fist into the air, stamping his feet and making violent and emphatic faces at the camera. It was a dramatic performance but confusing to my woozy intellect. What, I wondered, was Billy Idol being dramatic *about*? I'd just spent the past week in a burned-up, blown-up, looted city where there was no food or water, seeing mangled bodies and hearing stories of murder, rape, abduction etc. – pretty dramatic stuff. It made me get drunk and lie on the bed without taking my shoes off. But Billy Idol seemed to have experienced something much more dramatic, so much more dramatic that it made him strip half-naked, dye his hair platinum, wear a bunch of jewelry and jump around like an ape.

'Billy Idol concerts are,' I thought, 'obviously worse than war.'

Kuwait did have a better light show. There is nothing else in the world (I'm glad to say) quite like four or five hundred burning oil wells casting a lambent glow upon a nighttime desert landscape. The flames come up out of the wellheads in soft, thick, billowing shapes like clouds or turds or cake batter. The fires are scary when you glance at them but terrifying if you keep looking. That is, the fires seem to be big and close. Then you stare into the perspectiveless desert and realize they are fifteen or twenty miles away and are therefore enormous beyond comprehension. You can hear them across all that distance. There's no reassuring, ordinary crackle and roar in the noise the fires make, and no blast of heat. Instead the sound is a steady, sucking rumble of the whole atmosphere being dragged toward the conflagrations. And beyond the fires that you see are the fires you can't see, brightening the horizon on all sides like a dozen simultaneous dawns breaking on one very bad day.

I had a lot of time to look at the oil-well fires because on the third night of the ground war I spent six hours with forty-five other journalists and a half dozen British army officers being held at gunpoint in the middle of the Kuwaiti desert.

Not by Iraqis, of course. The Iraqi army was in high-speed rewind. We were under arrest by a Saudi colonel who was furious that the British didn't have the correct paperwork for escorting a convoy.

Our mission to bring pool journalists from Dhahran to Kuwait City was not moving with the same efficiency and precision as the rest of the allied Gulf War operations. The British military escort, an affable but clueless bunch – 'The Desert Squirrels' – did not have two-way radios or even maps. They put the eighteen-vehicle convoy together with the slowest things at the back so that the trucks all lost sight of the cars within minutes. The main purpose of the convoy was to get the British Independent Television Network's satellite dish into Kuwait. The first thing the British officers did was leave that dish behind. The second thing they did was take a wrong turn leaving Dhahran and head south toward Qatar instead of north toward Kuwait City. It took us eight hours to reach the Kuwaiti border, a three-hour drive.

It was dark by the time we passed through the well-shelled town of Khafji and its abandoned Saudi customs post. We could hear artillery fire in the distance now, and every few hundred feet we'd pass a burned Iraqi tank or personnel carrier. Saudi troops moving north had pushed these derelicts to the side of the road, and they sat like the cars up on blocks in front yards in certain parts of America. We seemed to be driving through a neighborhood of ultra-militant hillbillies.

Shrapnel was scattered everywhere on the road, causing a half dozen blowouts. And more time was wasted when young journalists – members of that generation so handy with keyboards, modems and electronic what-all – had their first encounters with screw jacks and lug wrenches. Then we got arrested.

The Saudi colonel, who looked like a cross between Omar Sharif and Mr Potato Head, had a platoon of soldiers line up across the road and level their rifles at us. 'YOU DO NOT HAVE THE PERMISSIONS! HOW CAN YOU BE COMING HERE WITHOUT THE PERMISSIONS WHEN I AM THE PERSON WHO IS MAKING THE PERMISSIONS FOR YOU TO COME HERE?! YOU MUST GO BACK TO DHAHRAN AND GET THE PERMISSIONS FROM ME THERE TO COME HERE AND GIVE ME PERMISSIONS!!!' shouted the Saudi colonel.

In vain it was explained to the colonel that this was an official

British military convoy, that the British were Saudi Arabia's allies, that this was Kuwait and not Saudi Arabia anyway and that we could hardly go back and get permission from him in Dhahran when he was here.

The electronic-minded young journalists fetched a Peter Arnett-style satellite phone out of their luggage and set it up in the middle of the road and phoned the Kuwaiti Minister of Information at his exile home in Tarif. The minister told the colonel the convoy could proceed, whereupon the colonel hung up on the Minister of Information and threatened to shoot the satellite phone with his submachine gun.

In the midst of this argument a metallic-blue Ferrari 328 came humming through our convoy, its thousand dollars' worth of tires and its three inches of ground clearance apparently immune to jagged metal fragments. This was just a couple of Kuwaiti refugees determined to get home before the liberation rush. They didn't even slow down for the gun-pointing soldiers, who jumped like quail to get out of the Ferrari's way.

In the end it turned out what the Saudi colonel wanted was a sufficiently abject and humiliating apology from the British officers for, I guess, failing to fill out, in triplicate, the Request for Permission to Help Keep the King of Saudi Arabia from Getting the Holy Kaaba Stuffed up His Butt by Saddam Hussein Form or something.

Apology delivered, the Brits led our convoy directly into downtown Kuwait before realizing that the city had not actually been reconquered.

Iraqi jeeps, trucks, armor and artillery pieces were lying on their tops and sides all along the Kuwait City expressways as though somebody had spilled Saddam's toy box. The Iraqis who'd been inside all seemed to be gone, in one sense of the word or the other. In place of the Fourth-Largest Army in the World we saw cruising teens. This was the Kuwaiti Resistance. One group of five pulled up in a Buick Park Avenue, happily brandishing AK-47s out the windows of dad's car. They were dressed just like teenagers would dress if the cool kids at the high school got to form their own partisan army – one guy

227

favored the Rambo look, another was dressed like Little Steven, two others were got up in Mutant Ninja Turtle garb and one fellow, who wasn't quite with the program, seemed to have stepped out of a J. Crew catalogue. They were hunting for Iraqis or people who looked like they might be Iraqis or people who had collaborated with Iraqis or had thought about collaborating. And I wouldn't be surprised if they were also keeping an eye out for the algebra teacher who gave too many pop quizzes. Small-arms fire could be heard coming from various places in the lightless city. It was a teenage dream come true: Bad guys invade your neighborhood and you and your best friends get to stay out late, kill them, skip school and impress girls. The Kuwaiti Resistance fighters welcomed us effusively. But when teenage dreams start coming true, sensible adults get out of town.

The Brits decided we should go to the International Airport even though we'd been hearing on the shortwave radio about a tank battle there. Fortunately, this was over but lots of jumpy US Marines were patroling the airport perimeter, and it was a shock to their systems when they came across us, totally lost, in eighteen civilian vehicles packed with camping gear, foodstuffs, bottled water and people in Banana Republic clothes. It must have looked like the Adventure Tour travel business had gotten completely out of hand.

Going back into the city at 6:00 a.m., we could see that the Iraqis had left in brainless panic. All their wrecked military equipment was pointed in the same, Baghdadward, direction. Allied air strikes had caused some of the destruction but traffic accidents had caused more. Jeeps had smashed into tanks. Tanks had rammed bridge abutments. Armored personnel carriers had rear-ended ambulances. A truck towing a howitzer had jack-knifed and collided with itself. And a T-55 Soviet tank came a cropper on a highway divider and wound up high-centered, three and a half feet in the air.

Iraqi defenses had been abandoned with the same comic haste. Guns, ammunition, canteens, helmets, even shoes were left behind. Tea kettles were still sitting on paraffin burners. I found somebody's uneaten dinner – a pot full of chicken and rice, or rice and cat maybe, white meat anyway. The defenses themselves were pathetic. The Iraqis had built miles of low dirt berms across the main road from Saudi Arabia. These were little more than speed bumps, and were supposed to . . . to what? . . . signal allied armor, 'Slow, War Zone'? In Kuwait City every highway overpass had a little pillbox built on it – four feet square and three feet high with no roof or back wall. These tiny redoubts were made of crumbly local bricks pasted together with a few dabs of mortar. Hundreds of them pimpled the city in places the Iraqis had, by some mysterious thought process, decided were strategically important. Thus the roofs of all the hotels had pillboxes but the roofs of other tall buildings didn't, and while expressways were defended, roads with two-way traffic were not.

Iraqi soldiers had made sad little nests in these emplacements – lined them with stolen blankets, chunks of foam rubber, old clothes and canned goods taken from local homes, pictures of pretty women torn from magazines and other bits of unmilitary junk. The local soccer stadiums and Kuwait's only ice-skating rink had also been fortified, the fortifications consisting of one row of sandbags placed in front of each principal entrance. The Iraqis must have thought that General Neal began every press briefing in Riyadh by saying, 'In excess of two thousand combat air sorties were flown in the Kuwaiti Theater of Operation yesterday, targeting continues to be travel and leisure facilities and small mounds of dirt.'

Members of the Kuwait Resistance showed me a twenty- by thirty-foot model of Kuwait City in the basement rec room of a mansion that had been occupied by Iraqi staff officers. The model was made of sand with blue-dyed sawdust for the Persian Gulf. Roads were indicated with gift-wrap ribbon and the principal buildings and military installations were represented by Lego blocks. Handsome navy-blue construction-paper arrows showed US forces coming ashore into conveniently located minefields, while much larger and more festively lettered red arrows showed

Iraq's reinforcements arriving from somewhere in the direction of the rec room's projection TV. It seemed Saddam Hussein had let the defense of Kuwait be planned by the prom decorations committee.

The Iraqis were better at destroying Kuwait City than they were at keeping ahold of it. But they weren't really too good at this either. Again their first concern was with the hotels, as if allied forces would never be able to effect a real conquest without room service. The Iraqis tried to set all the hotels on fire, but in many cases they used diesel oil, which is not the best of arson accelerants. The hotel where I found a room had survived pretty much intact except that a thick layer of greasy and insoluble oil soot had settled on every chair, table, towel, bedsheet and toilet seat. After a couple of days, all the reporters staying there looked like they had passed out in a tanning booth.

Downtown there was evidence of plentiful random artillery fire, like children had had tantrums with tanks. But the big cocktail onion-looking pointy water-tower things that are the symbol of Kuwait City proved too sturdy for Iraqi gunfire, or maybe just too hard to hit when whole sides of city blocks offered themselves as targets. The *suqs* with their flammable jumbles of shops had been successfully torched. And anything complex and vulnerable, such as power stations, desalinization plants and the main telephone switchboard, was thoroughly ruined.

But what the Iraqis were really good at was looting. Every store and office and an enormous number of homes had been sucked clean of all possessions. Nothing was left behind except the trash of deliberate vandalism and, in some cases, piles of human shit. The Hilton Hotel had been taken to pieces room by room. It looked like all the worst rock bands in the world had stayed there at the same time.

The city was not, however, extensively booby-trapped. The Iraqi soldiers were evidently so stupid and eager to leave that it was hard to imagine them having the forethought to wire up surprises. 'All boobies, no traps', was the consensus. And most of us quit worrying about dirty tricks. Besides, there was so much

230

untricky dangerous stuff lying around the city – live bullets and artillery shells, loose mortar rounds, unexploded American cluster bombs and so forth. An NBC camera-crew member lost some fingers fondling a land-mine detonating cap he'd picked up as a souvenir. And mines were going off on the city beaches with fair regularity, turning some unwary Kuwaitis into what the GIs call 'pink mist'. I was helping dismantle one of the small pillboxes on the Hilton's roof, getting bricks to level a satellite dish. There was a wooden carton sitting in the pillbox. I lifted the lid and found enough RPG – rocket-propelled grenade – rounds to put me, bricks and satellite dish in permanent earth orbit. I closed the lid carefully and extinguished my cigar.

The Hilton is next door to the American Embassy, and a couple of days later US Special Forces came and 'swept' the hotel to make sure a small thermonuclear device wasn't hidden in the basement or anything. I saw one of the Special Forces guys later in the hotel lobby. 'Hey, we found a booby trap!' he said in the perky, enthusiastic, pumped-up way nineteen-year-old Special Forces guys have of saying these things.

'Good for you,' I said. 'Where was it?'

'In a big box of RPGs, in that first gun emplacement on the edge of the roof. You know, the one with some bricks missing off it. There was a hand grenade with the pin out in there. Man, if anybody had jiggled that box . . . '

I briefly got religion. 'God spared me for a special reason,' I thought and felt very good about myself. 'I must be going to accomplish something very important in life, something that will benefit all mankind.' It was a couple of days before it occurred to me that there had been two dozen other people on that roof, also spared for a special reason by God. It's probably one of them who's going to invent a vaccine to prevent Jim Morrison revivals or whatever.

On Thursday afternoon, 28 February, about six hours after the US declared a cease-fire, the victorious armies began to roll into Kuwait City. The Arab contingents were firing their guns in the air and the Kuwaiti Resistance fighters responded by firing *their* guns in the air and then the other Kuwaitis picked up all the leftover Iraqi guns and started firing these in the air, too. People were singing, dancing, clapping their hands and beating on car horns. The women began their eerie ululation, that fluttering liquid animal sound made somewhere in the back of the throat, and the women's kids joined in with a more familiar plain screaming of heads off. An impromptu parade was begun past the American Embassy, but there really wasn't anyplace else that the crowd wanted to parade to so the parade turned in ever tightening circles in front of the Embassy and finally just stopped and became a crowd. The crowd yelled, 'George Push! George Push! George Push!' Someone had already spray-painted 'Thank you for George Push' across the American Embassy wall, and the 'P' had been carefully crossed out and the spelling corrected. A donkey was led down the street with an Iraqi helmet tied on its head and 'Saddam Hussein' painted on its flanks. The first American soldiers showed up and everyone had to kiss them and shove babies into their arms and get the soldiers to autograph Kuwaiti flags. Kuwaiti flags were everywhere and at least a dozen little girls wore Kuwaiti-flag dresses – one red sleeve, one green sleeve, white down the middle and a black triangular yoke at the neck. Their mothers must have been stitching these all through the war. There were plenty of American flags, too, one with a picture of Marilyn Monroe sewn over the stripes. And across one intersection downtown a thirty-foot banner had been strung, reading – in answer to the US and European anti-war protestors' 'No blood for oil' slogan – BLOOD FOR FREEDOM.

Then there was a great noise and wind, and descending from the sky into this melee came a huge American Army helicopter down onto the roof of the US Embassy. The helicopter disgorged a squad of Army Rangers to roaring, stentorious cheers. It was the fall of Saigon with the film run backward.

A lot of people were crying, and I was one of them. A young Kuwaiti came out of the crowd and he was crying, and he grabbed me by my notebook and, with that immense earnestness that you only have an excuse for two or three times in your life and usually that's when your mother is dying, he said, 'You write we would like to thank every man in the allied force. Until one

hundred years we cannot thank them. What they do is . . . is . . . '
– words failed him – ' . . . is *America*.'

Not everything was quite so saccharine as that in Kuwait City,
of course. Earlier in the day, on the other side of the Hilton
Hotel, some scores had been settled. Kuwaiti Resistance kids
shot up an apartment building that was supposed to be full of
Iraqi collaborators. The Kuwaitis dragged out three ordinary-
looking middle-aged men, one howling for mercy and two looking deeply bummed. 'They are Sudanese Intelligence,' said one
Resistance kid. Though any review of Sudan's recent history
would render that phrase oxymoronic. The suspects were shoved
into a Toyota Supra sportscar and taken off to I'd-rather-not-
think-where. Later I saw another alleged collaborator arrested at
bazooka-point. Let me tell you, that was a quick give-up.

Palestinian guest workers, many of whom had had the bad
taste to chortle over the Iraqi conquest of their Kuwaiti
employers, were a particular target of the Resistance. Roadblocks
were set up all over town to ferret out the Pals. The roadblocks
were manned – boyed, to be exact – by nervous kids with automatic weapons. It was like being back in Beirut in the mid-
eighties except these militants wanted to hug you for being
American instead of shoot you for it. Considering how sloppy
the Kuwaitis were about gun safety, getting hugged was probably
as dangerous.

Some of the Palestinians weren't playing things too smart. I
found one of them standing in line with a jerrycan at a gas
station. He was being insulted by the Kuwaitis on either side of
him. Instead of making excuses or becoming suddenly Syrian,
he jumped out of line and started shouting at me: 'Why you
Americans come here and do this, why you don't come to the
West Bank as we have been waiting for since 1962?!' I presume
he meant '67 but, whatever, it didn't seem like the most politic
tack to be taking at the moment. The Kuwaitis apologized to me
and pulled the Palestinian back into the gas line so they could
insult him some more.

233

As joyful as the Kuwaitis were, they were just that furious. It was a difficult frame of mind to understand at first, though happy anger is probably more common and less contradictory than it sounds. Every Kuwaiti I spoke to had had members of his or her family beaten, killed or simply taken away. The hospital morgues were filled with the remains of tortured Kuwaitis, many unidentifiable. Every cemetery had a swath of new graves, mostly filled with men, the birth dates on the tombstones painfully contemporary and the death dates beginning 2 August 1990.

I visited a mass grave where two-hundred-some Kuwaitis were interred and these were only the bodies that family members had been able to retrieve and bury by stealth. In another cemetery I found a man tending the graves of his uncle and his uncle's son-in-law. Each tomb had an improvised wooden marker and a bottle stuck neck-down into the dirt with a verse of the Koran rolled inside. The man stood between the bare-earth mounds with his hands at his sides and spoke very quietly. His expression was of enormous, almost hysterical resignation, a kind of smile of grief. He said his uncle's body had burns from a clothes iron and from cigarettes. There were marks of electrical wires. His fingers had been chopped off. His eyes gouged out. Finally he had been shot in the head. The son-in-law had been tortured with an electric drill, then scalped, then shot in each eye.

'They were taken away on 17 January,' said the man in the cemetery. That was the day the air war began. 'The bodies were left at hospitals on 19 January,' he said. 'These people were not resistance.' He paused and then said in the same quiet voice, 'Iraqi occupying soldiers should be given back to the Kuwaiti people.'

When the Iraqis tried to leave Kuwait City, early on the second day of the ground war, they headed en masse up the road to Basra using both sides of the six-lane highway. About thirty-five miles north of the city, near a low rise called the Mutlaa Ridge, this bug-out was spotted by US Navy A-6 attack planes. These

Navy pilots must fly New York City traffic helicopters in civilian life, because they knew exactly what to do. They went right to the spot on the crest of the ridge where the road narrows from six lanes to four and plugged that bottleneck with cluster bombs.

We've got a real tie-up, outbound on the Basra Road this morning due to explosion, incineration, mutilation and death . . .

The panicked Iraqis tried to drive around the burning wreckage and became bogged down in the sand. The traffic jam spread out and backed up until it was nearly a half mile wide, more than a mile long and contained at least fifteen hundred vehicles. Then all the airplanes that the US Navy, Marines and Air Force could muster came in and let loose with everything they had. One Navy pilot called it 'shooting fish in a barrel,' but it was more like sticking a 12-gauge shotgun into a goldfish bowl.

The wreckage was still smoldering four days later. It didn't look like a battlefield. There were some Iraqi army vehicles in the mess – tanks opened up like bean cans and armored personnel carriers turned into giant hibachis. But most of the transport had been stolen, stolen in a perfectly indiscriminate frenzy of theft that left the ground covered with an improbable mixture of school buses, delivery vans, sports coupés, station wagons, tank trucks, luxury sedans, fire engines, civilian ambulances and semi-tractor trailers. I saw a motor scooter, a Geo Tracker and – the vehicle that would be my personal last pick for something to escape in – a cherry-picker crane. It looked like a bad holiday traffic jam in the States except charred and blown up, as though everybody in hell had tried to go to the Hamptons on the same weekend.

Allied burial details were moving through the wreckage, but some bodies were still lying there crispy and twisted in agony. I felt sorry for the poor dead bastards, but it was a reasonable, detached kind of sympathy that came from the went-to-college part of the brain. I was intellectually obligated to feel sorry for them, but after seeing what they'd done in Kuwait City, I had more of an Old Testament feeling in my heart:

> Then did I beat them as small as the dust of the earth, I did
> stamp them as the mire of the street, and did spread them
> abroad.
>
> —2 Samuel xxii:43

Of course I didn't do this personally, but my tax dollars helped.
I caught myself giggling at the carnage. This supposedly formi-
dable and certainly ruthless army had not only run from a fight
like a flock of broiler hens, it had also tried to carry with it every
item of portable swag in the Emirate. The killing field here was
littered not so much with corpses as with TVs, VCRs, Seiko
watches, cartons of cigarettes, box lots of shampoo and hair
conditioner, cameras, videotapes and household appliances.
School desks, tea sets, stuffed animals, silverware, an accordion
and a Kuwaiti family's photo album were all being dragged back
to Iraq. I saw a pickup-truck bed full of women's ball gowns and
another truck stacked with Pampers. A hot-wired camper van
sat with two cans of club soda resting in the dash-mounted drink
gimbals. The camper bunks were filled with men's boxer shorts,
the price tags still on them, and the whole – camper van, club
sodas, underpants and all – was punched full of tiny holes like
a cheese grater from cluster-bomb shrapnel. What we had here
was the My Lai of consumer goods.

Six days after the liberation of Kuwait the Kuwaitis were still
celebrating outside the US Embassy, firing every available
weapon in the air, including the .50-caliber dual-mount machine
guns on the Saudi and Qatari personnel carriers. It's one thing
to get plinked on the head by a falling pistol bullet, but a .50-
caliber slug plummeting from the sky at terminal velocity could
go right through you to the soles of your feet. One American
marine told me that sixteen people had been killed by 'happy
fire' so far, but a US Army officer said it was more like a hundred
and fifty. All the press corps' telephone and television satellite
up-links were on the roof of the Hilton and rounds were beginning to land up there. One bullet came down between the feet

of ABC executive Neil Patterson, who started handing out helmets and battle gear to everybody on the ABC payroll. The most dangerous thing I did during the entire war was cook spaghetti sauce on a camp stove on the Hilton roof without wearing my flak jacket.

Finally, one of the ABC satellite technicians – a Brit and a veteran of the Special Air Services – could stand it no more and leaned over the roof parapet and bellowed at the trigger-crazed Kuwaiti merrymakers, 'STOP IT! STOP IT! STOP IT! PUT THOSE FUCKING GUNS AWAY AND GO GET A MOP AND A BROOM AND *CLEAN THIS COUNTRY UP!'*

I went out to the Kuwait International Airport, or what was left of it, to try to get home. While I was sitting out there next to the burned ruins of the International Terminal, a Saudi business jet arrived guarded on all sides by US Cobra and Apache helicopters. The Crown Prince of Kuwait was returning home after a comfy exile in Tarif.

The next thing I knew the tarmac was covered with sleek Kuwaitis in perfectly draped *disdashas*. They were shaved and scrubbed and their gold wristwatches sparkled in the sun. A US Air Force enlisted man, sitting next to me on a broken couch that had been dragged out of the rubble of the first-class lounge, said, 'When the fat guys in the bath robes come back, you know the war is over.'

I hitched a ride back to Saudi Arabia on a New Zealand Air Force C-130. The members of the flight crew were all in their twenties and filled with leftover joy of combat. They let me stand on the flight deck as they brought their 132-foot wingspan, 100,000 pounds of an airplane down to a hundred feet and began chasing camels and goats across the desert at 300 miles an hour. The scattered tamarisk bushes were coming at us like uncountable fastballs in a batting-cage nightmare. The camels gave out pretty quick but the billies and nannies and kids were inspired to remarkable sprints of terror – turbo goats. The vast destitution of the Dahna Sands spread out in an infinity around us. 'Wall-to-wall fuck-all, eh?' shouted the Kiwi pilot. He and his crew mates had smiles as wide as their skulls. This was the stuff that made it all worthwhile, to be in absolute charge of 17,200 horsepower, to have, gripped in your fists, the whole might of science, of industry, of civilization's mastery of the world – *our* civilization's mastery of *this* world. 'HOOOOO-AH!!!' as the Gulf troops say.

We popped over the top of a little ridge, and there was a Bedouin camp on the other side. I watched a boy about nine or ten years old come running out from one of the goat-hair tents. We were so close I could see his expression – thrill and fear and awe and wonder combined. His whole life he'll remember the moment that sky-blackening, air-mauling, thunder-engined steel firmament of war crossed his face. And I hope all his bellicose, fanatical, senseless, quarrel-mongering neighbors – from Tel Aviv to Khartoum, from Tripoli to Tehran – remember it too.